An Unconventional Woman to Restore his Faith

———— ⚬ ————

STAND-ALONE BOOK

A Christian Historical Romance Book

by

Olivia Haywood

Table of Contents

Table of Contents 3

Prologue 5

Chapter One 12

Chapter Two 22

Chapter Three..32

Chapter Four 40

Chapter Five 46

Chapter Six 57

Chapter Seven 68

Chapter Eight 75

Chapter Nine 79

Chapter Ten..86

Chapter Eleven 97

Chapter Twelve 110

Chapter Thirteen 117

Chapter Fourteen 127

Chapter Fifteen...136

Chapter Sixteen 141

Chapter Seventeen..149

Chapter Eighteen..154

Chapter Nineteen..168

Chapter Twenty 177

Chapter Twenty-One..189

Chapter Twenty-Two..202

Chapter Twenty-Three 213

Chapter Twenty-Four..224

Chapter Twenty-Five..232

Chapter Twenty-Six 237

Chapter Twenty-Seven 249

Chapter Twenty-Eight..257

Chapter Twenty-Nine 264

Chapter Thirty 272

Chapter Thirty-One..280

Chapter Thirty-Two..299

Chapter Thirty-Three 307

Epilogue 315

Also, by Olivia Haywood..337

Prologue

Pinewood, Arizona Territory, 1871

Lucille's vision was cloudy with unshed tears as she surveyed the room. It was a warm day, and sunshine filtered through the window, shining onto the neatly brushed floor. The air smelled of the carbolic disinfectant she'd used to clean the surfaces—the desk, the copper washbasin, the cupboard that housed the microscope, and other equipment. It should have been a pleasant scene, but Lucille could barely bear to look at it. Her heart felt entirely cold, like the barrenness of the desert was resting within her.

This was her father's workroom. But he was not working here. Not anymore.

He was with God now.

Her beloved father passed away last week after a brief fit from which he had not recovered.

She swallowed hard, trying to feel *something*. Despite her wishes to cry, she couldn't sense any emotion. When she eyed her father's books, the wooden desk with its piles of papers, and the neat notes stacked in the glass-fronted closet, she wished she could express something. Part of her was howling in rage, pain, and loss. The rest of her—the part that everyone could see—quietly listened to the voices outside the window.

"Poor man."

"He's at peace, now."

The lawyer, Mr. Tarrant, and the banker, Mr. Longford, told her they would be coming to speak with her. Lucille knew she would have to face those men and discuss his estate and belongings.

She didn't know how to start. Even at nineteen years old, she had never been without her father. She smoothed her black linen skirt and high-collared blouse. As she bowed her head, her dark hair remained in place, pulled back in a bun, away from her face. She shut her dark eyes, keeping the pain at bay for a moment before they knocked.

"Miss Newbury?" a hesitant voice said through the door.

Lucille stepped forward, letting the men into her father's workroom. "Yes. Please, enter."

Outside, Mr. Longford removed his top hat, looking uncomfortable. Mr. Tarrant, tall and somber, wet his lips. Lucille stood behind the desk while they remained in the doorway, seeming reluctant to enter and ill-at-ease in her father's workroom. But she didn't feel ill-at-ease—she simply felt weary, knowing she could barely bear to speak with them. She just wanted everyone to leave her alone.

"Miss Newbury. We need to talk to you about your father's, er...effects," Mr. Tarrant addressed her carefully.

"His belongings. Yes, I know." Her voice was tight and croaky. She stared at them, trying to stand straight.

This was *her* space. She and her father had worked here for hours at a time—he had taught her how to stitch wounds, clean the equipment, and make medicine for coughs and fever. He was the town physician, but she had been his assistant.

And now, he was gone, and these cold and confused men were in his workspace.

Part of her wanted to tell them to get out, to leave her where his things still filled the space. It felt almost sacred because it was just as he had left it. If she sat in here, she could pretend for a moment that he had just walked into the village to buy more supplies and would return at any moment.

"Miss Newbury," Mr. Longford said gently with his head tilted. The banker occasionally called at their house and was a friend of her father's. "We need to speak to you about an... awkward thing."

Mr. Tarrant, who was much taller, hesitated beside him. They were merely floating, earnest, pale faces; their black, somber suits blended with the door's shadow.

"Please, begin," Lucille said, annoyed by their caution. She only wanted the facts. While she knew they were doing their best, anyone's presence was too much to bear.

"Um, yes," Mr. Longford said. "Mr. Tarrant, perhaps you'd like to, er...outline the news?"

Mr. Tarrant glared at the shorter, rotund form of Longford with a wrinkled lip as if he did not wish to speak simply because Longford invited him to do so. The men didn't like one another; it was known to the townsfolk and was a source of some entertainment. Lucille might have found the asperity funny, but now, she couldn't find much amusement in anything.

"Miss Newbury," Mr. Tarrant repeated carefully. "There is a matter of a loan."

"A loan?" Lucille gaped at them, unbelieving. "What sort of—"

"Apologies," Mr. Longford said. "My dear girl, your father borrowed money of a considerable sum. It was unpaid, and now that he is...passed...he...well, his estate owes the money."

"I owe money?" Lucille asked in a whisper. Dizzy, she leaned on the desk. None of this seemed accurate; she couldn't believe it. She thought they came to discuss the distribution of his property. Since she was the only living relative Papa had, it would pass to her. As far as she knew, her father had no debt. One thing she knew was that they were comfortably off—they owned the cottage that appended the workroom where they stood now, the plot of land, and the cart with which they traveled. They were wealthy in comparison with many folks in the town. Her father did not *need* moneylending.

"*You* don't, my dear girl," Mr. Longford assured. "It is just, well, when a debtor passes, their debt needs to be paid, and so—"

"But how did Papa incur debt?" she asked, her voice like a small child's. She'd never felt so helpless, so weary, and confused.

Mr. Longford glanced away before speaking as if nervous to answer. "My dear, your papa was too generous. He didn't always take payment for his services. And he spent more than he had. He built up debts in every establishment, and, well...this is the result."

"Miss Newbury, the house passes to the estate, which passes to the bank. It will be sold to pay the debt owed to them." Mr. Tarrant sounded wintry. While Longford was doing his best to be kind, Tarrant was relaying the facts, which, in a way, were what she needed. She needed *something* to hold onto, something to understand. She had been raised to have an incisive, clear mind and found confusion hard to bear.

She leaned on the shelf behind the desk, too weak to support herself. None of this was real. She must be dreaming.

"My dear girl, I'm sorry," Mr. Longford repeated in a tight and strained voice. "I am so sorry. If there was another path, I would take it, but we cannot leave his debt unpaid. The—"

"Miss Newbury," Mr. Tarrant interrupted flatly. "I suggest that you contact any acquaintances to arrange lodging. I will delay if I can, but you need to find alternative accommodation."

Lucille's body shook, and her ears felt blocked with cotton as though going deaf. Nothing made sense. Slowly, her senses withdrew. Though the men were trying to remonstrate, a part of her was floating, unable to comprehend the words.

"Miss Newbury, of course, we will do everything possible to ensure that—"

"Please," she whispered. "Please. I can't understand you. Please, *let me think.*"

Mr. Longford glanced at Mr. Tarrant, and relief flooded through Lucille as he tapped him on the shoulder. "Let's leave Miss Newbury to think. I'll ask the neighbor to step in for a bit," he said softly.

"No," Lucille breathed. "I want time to think on my own."

Mr. Longford patted her hand. "You need company, miss. It's not good for you to sit here without a companion. Let me fetch the neighbor."

"No." Lucille knew he hadn't heard, but all that concerned her was the men were leaving. Once they departed, she slid into her father's chair.

Utterly drained, she rested her head on the desk and prayed. God would find a way forward for her where there seemed to be none.

She was still in her father's chair with her eyes shut when her neighbor entered, sent by the banker and the lawyer. Lucille sighed. She didn't want to talk to anyone and wished they hadn't sent her. She tried to smile, though—she didn't want to be unkind.

"Good morning, dear," Mrs. Powell said gently. "I brought you some fresh-baked bread."

Lucille nodded absently. Though she didn't have an appetite, what could she say? She appreciated the gesture, though she struggled to find words through her brain's fog.

"It's no trouble at all, my dear," Mrs. Powell said caringly as though Lucille had responded. "Now, I'll sit with you if you like. It's not good to be alone. I brought my Bible and could read it aloud to you...?"

Lucille shook her head, trying not to cry. "Thank you, but I would prefer the quiet. I have a lot to think about."

"Of course," Mrs. Powell agreed kindly. "Well, I'll leave the bread here for you. And remember, the Lord hears our prayers."

Even in her current state of numbness, Lucille knew that to be true. While she couldn't imagine how, somewhere in her heart, she knew that help would come from the Lord.

Chapter One

The smell of tobacco and coffee, sackcloth, and plaster floated across the trading store's counter. A line of people was already at the counter, and Lucille wanted to run. She wished to avoid the crowds, but she'd been busy washing her laundry.

As she stepped inside, she was aware of the eyes on her. Everybody found it necessary to remind her that her father had passed, eulogizing him like she had no idea who he was or how much they missed him.

Hands clenched in a fist, she wished they knew how she tried not to think of him sometimes. If she did, the pain would become unbearable.

The coins for flour and yeast were heavy in her hand. Though she wanted to buy soap, she couldn't purchase anything else if she did, and she so dearly longed for fruit. However, she was aware she had limited resources. If she didn't get a job soon, she wouldn't have any money.

But *how?*

Options for work were limited. Lucille considered taking in washing for neighbors, but that was already primarily taken by Mrs. Prester on the corner, who did all the washing for the ranch hands. Lucille had no skills in baking or handicraft, though most people did their own cooking. There was already a teacher for the schoolhouse, and other options like housekeeper or cleaner were limited. The few houses big enough to employ people were in larger cities, like Prescott, fifty miles away. Their housekeeper, Mrs. Whitestone, left weeks before Papa passed away. Now, Lucille understood it was because they could no longer afford to pay her, and her father concealed it from her. She had no idea what to do.

Some of the neighbors tried to help. Mrs. Powell, who had always cared for her, bought a paper from Prescott to help Lucille in her search, but being poor as well, that was the most she could offer. Except for Mr. Longford, Mrs. Powell was the only person she and her father knew well. Nobody else had even come forward to attempt to help her in her need.

She gazed around the crowded store. Most stood around talking while Mr. Rosegate, the owner, served Mrs. Paget at the counter. The shelves were stocked with farm equipment—hoes, rakes, plows, and bags of grain for chickens. All the other wares—soap, tobacco, flour, sugar, sweets—were kept behind the counter. Its high, wooden length festooned with bottles and the shelves behind glinting with jars and baskets of apples and pears.

Taking a breath, Lucille wished Mrs. Paget would hurry, as five people were waiting. Did everybody in the town do their shopping mid-week? Why had she not recalled this would be the busiest time?

She felt helpless and irritable, as though flies buzzed about her, settling, biting, and flying away. Though Mr. Tarrant and Mr. Longford tried to delay the debt collection for a week, she couldn't expect them to give her more grace than that. If she didn't move out soon, she would still be in the cottage when the bailiffs came to take her belongings.

"….and it's about Miss Newbury…"

The voice was low but distinct. She frowned, scanning the shop. *They are gossiping about me.*

The townsfolk knew about the debt; Tarrant or Longford told somebody, as she guessed they would, and word spread. Two shoppers glanced over their shoulders with guilt and speculation in their gaze. Shame was like fire on her skin.

Without thinking about it, she blundered through the door. She couldn't endure their eyes on her, their wagging tongues, sure that some folks enjoyed her helpless state. Her father had friends, but he also had enemies—more than they knew. He had been oblivious to those who resented him or were jealous of his popularity and good reputation. However, Lucille noticed the sullen glances. Now, they directed their anger and bitterness toward her. Lucille had thought that the townsfolk would remember how they valued her father and help her, but nobody bridged the gap. Perhaps, after all, they had resented the subtle status difference that being a doctor gave him, which was why they were reluctant to help.

She had been so sure of everything, so confident. When people whispered about her, she felt like an outcast, like she had a mark that made her less of a person. She would soon be homeless, but all those fickle townsfolk could do was talk about her. Constantly threatened and judged, it sapped her belief in everything, especially herself.

The dirt and paving were rough under her boots, smelling dusty and dry as she fled. The store stood on the main street, and six others roads branched off from it. Her house was on the other side of town. While she wanted to flee there, she was utterly overcome with emotion.

"Please, God," she whispered as she rounded the corner by the inn. "Please. I need Your guidance."

She had almost stopped believing He heard her prayers but reminded herself: *He does. I know He does.*

Though she didn't like being a doubter, she had never felt this flat, cold silence when she prayed. It genuinely felt like nobody was there, as if nobody heard her. Every time she didn't find jobs in the paper, every time she searched for inspiration, and no guidance came to her, a little of her faith diminished. But she hadn't entirely stopped believing. She took a deep breath and shut her eyes, trying not to cry. The stone was cold as she leaned on the wall. While it felt better than standing in the store, the wind cut through her clothes like ice.

She was utterly alone.

Footsteps approached and stopped on the cobbled street. Opening her eyes, Lucille saw a wrinkled, wise face with dark, somber eyes. "Mr. Chaffee?"

The short, older man grinned, showing yellowing teeth. "Look at you! Lucille Newbury, I'm so glad to see you."

"Mr. Chaffee," Lucille gasped, flooded with relief. "It's a surprise to see you here!"

Max Chaffee was her father's friend. He seldom visited because his ranch was many miles away, in the wilderness between Pinewood and Oxplains. Once a month, he came to town for supplies and to stock up on goods, some of which he sold in Oxplains. Lucille blinked at him, genuinely glad to see someone she knew. He was someone she had known all her life and somebody who understood her father. In a world where people were fickle, and gossip sprang up around her like wildfire, it was good to have someone she could undoubtedly trust.

"Yes, child. It's me, all right. Look at you! You'll catch a chill if you stand around without a coat."

Mr. Chaffee's laughter made her smile. He wore leather and homespun linen, his face tanned by the sunshine. He hadn't tried to commiserate by telling her how much he missed her father. He hadn't even mentioned her loss, though he must have known about it. Due to her father's popularity as the best physician in the region, his passing made the front page of the local Gazette.

His hazel eyes were filled with care. "How are you faring?"

Lucille sucked in a breath. "Not well, Mr. Chaffee." The road was still unoccupied, but she didn't want to talk where they could be seen—both because they would gossip and she needed to vent about her troubles and didn't want them overhearing.

"Would you like a cup of tea?" she asked. It was impossible to invite Mr. Chaffee to her home since people would talk if she entertained a man, even a family friend. But the inn was open, and nothing was stopping them from taking a cup of tea in the inn parlor. Though unconventional, it was not suggestive, not even by the standards of the most closed-minded.

He nodded. "I'd like that. And best if you get indoors." He coughed as he swore about the cold. "Sorry, miss. I'm not fit for polite company."

"Darn right." Laughing, Lucille followed him into the building, feeling better than she had in a while.

The parlor was empty, and Lucille was relieved to talk freely. After they requested tea, Lucille's heart surged. The interior was dark, except for the light that shone through the window behind them, a net curtain keeping out any curious eyes. There was nobody else inside besides them, for which Lucille was grateful; she expected any villagers seeing them would gossip. While it was reasonable for villagers to take tea there, most didn't, reserving the inn for the out-of-town guests who might pass through on their way south or traders.

Lucille grinned at him. "I'm so glad to see you, Mr. Chaffee."

He beamed. "I'm pleased to see you, Miss Newbury." The laughter-etched wrinkles in the corner of his eyes drooped with sorrow. "I am so sorry for your father's passing."

"Thank you." She sighed. "We both feel sorrow for his loss."

"Gerard was a fine doctor. A fine man."

Lucille allowed thoughts of her father to surface. She could share real memories with somebody who knew him as more than just the physician. Mr. Chaffee had known Gerard Newbury, a complex human with his own story.

They sat in silence while the proprietor brought tea.

"Listen, Miss Newbury," Mr. Chaffee said awkwardly, stirring milk into his tea absentmindedly. "If you need anything, tell me. You're a young lady, and I know it's hard.

It's not easy dealing with all that legality." He gestured in the direction of the office.

"I am trying to deal with it," she swallowed. "But it's not easy. I..." She tried to find the words to tell him the news. "Papa had debt and never told anyone. I only found out a week ago."

"Debt, eh?" Mr. Chaffee, who'd been sipping his tea, sat straight.

"Yes," Lucille murmured. As she shared the story, he nodded slowly, his expression gentle. Relief flooded her. After the whispering gossip-spreaders, genuine care was like a balm for her. She hadn't realized how much it wore her down, how those sly glances at the store had eroded her belief in everything, even—and especially—in herself. That, plus the fear of imminent homelessness, stripped her dignity away and left her raw and uncertain of everything she always knew.

"That's rough." Mr. Chaffee whistled. "You need somewhere to stay. How about..." he paused, rubbing his chin. "Your pa trained you?"

"That's right." Physicians never took women as apprentices—that was an absolute rule. Though it was almost unheard of, she had practiced. But her father told her that nothing could stand in her way. Her eyes flooded with tears, recalling how highly he'd spoken of her. Her voice wobbled. "He trained me."

"Well, then," Mr. Chaffee said thoughtfully. "I reckon I know someone who's looking for a physician. You could come with me."

"You do?" Lucille stared at him, flooded with delight. Unexpectedly, terror instantly followed. Nobody would accept her; she was a woman. People didn't go to women physicians—not usually. She could work as a nurse, though. "I suppose I could help a physician if he'd—"

"Come, now!" he chuckled. "Miss Newbury, you could *be* a physician. Why not? Your pa would say so."

"But..." Lucille sighed. She had always wanted to be a physician, but even her papa acknowledged that it was hard for a woman. Anyone else would say it was impossible. Her father was the only person she knew of—besides Mr. Chaffee, though she hadn't realized before—who would accept the idea. "But Mr. Chaffee...I'm not, well..." She gestured toward herself.

"You're not a man. Is that what you meant?"

She nodded, glad he hadn't made her explain further. Women could not become doctors. It was as well-known as fire could burn you or that it was cold at night.

He chuckled. "Honey! It's time people forgot about that. There was that lady...you know..." He flapped a hand, frowning as though the name refused to come to mind.

"Elizabeth Blackwell." Lucille nodded. Elizabeth Blackwell had practiced, but she was the only example she could name. A few years earlier, Elizabeth Blackwell had graduated as a physician in Geneva, New York. Lucille only knew because a late peer of her father's met her. Though Papa highly admired Dr. Blackwell, Lucille knew how terrible an ordeal studying had been for her—even her colleagues had laughed and scoffed.

"That's the one," Mr. Chaffee grinned "So, you see... It could be done. And anyone who says not is outdated."

Lucille swallowed. It was what she'd dreamed of her whole life. If someone asked her what her deepest longing was, she would hesitate to name it as being all too unlikely. She was no Elizabeth Blackwell, ready to defy all norms. People would ridicule and laugh at her. Lucille gazed at the tea forgotten on the table and tried to voice her feelings.

"I'm not certain..." She coughed, her throat tight.

He shook his head. "I don't believe that. Not for a second. I know you, Miss Newbury. You're like Gerard, so like him, I can barely believe it sometimes. And he would think it was no bad thought." He paused. "I knew him. He would say that the Lord works in mysterious ways."

Her eyes went misty, and for the first time in weeks, she thought she would genuinely weep. She hadn't mourned her father—she'd barely been able to feel. But now, talking with his friend, he seemed so vividly present, as if, for a moment, he stooped down from Heaven, and she could almost see him.

"He would," she agreed. "That's so typical of him, somehow."

"It is," he said. "And he would have said this was your divine calling. I know he would."

"Maybe," Lucille said carefully. Her father suggested that once, long ago, when she helped him. It was the highest praise he ever gave, and she kept that treasured memory a secret. She wondered about it now, hearing Mr. Chaffee's words.

They both sat silently for a moment while Lucille was lost in her father's memory. Across the table, she knew his friend was also wandering in his memory.

"If I can travel with you," she said. "Then I would be ready to do so. But I will need time to decide about the... other consideration." She couldn't even say that she was thinking about being a physician. It was too huge.

"Well, then!" he said, laughing. He clasped her hand and something thawed inside her. "I'd be delighted if you came with me. And you can take all the time you need." He paused. "I'm going to Oxplains tomorrow, but I'll be back in a week. You can let me know your decision then. Will you be safe until then? Will you be able to negotiate with the bank for another week?"

Unable to speak, she nodded. She hoped Mr. Longford could be convinced to give her that time, especially if she had the possibility of work. A mix of nerves and excitement filled her, flowing through and uplifting her.

For the first time in weeks, there was a glimmer of warmth within, and she was ready to take the step placed for her. Deep down, she knew that the Lord provided the opportunity. It was a terrifying yet exciting start to a new journey.

Chapter Two

Oxplains, Arizona Territory, 1871

Nicholas sat heavily behind his big desk with its cracks and chips, his head aching. His gaze rested on the small windows, the view blurry in his tired vision. While Oxplains was a small and far from prosperous town, the sheriff's office was luxurious compared to how many people lived.

Breathing in the familiar dusty smell, Nicholas wondered what he would do. The latest problems in town were like a weight. He was still contemplating them, mind hazy with weariness, when footsteps approached from the hallway.

"Sheriff Barnes?" Luke, his deputy, called as he ran in. "What should I do about Mr. Simmons?"

Running a hand through his dark hair, Nicholas narrowed his eyes with a growing headache. "Let him off. Like usual."

"Sir." Luke inclined his head deferentially, disappearing down the hall. Nicholas sighed as the door shut behind him. Luke was a good kid—eighteen, earnest and eager, with pale hair and big, brownish eyes. But he was one more weight on Nicholas' shoulders, as was Mr. Simmons.

There were far more significant problems to worry about than an octogenarian tying his horse up outside the bar, where it wasn't allowed. Nicholas always let the old fellow off with a reprimand and occasionally a small fee for cleaning the street. There were two severe issues on his mind at that moment: the bandits in the nearby cave system and the injuries they caused.

Nicholas had just returned from inspecting a break-in at one outlying home. The windows were broken, and the property was damaged. The elderly folks who lived out there for the last fifty years were terrified and traumatized. Fortunately, though, the couple was in their bedroom at the time, and the bandits left them unharmed. The last thing Nicholas needed was more people wounded, like what happened last week.

Mr. Simmons, the old man with the horse, represented the only help dealing with serious injuries. As a physician serving during the Civil War, he was the only person with any knowledge of healing in the town, even though he retired almost ten years before the war started. Serious injuries often happened because of the bandits' presence and the town's agricultural nature. It was just one more thing for Nicholas to face. Feeling inadequate, he wished he had someone besides Mr. Simmons and himself to deal with the injuries.

Luke reemerged, and Nicholas barely looked up. "What is it?" While he tried to make his voice less raw, it was hard. Luke's enthusiasm was draining. Nicholas was twice his age, but he couldn't remember when he had been as energetic as Luke.

"All dealt with, sir. Mr. Simmons is on his way."

"Good, good." Nicholas drew random lines in the margin of an old bill. Small, intricate lines that resembled a cage. Weary and exhausted, he needed time off.

"Should I check on the main road again, sir?"

With a yawn, Nicholas nodded. The temptation to shut the office and ride home to his ranch was overwhelming. But he couldn't do that—not yet. However, he could go get a drink. He stretched and departed with a murmur of his destination.

Nicholas was too tired to see straight. Though he was working himself to exhaustion, it wasn't too bad since it meant he'd sleep. He was sick of lying awake at night, his head full of problems.

He had never felt like this before—so forsaken, so without the reassurance that his faith gave him. Before, his world was tranquil and easy. The trouble with the bandits made him face a violent, tumultuous world. It left him orphaned, and he'd built so much in his life—his routine, his careful self-control—around keeping it distant from him. Nothing seemed certain anymore.

The bar was close to his office, just a short walk down the street, and he was grateful. His knee ached as he limped. It always hurt when he was tired—the result of a fall when he was eighteen and riding on Breakwater Ranch. The memory amused him. He'd fallen sideways off his horse due to a poorly fastened saddle; at the time, he'd been more concerned about how embarrassed he was than about the pain in his leg. The Radfords, who owned the ranch, more-or-less adopted him. They also hadn't made him feel like a fool for riding with a loose saddle, though he'd been desperate to prove himself and felt like everyone would laugh at him.

Those were hard years. Nicholas could barely remember his parents, who passed away when he was three. Shortly after, he moved to Breakwater Ranch. The Radfords—distant family friends—took care of him like he was their son. Even as a child, he knew full well that he was granted help and would never stop trying to prove he was worthy of it. It could have been a burden, but the Radfords were kind.

Nicholas smiled when thinking of Mrs. Radford's sweet face, the only mother he could honestly remember, and his father figure, Mr. Radford.

***

Once he reached the bar, he scanned the room wearily. The narrow rear windows were covered with thin velvet curtains and a few tables and chairs in front of the bar. As he sat on a hard barstool, he smelled the spirits and the food, reminding him he hadn't eaten since the morning.

The barman's squarish face lit up with a grin, his baldpate shining in the lamplight. "What're you having?"

"Brandy. And whatever that is." He jerked his head to the table where a man sat facing away so Nicholas couldn't see what the plate contained.

"Sure, Sheriff Barnes," the barman, Mr. Elwood, said. "Right away."

Nicholas noticed the scuffed floor, thinking that so many people must have walked here over the decades—he didn't know how old the bar was, but he was sure it was one of the most well-worn buildings in town.

Once the brandy was poured, Nicholas drank it, making a face. He was fond of the taste of good brandy; the Radfords were prosperous, and the food and supplies were fine. But this brandy was horrid—rough and sour. He shivered and set down the glass.

"Plate of stew, sir."

"Thank you," Nicholas said absently. He breathed in, appreciating the warm smells of onion and spice. The stew was not necessarily appetizing—a grayish mass of thinnish soup-water and rough-cut meat—but he was hungry and ate it fast. Leaning back, eyes shut, the food and warmth eased his mind.

Relaxing his neck, he sat for a long moment with his eyes shut, his head tipped back. It was relieving, the first rest he'd had for days.

"Sheriff Barnes?"

He jumped in surprise, glaring at the person who'd spoken. *There's no need to give a fellow a fright like that!* He was angry enough not to recognize the person for a moment or two.

"Mr. Chaffee?"

Not seeming distressed by having affrighted him, Max Chaffee grinned unapologetically. "Hey, Nicholas." He smiled fondly, heaving himself onto the stool beside him. "Sorry. Didn't mean to disturb your contemplations."

With a deep breath, Nicholas calmed down. Max Chaffee was one of the few in the surrounding district whom he trusted and liked—besides the Radfords, who passed away years ago, leaving him their ranch. Max was also one of the few living people who knew his father.

"Good afternoon," he smiled politely, feeling calmer already.

"It is," Max agreed pleasantly. "A fine day. Did some travel lately. Went all the way to Pinewood." His face was lined with years of exposure to sunshine, his hazel eyes mild as he watched Nicholas thoughtfully.

Nicholas had always liked Max. Max's trading visits brought him to Breakwater Ranch when Nicholas was a child. Nicholas recalled how Max would visit with his cart of goods, to the delight of Mrs. Radford, who would buy silk ribbon and other fine things. Max's visit had always lifted everyone's spirits.

"Oh?" Nicholas returned from his memories to focus on what Max was saying, trying to draw a mental map of where he'd been. Pinewood was a reasonable distance away. "Did it take long?"

"Just two days," Max confirmed. "The usual," he gestured to Mr. Elwood, who nodded.

"Good, good." Nicholas frowned. "And you didn't have to fend off Rider's gang?"

"No," Max said. "I wasn't bothered by anyone. Saw some fellows I didn't recognize in the distance, but they didn't approach."

"Oh." Nicholas's headache pressed in on him. "Whereabouts?"

"About four miles out from my place. They didn't do anything. Just watched me. I think they reckoned I'd be armed. Thank the Lord they didn't approach," he added fervently.

"Me, too, Max," he nodded sincerely before frowning. "Rider's gang haven't been going out that far."

Max's ranch was one of the furthest from the town, closer to Pinewood than Oxplains. His work would get more complicated if the bandits ranged that far afield. If they were attacking the main supply road, it would be a significant problem in the region. His stomach twisted painfully, a frown flitting across his brow.

"You look like the woes of the world are on your shoulders, Nicholas," Max said gently.

"A bit. It's the bandits," he explained. "Since more were recruited, they're becoming more troublesome every day." Longing for sleep, he ran a weary hand down his face. Privately, he sometimes felt God had forsaken him—he felt so alone.

"Didn't shoot nobody, though?" Max asked, his wrinkled face a picture of worry.

"They shot a fellow last week." Nicholas dipped his head in shame. "He's not dead, but I don't thank myself for that. I didn't help him much."

The pain, fear, and helplessness of facing that injury haunted him. His nausea grew worse as he remembered the blood, the pale skin, and his own uselessness. He had prayed for guidance, and God's abandonment had grown with each passing second.

Max looked at him kindly. "You're a sheriff, man, not a doctor. What were you supposed to do?"

Nicholas sighed, running a hand through his hair. "I should be able to do something. I can't, though. I don't know where to start. I've never even seen someone remove a bullet." The former sheriff, Mr. Rowell, was better with that. He felt inadequate just thinking about it.

"I guess." Max rubbed his chin, a habit when he was thinking. "You know, I think I know a physician."

"*You do?*" Nicholas gaped at him. "You really do? Tell me about him. Where is he? How long would it take him to get here?" Excited energy flooded him. It was an answer to his nightly prayers. If there was a physician here, half his worries would be addressed.

"*Her,*" Max said, chuckling. "The physician's a woman. She's unlicensed, mind, but I can vouch for her. I knew her pa, and he was the best physician I ever did see. Fine man." Max shut his eyes, face strained, and Nicholas guessed that the physician must have passed away.

The fact was negligible compared to the revelation of her gender. *A woman!* There was no such thing as a female doctor in Nicholas' world. He'd never heard of one and doubted if anyone else had. That was even more of a concern than his own shock.

Nicholas shook his head. "I can't have her here. Folk wouldn't trust her." He had been so relieved and was almost angry with Max for offering him a solution and then pulling it out from underfoot.

"You're assuming. You don't know." Max frowned.

Nicholas just stared at him, green eyes skeptical. "You know these folks."

Max appeared unbothered. "But, as you say, they need a physician, and—"

"No, Max," Nicholas said carefully. "No. Don't even think it. The last thing I need is some unlicensed lady wandering around town. I have enough trouble on my hands without half the folks rebelling."

Max shrugged. "It's for you to decide," he said. "I just thought... that poor girl has enough trouble on her hands. She needs a place. While she can stay with me for a bit, you know how people would tongue-wag."

"I know," he sighed. "And that's half the trouble." People would assume Max and the woman were involved with each other and that the woman was...of low moral character. Most folks would be railing to get rid of her, and others would be clamoring for her to stay. He had enough problems on his hands without a woman igniting more trouble.

But Max said the woman was facing hardship. Though Nicholas felt a need to help, what could he do? That was one of the things that made his job so hard—he genuinely felt called to help those in need, which meant that he spent every day in Oxplains. Yet, he still felt inadequate because so many people needed help whom he couldn't assist.

Max looked disappointed, but Nicholas pushed the thought away. He had enough on his hands without feeling more useless or guilty for not being able to help this woman or Max. He didn't need the weight of those emotions, and Max wasn't helping.

"I need to get back to the office," Nicholas said as he stood.

"Sure thing." He paused. "Think about it, Nicholas. It could be a solution. The Lord works in—"

"Mysterious ways," Nicholas agreed wearily before leaving Max at the bar.

Outside, he stared at the spire on the church tower, so like a finger pointing heavenward, and he wished that he understood what the Lord expected of him. "Lord, give me strength," he murmured.

He turned the problem over and over in his mind. He could just let Max bring her. Though he might not be able to let her take over as the physician, maybe he could take her on at the ranch if she needed work. There was plenty of cleaning to do. His housekeeper—who he more or less inherited along with the ranch and couldn't possibly dismiss her—was getting too old to tidy the place by herself. If he hired this woman to do that, nobody in the village could say anything. It would give him a chance to find out more about her, and it would also salve the weight that pressed on his conscience.

He could curse Max for giving him another problem to worry about. Even though he couldn't see the villagers accepting a female doctor, his conscience would not let him shirk his Christian duty to help her.

If the townsfolk rejected her, he could offer her work on the ranch. He would see what happened.

Nicholas limped to find his horse and head home. His headache was still there, pressing in on his eyes—Max offered him a solution, but it could ignite even more trouble, and he didn't know what to think about it. All he wanted was to sleep and hope he would have a clear head tomorrow.

Chapter Three

As Lucille stepped down from the wagon, nausea squeezed her stomach. She took Mr. Chaffee's worn, warm hand, clutching it for familiarity and because her balance was gone. Her head spun. She told herself it was the wagon ride, the dry air, she was dehydrated, and it was already nightfall. It explained why she felt ill, but it wasn't just that.

It was the fact that she was embarking on a new journey.

Two days ago, she climbed into the wagon with a suitcase of her dresses, one or two pieces of sentimental jewelry, her medical books and Bible, and a second, smaller bag of surgical equipment. She didn't think of the home, the village, and all the familiarity of the place. If she thought about that, she would not be able to avoid tears.

She held grimly onto Max as he held her up for a moment. Apprehensively, she peered up at the building before her among the barren landscape.

"It's getting late, so I'll have to head home," Max explained. "I'll leave you at the trading post. You won't have to wait long. Nicholas said he'd meet us at six o'clock."

Guessing the time from the lengthening shadow was something Lucille could do as a child. The skill was valuable playing out of doors and using it to estimate the time before dinner. Lucille had never been particularly good at it, but she guessed it was already around six o'clock.

Unsteady, she stumbled, and Mr. Chaffee caught her hand. Lucille murmured her gratitude, too drained to talk. She licked her parched and cracked lips, knowing she needed fresh water.

Her gaze drifted to the ox-wagon, a flat, wide cart-like structure with two seats at the front, a seat at the back covered by a cylindrical framework over which thick sailcloth was strung. The rear was protected from the worst of the sunshine, was where she sat for most of the last two days and where she slept when they stopped one night.

Mr. Chaffee had gallantly slept beside the cart under the stars—a position which terrified Lucille. There were coyotes and other dangerous predators in the desert. She had lain awake for an hour, watching the sky and thinking about how helpless she would be if he were attacked. Once she fell asleep, she had a dream in which her father tried to reach her, calling out to her through the fog.

She smoothed down her finest black skirt. She also wore her best dark gray blouse, with a high collar and ornamental buttons, the sleeves tight at the wrists and decorated at the cuff with lace and ribbon. With her hair in a bun, the clothing looked austere, covered with her long traveling cloak. She hoped she looked presentable, but the bun had fallen a little at the back, and it was difficult to be sure without a mirror. She wanted to make a good impression on Nicholas Barnes. Mr. Chaffee remained vague regarding his conversation with the sheriff earlier that week, only telling her to "expect some resistance." And she was going to combat that resistance. If he was too arrogant to entertain the notion of a professional female physician, she already knew she didn't like him.

Pushing the thought away, she surveyed the landscape. The sunset was red on the horizon, with cactus and scrubby brush on one side and dry, arid desert. It was the same landscape they had seen for the last day and a half of journeying, except she was now on her way to an utterly unfamiliar destination. Though she prayed every night for guidance, she was still afraid. She sent a silent prayer toward the darkening sky.

Please, keep me safe.

"Here we are," Mr. Chaffee announced fondly as he carried her bags through the door. "Now, you'll be perfectly safe inside the trading post. The owner, Mr. Stretton, is on the property. I'd not let you wait here unwatched. I don't like to leave you, but I must get home before it's too late."

Oxplains was too far from his ranch for him to drive there and back at night. However, at the same time, fear crept up her spine. The surroundings were vast and empty. Bandits or predators could lurk unnoticed, and a shiver coursed through her. She had felt so strongly that she was following God's plan for her when she embarked on this journey, but her fear made it hard to connect to strength and assurance right now.

Lucille swallowed hard, grateful for his forethought. "Thank you, Mr. Chaffee. I promise to stay indoors." The terror was tight in her chest and plain in her voice.

"It's my honor. You're a fine young lady," he beamed, setting her bags down. "Gerard is so proud of you, I'm sure of it."

Her heart jumped at the sound of her father's name. "Thank you," she whispered again.

After a brief and heartfelt goodbye, Max closed the door softly behind him, leaving her in the near-darkness.

"There's nothing to be afraid of. I am *not* afraid of the dark."

It was a desperate plea to convince herself it was true. Lucille didn't care that the store owner was somewhere on the property. Recalling Psalm Ninety-One, she tried to remember that God was always watching over her, keeping her safe. The repetition of the psalm of protection made her feel a little better, a little less afraid of the shadows. A little safer.

The sky, which had been dark blue with dusk, was entirely black. The stars were shining, one or two tiny points of light, but she was sure that soon, predators would be about. Pushing all fear away, she focused on the light of the stars, appearing so small yet so huge. They were like suns, magnificent and bright, thousands upon thousands of impossible distances far from Earth. *Such a miraculous universe!* A creation that evidenced the Divine Intelligence. Her father's voice echoed in her mind, talking of how bright the stars were, how far away, and the names of the constellations.

Orion. The Bear. The Scales. The Crown.

She named them, and when she ran out of names she remembered, she recited prayers and hymns.

It was the only way to keep out the fear.

After an hour—from what she could guess, the only illumination came from the last flickering of an oil lamp providing a wan light—she was no longer scared. However, she was enraged. She was also cold, hungry, and tired.

"Where is that wretched man?" she groaned, angry and affronted.

She disliked him already—after all, he had been dubious about letting her come to his town. Mr. Chaffee told her that much only very reluctantly, which made her believe it. But leaving her alone in the dark countryside when he'd told his friend he would be promptly here at six o'clock...that was worse. She would've been able to forgive his bias. This was impossible to overlook.

No longer content with sitting still, she paced, her boots loud on the worn, wooden floor before falling unnoticed as she walked. She called Barnes all the insulting things she knew under her breath. It made her feel less scared.

"Unprofessional, rude, intolerable..."

"Miss?" a deep voice called through the door. "Miss? You there?"

Lucille froze. She thought it was the trading post owner, but the words were coming through the front door rather than the back where she assumed the man lived. She reddened, straightening in shock.

It must be Mr. Barnes.

"Yes?" she called. What if he'd heard her? Her cheeks flooded with heat. Surely, he hadn't. And even if he had, how would he know she was angry with him?

When Lucille reached the door, she was still angry, still offended. She expected Mr. Barnes to be tall and sour like Tarrant. While she sat there in the dark, waiting for him, she visualized him so clearly. She imagined him scowling and bitter, with a jutting chin, missing teeth, and a wart or two for good measure. After a deep breath, she stepped back and opened the door.

A man stood there with a lantern. He was tall—much more so than she'd expected—with leather boots and good linen trousers, a fine white shirt, and a hat. Though he was clean and smelled fresh, that was not what captivated her.

The gentleman had high cheekbones and dark locks. His face was long, well-formed, with a fine nose and a firm chin that was slightly marked with stubbly dark hair. In the lamplight, his eyes were an intense green. Slightly hooded, they peered down at her, and her heart thumped. Her anger was replaced with indignation, mixed with a strange feeling she didn't recognize. She glared up at him, determined to be angry.

"So," she hissed. "Here you are." Her tone was as frosty as possible, trying to assert her wavering dignity.

"My apologies, miss," he said carefully with a raised brow. He inclined his head, and the fluid beauty of his movements caused her throat to snag. "I worked later than anticipated." It was impossible to tell if he felt guilty, offended, or anything—his face remained perfectly neutral, his tone flat.

"I am sure," she said thinly. She was angry, but it was proper. Nicholas couldn't just treat her like a chore that he could put off. Leaving a young lady in a desert outpost, unable to defend herself, was no joke. He was undoubtedly aware of that, and the blankness of his response was frustrating. It was as though he was ignoring her, treating her as less than himself.

"I am sorry."

His apology only made her angrier. She was exhausted, thirsty, and cold; she'd been waiting for an hour, terrified and alone. And he waltzed in here, with no real explanation, thinking his apology would make it better?

Turning away from him was better than unleashing the anger inside her. She wasn't going to lose her dignity by shouting at him—even that would show him familiarity he didn't merit.

His boots clicked on the floor, and she tensed as he approached. Whirling to face him, she was ready to defend herself.

"I'm just picking up your case," he said defensively.

A vein pulsed in her temple. "I am a woman here alone, sir," she protested. "You do not seem to understand my legitimate fears."

His jaw tensed as he glared down at her from his considerable height. "Please, Miss Newbury," he said through gritted teeth. "I came to fetch you. It's late. I had a busy day. All I want to do is get into the cart."

"As you wish." Her voice was tight. She felt as though he'd slapped her. What sort of a day did he think she'd had? He, at least, had slept in a bed last night and woken in his own home! She didn't even have a home, a job, or a secure future. *How dare he?*

Lucille's anger drained at the thought of her home, leaving her sad and very tired. She bowed her head with no strength to fight. "Let's go."

He followed as she walked to the door, the lantern still in one hand, casting wavering light by the steps outside.

Though Nicholas was silent, it was evident he was still agitated, tightly gripping the case, walking briskly to a covered wagon but with a slight limp that suggested an injury. He offered her a hand, but her anger and pride were too much to permit her to accept. She struggled with as much dignity as she could and settled in the back of the cart.

The sheriff put her case into the back beside her before climbing into the driver's seat. Her eyes were already closed. What purpose was she here for? Why had God brought her to this forsaken place where the sheriff seemed set on mistreating her? It made no sense, but then, she was too tired for anything to make much sense. Too exhausted to think, her mind drifted, thoughts becoming less coherent as she eventually fell asleep.

Chapter Four

Though Nicholas hung the lantern on the wagon's hook, he didn't need it—he could follow the pale outline of the road back to the ranch by ear. He knew every rattle and bump, every curve that led around stony ground and hillock from the trading post to Breakwater, and he could have described it without looking.

However, he was glad that he didn't need to see or think because there was so much on his mind that it would have been a struggle had he needed to concentrate.

He could not stop thinking about the woman in the back of the wagon.

A glance toward her told him she was asleep. He felt as though she still watched him, her presence like the warmth of a fire on his back even when he could not see her.

He had already decided not to like her, but she was beautiful.

Stop it.

He had enough on his mind without his attention drawn toward a lovely young lady. Even if she was the most attractive young lady that he could imagine.

What was so special about her? She had a soft face, dark hair, and a fine figure—what he could see of it under the traveling cloak she wore, at any rate. While her features were neat with a well-shaped mouth and a fresh smell, all those things were secondary. Her big, dark eyes, like pools the color of tea, were what drew him.

She was so beautiful, so full of a mix of gentleness and defiance.

After apologizing for being late, her frosty acceptance amused and stung his heart. What was he supposed to do? Ignore the callout to the ranch where Rider's bandits were stealing food? Just forget he was sheriff for an hour or two for her convenience?

Sighing, he realized he was judging. She was scared, and it was not a matter of convenience or inconvenience. The countryside was dangerous, and how much more so was it for a young lady than for him?

It's not unreasonable.

Grown men were afraid in this countryside. A pile of old fabric concealed a rifle in the back, and he had a pistol on him, its familiar weight by his leg. Though he didn't like to use it, he was more confident when it was nearby. In this countryside, one needed it.

The cart rattled along. Nicholas seldom required the old, covered wagon. He traveled everywhere by horseback and didn't need to transport goods large distances. But he'd brought it anyway, having no idea what to expect. He had imagined a fragile, sorrowful young lady with a few luggage cases. He had not expected someone furious, upright, and angry, with dark eyes that cut through him. The one small suitcase and the even smaller yet heavy bag also surprised him. Mr. Chaffee did say she needed paid work, but he hadn't realized how dire her need could be.

While he lived modestly without excess possessions, he had more goods than she did.

The oxen plodded ahead as his mind drifted to town. Tomorrow, he would call a village meeting, discussing additional protection for the townsfolk and the outlying ranch-owners and households. Many townsfolk were infirm and fell under his caring protection, and he worried for them.

The more he tried to think—arming the townsfolk, borrowing men from neighboring towns, and leading them to the caves—the more he realized how dangerous it was and how he would risk multiple people getting injured. But he had no idea how to solve this problem. The only plausible way to address matters was to discuss them with wise folks.

His eyelids drooped. "Almost there." The words were as much for the oxen as himself; the creatures must be tired. It would be a while before he could settle them back in their stall.

Sometime later, half-asleep and swaying, he rattled the wagon toward the barn. Distant lights were in the outbuilding where his three ranch hands slept, and the lamp in the kitchen still burned, meaning the housekeeper had only just gone out to her room in the back of the house. The lamps in the windows made small, still squares of light on the vast, dark landscape—tiny beacons that showed the presence of human life. Staring out over the ranch, he breathed in, deeply moved by the scene.

Oddly, in the silence, with Miss Newbury close by and the tiny points of light wavering in the desert, he felt closer to God than before.

"Here we are," he announced. "Miss Newbury?" he added after a moment.

Hearing no answer, he climbed to check, but she was fast asleep. The lantern shone on her pale skin, highlighting its contrast with the inked strands of her hair. Some strange softness settled on his heart. She was so small, so harmless.

He wanted to laugh, to dismiss his feeling. Miss Newbury was certainly not defenseless—he already knew that. She would have hit him if she could when he arrived; she had done little enough to hide her fury. He carried the suitcases to the house and shoved them inside before returning to the wagon.

Though he knew he should wake her, he couldn't. He stared at her dark eyelashes and pale weariness. It reminded him of when Mr. Radford showed him a porcelain figure when he was a small boy. He had felt intimidated, afraid to touch it in case it smashed in his hand.

Sighing, he gently touched her arm. "Miss?" he called softly. "Miss Newbury? We're here at Breakwater Ranch."

She was so lovely that his breath caught in his throat. His fingers were cool as if she truly was made of glass, each part of him aware of the feel of her shirt and the skin below it.

"We're here?" she murmured, clearly exhausted.

He nodded. While he ached to help her, something compelled him to avoid contact. If tapping her upper arm could make him feel that way, he would not risk lifting her from the wagon.

She staggered out, her boots stumbling on the wood porch as she reached the door and went into the house.

"Your bed-chamber is upstairs," he said carefully. It was the furthest room from his, one that had been a study.

He followed her three paces behind, and his heart filled with a strange, unfamiliar feeling as he watched her struggle up the stairs. It was like water welling up in a desert, one that felt new and exciting and a little bit frightening because he had not felt it for so long.

"Here," he said as she reached the room. "Here are your things."

"Thank you," she murmured.

Desperately awkward, he stood there. In the doorway, her big dark eyes watched him with a mix of weariness and exhaustion. There were so many things he wanted to say—to apologize, offer her comfort, and welcome her. But none of the words were at the forefront of his mind. So few words could express those niceties.

"We could have some bread and cheese for supper...?" he suggested hesitantly.

"Thank you," she sighed, voice raw with exhaustion. "But I'm so tired. All I want right now is to sleep."

"Of course," he said, rubbing his neck. "Of course. I'll let you sleep." As he left, she collapsed onto the bed.

In his room, he tugged off his boots and undressed, barely able to move. It was a long day for him, too, and he was almost asleep as he rinsed his face and hands in the bowl on the washstand. His mind was a jumble of pictures and notions. In some respect, he was oddly calm, though part of him was a tumult of new questions, new queries to his faith, and parts of himself he thought had passed away.

It surprised him that he didn't immediately sleep once he slipped under the covers. Images of Miss Newbury occupied his mind, which was disconcerting and uncomfortable. The struggles with his faith intensified, too. It was as if that wellspring of emotions thawing inside him heightened the conflict between the side of him that believed and the side that just wanted to forget all about love, faith, and the good things in life. Good things could cause such pain. He was still trying to understand all these new feelings and confusion when the thoughts spun out and wandered, and he drifted to sleep.

Chapter Five

After two weeks in the cottage with no money for wood or coal, Lucille was grateful for the sunshine on her face as she woke. And she was lying on a cushioned surface, which was even better than the night spent in a wagon. It was such a relief to be in a bed.

Yawning, she rubbed her eyes and scanned the room. The ceiling was paneled, and there were whitewashed walls. The wooden floor was clean and well-made. The warm mat on the floor comforted her tired feet as she rolled out of bed. It was a plain enough space, with undecorated walls and a single window to let in the light, but it was heavenly after being on the road.

Someone thought to leave a dish of water on the table, and she splashed her face. Despite this pleasant surprise, she was unimpressed by Mr. Barnes—he was rude and unmannerly last night, and she disliked him instantly.

While he might be fiendishly handsome, he was obnoxious.

As she dried her face on a flannel, she remembered Mr. Barnes had carried her bags to her room. She stretched, aware she still wore her travel clothes. The skirt was travel-dusty and rumpled from sleeping in it and would need to be put outside to air. She withdrew a long, brown dress from her bag. All her clothes were dark colors, still in mourning for Papa.

Once she was dressed and straightened her collar, she padded lightly down the stairs, passing the kitchen doorway.

"Morning, Miss Newbury," Mr. Barnes greeted her from the bright interior. Her breath caught upon seeing him in the sunlight for the first time. Without the shadows cast by lanterns or moonlight, he was even more handsome than she realized. He sat at the table, his shirt neatly buttoned, expression unreadable.

"Good morning," she said, swallowing hard. She kept her distance, drawing out one of the wooden chairs at the other end. The room was bright with a few windows, a good wood stove was on the right side of the white-painted space, and the wooden table and chairs were on the left. Though it was a fine house, far more spacious and grander than the cottage where she'd grown up, she was surprised that he chose to eat here. There must be a parlor or a dining room. It was undoubtedly the proper place for a ranch-owner like Mr. Barnes to take his meal.

"Will you take coffee?" he asked, offering a pot.

Lucille nodded, her head pounding with the ache of how much she wanted some. "Yes, please." She hadn't had any at home for weeks due to the expense.

As he poured her a cup, her fist tensed at her side. It sat badly with her that he was being magnanimous. Despite his kindness, she wanted nothing more than to be a physician.

Taking a calming breath, her eyes wandered the kitchen. She was relieved to see signs of someone else on the property. If the pair of boots by the back door—far too tiny for the sheriff—was evidence of anything, it was that a woman must work in the kitchen. It meant she wouldn't be there by herself, which was good. Staying under his roof and taking meals alone with him could become terribly uncomfortable. But the idea of being there longer tightened in her chest.

Managing to find her voice, she asked, "When will I start?"

He scratched his chin. While she couldn't help noticing what a fine chin it was, a part of her felt uncertain of him. Yet, she didn't understand the strange warmth that radiated in her cheeks as she studied him. Nevertheless, it would take more than coffee and a water dish for her to forgive his unmannerly tardiness and demeanor the night before.

"Today?" he asked absentmindedly. "I'll take you to the old doctor's space. There's a room above for you to stay and a kitchen out back."

If she was intended to stay above the workroom, why had he brought her out to the ranch instead? "Well, then," she replied carefully. "Surely, we could have gone there yesterday..."

His eyes never wavered from the table, avoiding her gaze. "You could, but you see, the doctor's rooms have been vacant for a while, and they need to be readied for you."

"I see." Though daunted, she wasn't going to mention that. She'd expected that his reluctance—and the reluctance of others—would be the only challenge ahead. Clearly, there were more obstacles. "So, it could be done in a day?"

"Possibly."

"And then I can stay there?"

"Yes."

Relief washed through her. Having her own home again delighted her more than she could describe. Leaning back in her chair, she relaxed for the first time in weeks. She inhaled the smell of fresh-baked bread, preserves, and milk on the table with a deep breath. It was a feast compared to the last weeks as she'd stretched her last few dollars.

They sat in silence as she eyed the food in between sips of coffee.

Clearing his throat, he stated, "Please, help yourself," before pushing back his chair and excusing himself.

Hesitantly, she helped herself to a slice of bread as he departed. Lucille frowned, having no idea how to comprehend the man's behavior. But she was well-rested for the first time in weeks and one step closer to her dream, so she decided it was best not to speculate.

God had brought her thus far safely, and soon, she would be in her home. It was truly wondrous, and she was grateful.

Once she was comfortably full, she rose to search for Mr. Barnes, surprised to find him at the front door with her bags.

"I brought them for you," he said with a slight bow of his head. "We need to get to town."

"Oh." His kindness to fetch her things collided with the excitement about seeing the town, mixed with a tiny wistfulness about leaving. She was glad to not have to stay here or share another awkward meal with him. So why did she feel reluctant and slightly sad that they'd not talked longer?

Impatient with herself and the feelings she didn't understand, she stood tall as she passed him out the door. He loaded her bags into the cart. This wagon was a flat, low-sided cart, different from the previous night. Clambering up, she winced as she hit her leg against the wood. She rubbed her shin through her skirt, knowing a bruise would quickly form.

"Ready?" he asked, face inscrutable.

"I am," she answered, trying to sound dignified. Back straight, she tried to look like the town physician. But her hair was already ruffled, and it was impossible to read his expression.

Her annoyance was replaced by eagerness and a tiny touch of nerves. She had never gone into surgery by herself and only practiced as a physician once when her father had fallen and needed help. Papa beaming as she recounted her days was one of her most precious memories. Lucille prayed he would still be proud as they set out for the town.

***

The cart rattling down the road distracted her as houses grew nearer on the horizon.

"Here we are, Miss Newbury," Mr. Barnes sighed, looking relieved. "This is Oxplains, my town."

While he sounded nervous yet glad to have arrived, Lucille wished the place inspired her as she surveyed her new home.

A cluster of dusty houses emerged from a slight rise in the arid landscape. They were drab and lackluster and made of mud-faced brick, their thatched roofs gray and sun-damaged under the heat. The road wavered even though it was still early in the morning, warning of a terribly hot day.

Even as Mr. Barnes drove closer, the houses were old and patchy, some with broken windowpanes, seeming desolate. It was upsetting. This town was so unlike any she'd seen. She had expected prosperity similar to Pinewood, which, if not prosperous, was at least habitable. This place appeared terribly neglected.

"Mr. Barnes..." she began, about to inquire if this was, in fact, the town where she'd practice. Before she could, he slowed and then stopped the cart.

"Here we are."

This was the workspace? She would not have thought so. It was an unmarked, whitewashed two-story building on the corner of a small, narrow street of cobblestones. It had a thatched roof, and a lone window showed the upper floor. The fence around it needed repair. The door was scuffed and old. At least the windows were intact.

"Mr. Barnes?" she said carefully, aghast. "This is where I am to work?" He'd mentioned it needed time to be prepared, but that was an understatement compared to its state.

He nodded. "As our physician, until I can arrange another."

Lucille's mouth hung open as though she'd been hit. If she was not so enraged, so insulted by his comment, she would have been ready to see the office and the room overhead. She could've ignored some cosmetic concerns if the inside still functioned as a workspace and lodge. But he insulted her.

As he took her bags with a simple gesture toward the door, she followed, glaring at him as she opened it. Heart dropping, she stopped in the doorway. Every inch was thick with dust. The floor creaked, and the wall sported a big crack, allowing sunshine to peek through. Feeling something beyond disappointment, she pushed the hot, angry tears away.

The place was unusable. The paneled ceiling was thick with cobwebs, the floor was dirty, and the window was ill-fitting and old. Lucille *couldn't* work in this place.

Looking around, the thought of seeing patients in there dismayed her. "I can't work here."

He paused in the entranceway, her bags still in hand. "Why?"

Whirling to face him, she could no longer contain her rage due to his ignorance and insensitivity. "*How* can you even ask me that?"

His brows furrowed with genuine confusion as his green eyes scanned the room. Though a voice in her mind reminded her he was not a physician—*how could he know the importance of a sanitized workspace?*—she was too angry to care. This place had been promised to her, so it was where she had at least some authority to speak.

When she only fumed, he raised a brow, studying her with the same bland expression from earlier, except there was curiosity in his eyes. Despite her attempts to suppress her rage, it finally became too much.

"Come in here," she hissed. To her surprise, Mr. Barnes obeyed. Though his limp was even more apparent, she would have marched him inside regardless. "The ceiling is filthy. I can't operate with clouds of dust falling through it! And the floor, too. How do you suggest I get it clean? And don't even get me started on the wall." She pointed stiffly at the hole where dust floated in the rays of the morning sun.

"Pretty dirty, eh?"

"Yes!" she shouted. "Yes! That's what I've been saying. It's not just dirty; it's unsanitary. I can't have patients in here—they'd die of infection in a week." She glared at him impatiently. "Something *must* be done."

His head titled as though considering. Dark prints rested under his eyes, and his skin seemed paler than she'd thought; she realized just how exhausted he was. But she couldn't excuse this foolery. How could he hire a physician when there was no space where one could practice?

It was inexcusable.

"I'll find out," he stated.

Heat flooded her cheeks, boiling her with fury. When she opened her mouth to object, he held up a hand to stop her.

"Look, miss," he sighed, annoyance bubbling in his tone. "I have a town that needs running, people to help... This is all we have. I don't have time to run around today."

Lucille gaped at him. Nobody had ever addressed her like that. Even in Pinewood, most people whispered behind her back, their fake smiles empty beneath judgmental stares. He was dismissing her, clearly unconcerned with the well-being of his citizens.

I cannot perform operations here.

The thought was heavy on her mind, but she pushed it away. She had an office and a house of sorts. She shuddered to think of the state of the room over the workspace. If that was where she would stay, then so be it.

As he put her suitcases down and walked to the door, she rubbed her face.

"Well?" he said. "You want to see the town?"

Her head shot up. "You mean...you're going to escort me?" His courtesy was even more perplexing than dismissiveness and that strange, aloof manner. "You have time for *that*?"

"I can't just expect you to find the inn and trading store, can I?" He shrugged, ignoring her tone. "I can't go to work until I'm satisfied you at least know where to purchase something to eat."

She blinked, struggling to find words in her mind's cloud of confusion. "Um, thank you."

For a moment, she thought his expression was tender. Why would he stay if he didn't even respect her or care about her discomfort? And if she was such a trial, why did he look so kindly at her? Nothing made sense. Nevertheless, she followed him down the cobbled street and toward the center of the town.

As they walked, her stomach twisted. Oxplains was small, but the intense griminess and poverty of the place were troubling. There were broken windows and weeds on the sidewalk, the hitching post knocked over at the corner, the postbox looking as though nobody had used it for a long while. With deep breaths, she tried not to let herself feel overwhelmed.

Mr. Barnes stopped on the wooden platform outside a store. "This is the inn. You could get a hot meal here this afternoon. General store's a bit further out, but I'd advise you to go when your neighbor goes—I believe she does her shopping on Tuesdays."

"Why would I need to go with someone?" she asked, brow raised. While Pinewood had also been small, she had never felt afraid to wander about alone.

His jaw clenched, not meeting her gaze. "Well, let's say it's better."

Before she could probe him for more details, he continued up the sidewalk a few paces. "Miss Newbury, I must get to the office. I'll drop past the house later this evening to see if you need anything."

"Why?" It felt childish to ask so many questions, but she was bewildered.

But he didn't answer, already walking away, his limp giving him a characteristic gait toward a building across the road. Lucille sighed.

Lord, what do I do?

With his words about safety echoing in her mind, she strolled toward her office. She paused at the bakery, thinking it would be best to buy something while she was outside. Considering the amount of cleaning to do, she didn't know when she would have time later.

After buying a loaf of bread and an iced bun with her last few cents, she returned to the house. She ate the iced bun on the way, the rich, sugary flavor delicious and sticky in her mouth. Once inside, she dusted a space on the stair and sat, exhausted and weary.

With watery eyes and a heavy heart, she prayed. "God," she murmured in the empty space. "I know that You brought me here. You intended me to do something in this town, but I have no idea what. It's too dirty to even practice my craft here. And the sheriff is oppositional. But if You willed me to be here, I know it's because it's what's best for me."

Bowing her head, a sense of peace descended onto her, lifting her spirits.

She was here. This was *her* space, *her* office. If she could fix it, she could realize her dream of being a doctor. The Lord had brought her here, and He provided her with just what she required: A home, a place to stay, and the opportunity to work.

Grinning as she stood, fresh energy coursed through her. It no longer seemed too overwhelming; she was ready. After she rolled her sleeves, she grabbed a broom she'd spotted in the corner. Before she began, she sent another prayer of thanks for the energy the iced bun gave her—she was going to need it.

Chapter Six

Nicholas absentmindedly stared at the cracked panes in his office window. Shaking himself in annoyance, he tried to concentrate on a stack of papers regarding the laws of a boundary dispute. Though he needed to read them today, he kept thinking about Miss Newbury and wondering how she was getting along.

He replayed her shock and disgust at the doctor's rooms. The building had been raided, one of the first to be so, since it had stood vacant for many years, but he was too embarrassed to admit it. Telling her would've made him feel like an incompetent sheriff, and he didn't want her to think badly of him.

Miss Newbury was an unusual woman—she wasn't tearful, as he might have expected. He remembered how she'd settled and accepted the place after a moment of rage. Mrs. Radford, the dearest woman he knew, was much more delicate than Miss Newbury. He'd never met a woman like her. Most women were the gentle, retiring sort, which was partly why he was uncertain of a female physician. After seeing her, he wondered if she really could do what she claimed.

Shaking his head, he chastised himself. If *he* couldn't face the sight of blood, she certainly wouldn't manage it either. Once again, he'd let his thoughts stray to her. Annoyed, he refocused on the documents and read:

Article Eleven: When a boundary stone is disputed, and the stone appears to have been relocated, it is essential that...

"Sir! Sir?" Luke's voice cut through Nicholas' concentration just as his mind settled. Luke stood in the doorway, and the distress on his young face made Nicholas instantly forget his irritation.

"What is it?" he asked, already on his feet.

"Come quick! It's Mr. Leeson, sir! He's just come in from the farm. He's—he's—" The younger man's face was white, and he sounded queasy.

"What is it?" Nicholas strode to the door, boots loud on the floor. As he limped down the hallway, Luke hurried beside him.

"Mrs. Leeson brought him in from the ranch. He's injured, and there's so much blood..." Luke shuddered as though he might throw up.

Nicholas was numb with shock. Bert Leeson was a good friend and didn't live far from Breakwater Ranch. He thought of Rebecca, Bert's wife, who must be terrified.

"Where are they?"

"Their car is just outside the office, sir. She didn't know where to bring him, so she brought him here. The bleeding's bad," Luke repeated. "I tried to fetch Mr. Simmons, but he's visiting family. Nobody knows when he'll be here."

Outside, Nicholas marched around the corner where a small square allowed carts to park. When he considered summoning Miss Newbury, he dismissed it instantly. Why would he send for her if he didn't believe her capable?

A small crowd had gathered around the cart. Rebecca Leeson was in the back, beside a man so pale-faced, it made Nicholas ill.

"Bert?" he gasped. "Let me get to him!" he shouted to the crowd. Though Bert was not a particularly big man, he was strong. Seeing Bert lying so helplessly in the back of the cart, his white flannel shirt dirtied with dust, his honey-brown hair matted with perspiration, alarmed Nicholas. Eyes locked on Rebecca's terrified face and Bert's pale figure, he didn't notice the woman beside him until she spoke.

"Bring him to the office."

Blinking and shaking off his nerves, he recognized Miss Newbury in the crowd. With her traveling cloak and her hair arranged, she seemed different. Perhaps it wasn't her hair, but something about her expression made her firm and strong in ways he hadn't noticed before.

"Miss Newbury," Nicholas said briskly, "you said yourself it's not fit for work." His stomach heaved when he looked at the man's leg, where his wife was trying to tie bandages. The cart was slippery with blood, a pool forming under his leg, dark and coagulating.

"He's lost so much blood," Rebecca whimpered.

"Let me lift him out," Nicholas said, clambering into the cart and wrapping his arms around the prone fellow, wincing as he did so. The stench of blood was pungent, turning his stomach when he touched it.

"He was chopping wood in the yard," Rebecca explained as Nicholas strained, holding the prone weight of Bert in his arms. Although Bert was shorter than Nicholas, a fully-grown man was a heavy weight for anybody, and he was relieved when two men in the crowd came to help.

Nicholas glanced at Bert's thigh, sticky with blood, grateful the wound was covered with bandages; he didn't want to see. He passed Bert, groaning and weak with pain, to his friends.

"I didn't know what to do," Rebecca cried. "I could only think of finding you. Please, help him."

"I'll try, ma'am," Nicholas grunted, attempting to sound kind and calmer than he felt. He swallowed hard, chest thudding.

Bert groaned while two men carried him toward a bench. Nicholas froze as Miss Newbury approached the men, one of them gestured angrily.

Hopping off the cart, he hurried over, hearing raised voices between them.

"I'm a physician," Miss Newbury demanded. "Let me see him."

"Keep away from him," one of Bert's friends, Lewis Canfield, snapped. "We don't need busybodies here when a fellow is suffering."

"Maybe I could ease his suffering," Miss Newbury retorted.

Nicholas sucked in a breath. While he was livid with her for interfering, he could see how hurt she was, and he disapproved of Lewis' rude tone.

"It's all right," he said to Lewis, positioning himself between him and Miss Newbury. To her, he said, "He's overwrought, miss. Best you get back home."

"I am a physician!" Miss Newbury cried, tears welling in her eyes. "Please! I could *help* him. Let me see the wound."

Bert's friends eyed him helplessly, Bert was almost unconscious, and a crowd of curious onlookers stared. He couldn't back down; the town would lose all respect if he acceded to her over his friend. At the same time, he wanted to let her try. The wound was severe. He'd seen enough to know it needed stitching, and that was a skill he simply didn't have. He could bandage something to stop the bleeding, but that was the limit of what he knew.

If Bert wanted a good chance, it might be best to let Miss Newbury try.

Clearing his throat, Nicholas tried to reason. "Lewis, Radley...this lady is what she says, and maybe it would be best if we let her—"

Bert sat up and struggled to speak. "Don't...want her touching me. She might...make it worse."

Nicholas shut his eyes. If Bert refused her help, there was nothing he could do. It would fall to Nicholas to try and tie off the wound, and he wasn't sure it would help. A bloodstain soaked the sand, and though Bert was pale, he didn't even know how to start.

"*Listen*, all of you—" Miss Newbury demanded, but Lewis stepped around Nicholas, jaw set with rage. Nicholas whirled to protect the newcomer, but just as he opened his mouth to talk sense to the younger man, a familiar voice shouted from behind them.

"What in Perdition is going on?" an older man hollered.

Relief washed through Nicholas. *Max Chaffee!* As the man approached, his eyes darted around the scene.

"Max," Nicholas sighed, tension draining. "Look, this fellow's hurt and these men are—"

"Mr. Chaffee, this man needs my help," Lucille stated firmly.

Max came beside Miss Newbury with care in his expression as a father would for a child. He rested a hand on her shoulder, concern lining his sunburned face. "What's happening?"

"Mr. Chaffee...that man is bleeding. I need to stitch his wound. These men are obstructing me." She gestured at Lewis and Radley, who glared back at her.

"Max, I—" Nicholas began, trying to avoid the situation escalating. But Max was not inclined to avoid an argument.

"Look," he huffed, walking right up to Bert's friends. Max was short, stocky, and well-built, despite his age. "I know this lady," he continued. "Her father was the best physician I ever did see. If anyone can help young Bert here, it's her. I can vouch for her. If she hurts him, you can take it out on me."

Nicholas drew a breath. While he had limited faith in Miss Newbury, Max was a dear friend. He didn't want to see him beaten or killed by enraged townsfolk. Before he could protest, Radley shrugged.

"Bert?" he asked his friend. "What would you say?"

Pain lined Bert's face. Rebecca watched him with an agonized expression, hand on his arm. Nicholas couldn't tell if she trusted Miss Newbury or not.

Bert drew a gasping breath. "Let her...try."

As the words left Bert's lips, Nicholas felt weak with relief. Bert slumped onto the bench, and Rebecca stroked his hair. The two friends were silent as the townsfolk whispered.

Max nodded. "I'll help you carry him."

"We'll do that," Lewis interjected. Comforted that the atmosphere had changed, Nicholas watched as the two men lifted Bert's prone figure. Nicholas thought he was almost passed out; his head lolled, and, though he gave a cry of pain as Lewis lifted his legs, it was the only sign Nicholas could discern that he was living.

"Carry him into the sheriff's office," Miss Newbury called. "I'll work on him there."

Nicholas frowned. "You don't have your things."

Miss Newbury raised a brow. "Then you must fetch my bag. This man is too weak to carry across town."

If the situation were less demanding, Nicholas would have laughed. Her proprietary manner, the way she ordered him to fetch her bag, was refreshing.

He ran down the street, heading for the doctor's office. When he arrived, he was astonished by how orderly it was. *She must have spent the morning cleaning it,* he thought. She was a most remarkable woman. When she'd fussed about it oo badly, he imagined she would be too afraid of a bit of dirt to clean it. But he'd made a misjudgment. She had swept, tidied, and even moved the table across the room. His lips lifted in a slight smile.

Remembering the situation's urgency, he located her bag and ran back to his office.

Voices came from the room next to his own. "How much blood would you say he lost? About a cup, say? How fast did he lose it?" Miss Newbury asked Rebecca.

Rebecca murmured an answer too low for Nicholas to hear in the doorway. She remained beside her husband, holding his hand. Bert lay on a desk, his injured leg stretched out, his torso flat on the wooden surface. Miss Newbury was carefully cutting the bandage with a pair of shears. Lewis and Radley helped, one holding a towel and the other leaning on Bert's leg, pressing as Miss Newbury instructed.

"Press there, Lewis. Lean into it and keep pressing until I say stop."

"Yes, ma'am."

It amazed Nicholas that Miss Newbury had taken charge quite easily. The two women tended to Bert; Rebecca spoke softly to him while Miss Newbury swiftly clipped at the bandages and the remains of Bert's trouser leg, stiff with dried blood. Though her hands were red up to the first joints of her fingers, she didn't seem overly bothered.

"Here," he said, offering the bag to her.

"Put it there on the chair," Miss Newbury said. "And open it. Thank you," she added as she glanced at him. She was frowning, deep in concentration, and Nicholas stepped back as she selected what she needed from the bag. He felt oddly useless, oddly respectful as he watched her work.

Miss Newbury withdrew a small vial of needles and a length of suture in another. She threaded the needle neatly before removing a small pair of scissors and a roll of bandage. If she was nervous, it was almost impossible to see.

"Now, Lewis," she said. "You need to keep pressing. Radley, hold his hand. He's going to need to grip on something. Give him this if he needs it," she added, passing a strip of leather. Nicholas guessed it was for him to bite on but thought Bert was too close to passing out to have the energy for anything like that. Miss Newbury approached the wound with the needle in hand.

Nicholas's stomach contracted, and he thought he might be sick. He'd seen plenty of wounds before, some just as bad, but he always felt nauseous. A deep, straight cut about the length of his finger was across the man's thigh. It gaped in the middle, shallower at the edge, and the blood had crusted black around it while more trickled out. Glancing away, Nicholas heard Bert draw in a breath as Miss Newbury started stitching.

"Easy, there, it's all right," Rebecca murmured.

Despite his stomach, he couldn't help watching Miss Newbury. She was focused on her work, lines on her brow where she frowned. She threaded the suture through once, pulled the wound shut, and tied it off. Nicholas had seen wounds stitched once or twice by Mr. Simmons and knew that she would place each stitch individually, tying each one off separately, unlike when one darned a hole in clothing.

After Miss Newbury cut the suture, a slight gasp escaped Bert as she stitched again. Nicholas hadn't noticed if she had given him brandy for the pain. Five stitches later, she straightened.

"You can carry him to a couch." The men watched her with absolute awe. Nicholas would have laughed had he not been so relieved.

"Yes, miss," Lewis nodded.

They carried their friend and his bandaged leg out of the office. Nicholas watched approvingly as they placed him on the long, padded seat in the hallway. Rebecca sat with him, her hand gentle where she touched his head. Bert had slipped into unconsciousness as Miss Newbury worked, but he would live and walk around.

Lewis and Radley collected their coats, muttering thanks to Miss Newbury before leaving. Nicholas hadn't noticed Max in the doorway across the corridor.

"Well done, Lucille," Max said proudly as he entered. Nicholas wished he could say that to her—he reckoned she wouldn't want him to. All the same, he admired her, and he wanted to tell her so.

She looked to Max, swaying on her feet, and Nicholas stepped forward. She was bone-weary. As he went to catch her, Max drew out a chair.

"Here, sit," he said gently.

Nicholas froze, helpless and stupid, as Max went to the water pitcher on the windowsill and poured some for Lucille. She thanked him, drinking deeply.

Lucille was pale, a smudge of blood on her neck where she'd pushed a stray hair away after the operation before wiping her hands. She was clearly fatigued, and he wished he could tell her what a terrific job she'd done.

"You need to rest," Max said. "Gerard would be so proud of you."

"Max... I'm just so tired," she murmured. Max took Lucille's hand as she sniffled. Watching them, Nicholas felt unwelcome, so he left.

Though he wished he could help Lucille, he had already made her mistrust him. He could only guess it was because of his reservations about her fitness to be the village physician. It was apparent she did not see him in a positive light. He drew a deep breath. She was clearly competent—at least as far as sutures went—and he felt stupid for having doubted her. But he had no idea how to get on her good side.

Pushing his thoughts aside, Nicholas went to find Luke and check on Bert in the hall. His sorrow for letting Lucille down didn't matter anymore—all that did was how he would make it up to her.

Chapter Seven

Lucille's back ached, her head swam, and she was utterly drained. She'd felt something like this the first time she'd stitched a wound—the intense focus and the need to stay calm and self-contained drained her like she'd been awake for days. She'd been weary after all the cleaning; now, she was entirely exhausted.

At least the exhaustion blocked out a lot of the other confusion in her mind—the insult of being dismissed by the farmer's friends, the concern for the man, and the elation of saving him. Lucille sat on a weak chair in her office. Leaning back against the wall, she shut her eyes. Though she needed to cook, clean, and make some sort of order out of the filthy room she was supposed to live in, she didn't have any energy left.

She remembered her father so clearly. He had got tired like this, too—admittedly, not after something simple, but after a complicated operation, he had been completely and utterly drained. His lined face was vivid in her mind, his dark eyes ringed with gray from lack of sleep, his mouth tight at the corners. Recalling his smile, her heart ached. She wished he was there and could tell her what to do, how to cope with all her feelings.

Out of all the things that occupied her mind, her thoughts could not release that she had completed her first job as a physician in Oxplains. She couldn't deny it to herself anymore—she really was a physician.

"God, thank you," she whispered. Beyond all other emotions, she was awed by that fact.

She was a practicing physician.

Lucille grinned, too tired to do anything else. When she rose to clean the room upstairs, her head pounded, so she sat again. She couldn't recall eating anything beyond the iced bun mid-morning. It was suppertime, but she couldn't think of finding the energy to make food, even to cut some of the bread she'd bought and left somewhere in the kitchen.

"Miss? Miss Newbury?" a man called, followed by a tap on the door.

"What is it?" she replied, her voice like a whisper. As she rose to open the door, she felt as though her body was carved from stone, each part so heavy that she could barely walk. Someone opened it from outside, and she froze, remembering dimly that she hadn't locked it.

"Miss?" the voice repeated, and she recognized it as Mr. Barnes.

Her jaw set as he entered, feeling as though she had to defend herself. She expected him to insult her, to tell her that she had to leave Oxplains. Her heart raced and, despite her exhaustion, she wanted to run away, far away, where he couldn't threaten her.

"Miss, I came to see how you are," he said with a gentle smile. "You had a long afternoon, and I wanted to check you're all right."

"Oh." Lucille stared up at him, his green eyes full of concern. Why did he want to check on her? When she tried to see her patient, he'd supported the townsfolk. He'd been impatient with her opinions about the doctor's workspace and barely listened to her when she tried to explain how she couldn't work there. Why was he acting like he cared what she felt like?

"I needed to check if you're all right," he repeated softly. "You worked so hard this afternoon."

Lucille raised a brow in surprise. At that moment, she wanted to take refuge in sarcasm. He hadn't even believed that she could perform a basic operation like stitching a wound, so why was he acknowledging what she had done?

"Thank you," she muttered. If there was sarcasm in her tone, Mr. Barnes didn't notice.

"I wanted to ask if I could bring you something," Mr. Barnes added, "since you will need to prepare your own meal tonight." He scanned the room as though taking in the cleaning she'd done, but her exhaustion could no longer hold back at the mention of staying there.

"I can't clean upstairs," she whispered. She plopped in the chair, covering her face with her hands. "It's *disgusting* up there. I can't sleep there. And there's no food in the house, and I have nothing for the fire."

She hadn't expected it, but she cried, noisy tears that ran down her face. Now that she was too drained to push it aside, all the strain flooded in: the pain of losing her home, the terror of those uncertain weeks, the sorrow for Papa. All of it burst through the dam of her reserves.

Lucille rocked and sobbed. As she sat there, footsteps crossed the floor. She expected him to storm out, to tell Max that he couldn't possibly have her as the town's physician. But she couldn't do anything to hold back anymore; the tears were flowing, and she couldn't stop them, not for anybody's opinion.

"Miss? Miss?"

Tears streamed down her face, shoulders shaking. She couldn't sit still, and she couldn't stop crying. Weeks of grief, anger, and shame possessed her, begging for release, needing acknowledgment.

After a few minutes, she realized that a figure kneeled in the dust before her, one hand gently on hers where it rested in her lap. Her brain worked so slowly, trying to comprehend it.

"Miss?" Mr. Barnes repeated gently, his face a picture of tenderness. "Miss, please. You don't need to stay here. You can stay at the ranch. You can work here when I come into town. You don't need to live in the town to be our physician."

The words didn't seem to mean anything, her mind driven to a place where speech didn't make sense anymore, only her pain. But as he squeezed her hand, repeating the offer gently, it cut through the exhaustion.

"I don't need to stay here?" she whispered as if she had misunderstood him. It seemed almost impossible, too good for her to believe. She watched his face, trying to see if he meant what he promised.

He smiled, green eyes crinkled at the corners. "Yes," he said. "Yes. You can stay in the attic, where you slept yesterday. There's no reason for anyone to think anything about you staying under my roof because my housekeeper would certainly tell people if there was." He chuckled.

Lucille couldn't help but laugh. For a moment, laughing took her mind off her sadness. "You really think I could?" she asked.

Mr. Barnes nodded. "Of course, you can. You helping around the house would take a weight off me, too. I know you're a physician, and it seems a bit...well, rude of me to ask, but if you could do the washing, and..."

She sniffled. "I don't know how good I'll be at starching shirts. I've never actually done that."

He laughed; it was lovely, low, and melodious. Sitting on the floor, his arms rested on his knees as they talked. It struck her that he must've kneeled for quite some time, and she wondered if his injured leg was sore. Still, his eyes were kind when he smiled.

"Well, I might be the sheriff, but I am not fussy about starched shirts. I don't look that formal—no need around here." He gestured, encompassing his thick cotton shirt and leather trousers. His coat was of superior quality, but aside from that, he really dressed no better than most farmhands.

She giggled, and neither spoke for a moment. Mr. Barnes' expression was friendly as he rose to his feet. It was as though they became aware of where they were—that they were alone in her office.

Too tired to care too much about propriety, she stood as well. "I'll wash my face," she sighed.

She was grateful she filled a pitcher earlier at the pump. The injured farmer interrupted her plans of a late lunch and a trip to the general store to purchase soap and lye to disinfect the surfaces. Splashing her face, the water soothed her enough to do it several times.

"Here," Mr. Barnes said once she faced him, holding a linen cloth. "You can use this."

Lucille smiled and accepted the cloth, which was stitched neatly around the edges and had something embroidered on it. Her fingers brushed his as he passed it to her, and she drew a deep breath at the contact. Warmth rushed up her arm and into her face, and she blushed.

After she dabbed at her face, Mr. Barnes cleared his throat.

"I can take you out to the ranch now if you want."

"Yes. Thank you," Lucille murmured, noticing it was getting dark fast. She'd lit a candle earlier, and it supplied the only light which shone on his face. His eyes were tender as he watched her. "I'll get my workbag."

"I'll fetch the cart," he said.

Lucille watched him leave, and she looked around the darkening room, blindly reaching for her workbag. Her suitcase was in the corner too, the weight impossibly heavy as she gathered it up. She carried the bags to the door and waited. A few minutes later, there were footsteps on the entryway and a gentle knocking.

"Are you ready?" Mr. Barnes asked caringly when she greeted him.

Lucille nodded with a grateful smile. She carried her case but didn't comment as he picked up the work bag, which was too heavy for her. He effortlessly put it into the cart, and she clambered unsteadily into the back. She was too tired even to sit on the front seat beside him, uncertain if she could maintain her balance.

Mr. Barnes snapped the reins, the horse snorted, the cart creaked, and the wheels rattled. Rocked by the sounds and motions, Lucille fell into restfulness, her father's face at the forefront of her mind.

Chapter Eight

The harder he tried to forget Miss Newbury's presence in his house, the more his mind returned to it. As he sat alone, his bed-chamber and mood darkened.

"Have I been stupid?" he groaned.

Almost giving up on anyone answering, he was surprised by the positivity that returned to his thoughts. He didn't feel that terrible dead emptiness that responded to his prayers; instead, warmth radiated through him.

Sitting by the fire, he noticed the lengthening shadows where the firelight flickered in the grate. Though he knew he needed to sleep, his mind kept worrying about the problem of Miss Newbury under his roof. Max Chaffee would be the first to mention if there was any hint of impropriety. After all, he clearly cared deeply for Miss Newbury. In any case, Miss Newbury could not stay with Max—he had no housekeeper and nobody else besides one itinerant worker on his ranch, which would look truly terrible for Miss Newbury's reputation.

No, staying with Nicholas was the only possibility that made sense until such a time as the rooms above the doctor's office could be satisfactorily repaired and renovated.

Nicholas ran a weary hand through his thick, dark hair, deciding to ponder those problems tomorrow. He couldn't waste more time on them tonight.

He changed into his nightshirt, wincing at the pain in his knee. Even minor things made it hurt, exhaustion, standing too long, and when he was bothered about something.

This matter with Miss Newbury weighed on his mind.

After he washed his face and rinsed his mouth in a bowl of water on the nightstand, he lay in bed.

He fell almost immediately to sleep, thoughts filled with Miss Newbury. He was confused by how he felt—both deeply protective and strangely resistant—and didn't understand it.

***

The following morning, he woke before the light, a habit that developed when he was young and helping with the horses and other animals on the Breakwater Ranch. Now, with his duties as sheriff, he left that work to the three ranch hands who looked after the horses and cattle for him. He hadn't slept deeply, and he reckoned it was all the worries on his mind—his dreams were taken up with the bandits and the other problems.

Stiff and drained, Nicholas rinsed his face and changed into his white cotton shirt. The curtains were half-open, and he could see his reflection in the small round mirror on the wall over the nightstand. He needed to shave, and he looked tired as well.

When he was dressed, he half-stumbled down the stairs and took a deep breath, inhaling the tasty aromas coming from the kitchen. He also heard voices coming from the kitchen, which was unusual for this hour in the morning. Blundering into the candlelit space, he found his housekeeper, Mrs. Grierson, and Miss Newbury.

"How long should I cook it for?" Miss Newbury asked.

"It's cooked," Mrs. Grierson replied.

Nicholas wanted to grin warmly at the smell of burning toast but kept a straight face as he went to the table. Miss Newbury looked tense, and he didn't wish to offend her. Her long brown hair was loose from its simple style, the locks curling in the kitchen's heat. Still, she looked astonishingly pretty—her cheeks flushed, and her soft skin was pale in contrast.

Nicholas was still staring at her when she brought a plate of toast and eggs to the table.

"I tried to cook breakfast," she sighed.

He couldn't conceal his grin. The toast was blackened, the eggs were crisped on the outside, and the yolks were hard and crumbly. But by the hopeful expression on her face, he couldn't bring himself to traduce her efforts. "Thank you. It's good."

Miss Newbury's beautiful eyes searched his face, and he knew that he wasn't fooling anybody. She knew what toast and fried eggs looked like, and what she'd made didn't look right. But at the same time, she looked as though she hoped he wouldn't spot it.

"Thank you," she smiled slightly.

He waited for her to sit. They had eaten breakfast together just yesterday, but she went to the copper washbasin where the pans were stacked. Mrs. Grierson was busy cleaning the stovetop, her long black, graying hair tied back in a bun.

Self consciously, Nicholas ate his eggs and toast. The toast tasted like charred wood, and the eggs were almost tasteless, the yolk powdery and dried. But when one was hungry, anything tasted good, and Nicholas was hungry, so he ate.

Eating in silence, he noticed Miss Newbury's face. Her jaw was stiff, and her expression sorrowful. Some strands of hair stuck to her neck. He wanted to console her but had no idea what was wrong. *It must have something to do with her past.* She had just lost her father. He realized he knew nothing of her story—he only knew that she had been in dire circumstances and needed help.

"Miss Newbury?"

Tears were in her eyes. He didn't want to upset her further, but she dashed to the door before he could say anything.

Not knowing what to do or say, Nicholas remained in his seat, breakfast cooling fast. After a long moment, Mrs. Grierson went to the sink.

"Go after the girl." Mrs. Grierson had a strong accent due to her Hualapai ancestry.

Nicholas waited, but the housekeeper didn't seem like she would enlighten him about what happened.

"She's just tired," he murmured; whether to inform Mrs. Grierson or reassure himself, he didn't know. Mrs. Grierson continued cleaning, so Nicholas went to find Miss Newbury. Her boots had been by the front door, but they were gone. Wondering if she was outside, he fetched his boots and coat, praying he wouldn't make things worse when he found her.

Chapter Nine

The yard was still a little dark with the morning, and Lucille blinked, unable to focus on her surroundings. Lights flickered in the windows of a long, low building. Too sad to care or think about who might be watching, she leaned against the cold stone wall and let tears fall.

I am so useless.

It was silly—she knew she wasn't useless. She just hadn't cooked before—at home with Papa, Mrs. Whitestone did the cooking. But on top of the townsfolk's attitude yesterday and being too exhausted to work, she was frustrated and sad. Could she not even make food?

The wind ruffled her skirt. Though it was still cold outside, she didn't want to go back into the kitchen. She didn't want to face Mr. Barnes again. He must think she was so stupid! She couldn't even cook a plate of food. He'd already saved her by bringing her here, and now, she was proving that she couldn't even do the basic tasks he requested.

Her heart ached as she cried. Why did she come here? There was no reason for her to be in Oxplains or on this ranch. She'd let herself believe God had brought her here for a purpose, but now, it was hard to hold onto that belief.

"Miss?"

She tensed. Mr. Barnes was at the kitchen door. Having gone around the corner, she remained perfectly still, hoping that nobody would hear her.

Go away, she thought. *Let me stand out here and cry, at least.*

Footsteps approached, getting closer as she stared at the horizon. She didn't want to talk to Mr. Barnes—she could see him just at the edge of sight, standing at the corner of the wall. He stayed where he was, speaking in a faint voice meant for her ears.

"I know it's hard," he said gently. "You did so well. It's your first day on the job. You know, my first day on the ranch was funny. I was kicked by a horse, slapped in the face by a cow's tail, and fell into the trough. You should have seen the other fellers laugh."

Despite her resolve to ignore him, Lucille chuckled as she imagined it.

"You, see?" he soothed. "It's always hard, learning something new. I know it's disheartening, especially when you're good at your job."

She sniffed. "I'm no good at that, either. I'm only here because I can't even do that." Tears poured down her cheeks. Silently, she let them slide into the collar of her shirt. Why did he have to stay here and watch her? Crying was embarrassing enough without someone watching.

He spoke so softly that she could barely discern his words. "It's all right," he continued tenderly. "It's all right. You are good at your job. Bert is fine. He could have died—he would have, even, if you hadn't been there. You saved his life." He took a deep breath. "Nobody else in the village could have done what you did. I am so glad you were there. Truly, I am." Lucille was amazed, but he continued. "You are particularly good at what you did, and if it wasn't for the rooms being filthy in town, you'd be there, doing your job."

The care in his words was apparent, and the fact that he was outside in the chilly air, missing out on an early ride to work, was enough to show his support.

"Thank you," she sighed.

As he stepped closer, he tilted his head, studying her with a slight grin. "Miss, you don't need to thank me. I am glad you're here. Now, it's better if we step into the warm kitchen."

Lucille nodded. His green eyes were so tender as he met her gaze. Even as she tried to be strong and ignore the sorrow and gentle feelings that crowded into her heart, her heart melted.

Seeing his gentle smile, she couldn't help smiling back before quickly looking away. She didn't understand the warmth that flooded her heart when she looked at him, and it was confusing. She'd gone from desperately trying to hold back her tension and unhappiness to being angry and sad, and now, she wasn't sure how she felt. While she still felt awkward about the breakfast—it wasn't how she'd intended it to turn out—she knew he wasn't angry or disappointed, which soothed the feeling of uselessness that had settled on her chest.

At least he didn't think she was useless.

Mrs. Grierson was cleaning the dishes when they returned.

"I'll help with those," Lucille said caringly. Mrs. Grierson smiled at her and stepped back to check the fireplace. As

Lucille washed the dishes, she exchanged shy glances with Mr. Barnes.

"I'll be back around seven o'clock," he announced. "I'll see you two ladies then."

"Have a good day's working, Mr. Barnes," Mrs. Grierson called.

"Have a good day," Lucille echoed.

Lifting his hat, he grinned at them both before hurrying out. Lucille bent her head over the basin, scrubbing a pot with burned remains of breakfast clinging to the bottom. She couldn't help thinking about Mr. Barnes and his handsome face as she did so, those green eyes gentle with concern as he looked at her.

That man might be kind, but he opposed you being here.

She tried to make herself angry with him, but there was none. She couldn't help liking him. He had been so kind to her, so understanding. It was new to feel like this. The one or two times she'd met men close to her age were brief. While she had no idea how she felt about him, try as she would, she couldn't sustain her frustration with him for not wanting her to practice as a physician. He'd been so kind and supportive since then that she had to forgive him that, at least.

Wanting to aid Mrs. Grierson with as many chores as possible, Lucille was relieved when some didn't take as long as she expected.

"Right," Mrs. Grierson said when Lucille was drying the plates. "Now, we need to do the laundry. You go upstairs and get the sheets—Mr. Barnes will have left them outside his door—and we'll wash them together."

Lucille's throat tightened. It was something she hadn't considered, but, being his housekeeper, she would be in contact with his sheets and other intimate things. It made her feel a strange shyness. She had seen men without their shirts in her father's office for checkups and should not feel bashful at the thought of somebody's sheets. At the same time, she couldn't help it. The idea of washing Mr. Barnes' clothes and linen seemed so odd.

After a deep breath, she found her courage. She would take the position of housekeeper seriously. Though she might never have done it before and might not know much about it, she would learn as much as she could and do it as well as possible.

Her footsteps were quiet as she climbed the stairs, and she spotted the pile of sheets neatly outside his door. Collecting them, she inhaled the slightly musky scent.

Stop it. Don't think about it.

Lucille pushed the thought of Mr. Barnes away, his smell strong in her nose. She had not noticed before that he had his own smell—leather, mixed with a scent she couldn't describe that made her think of wood or the rich aroma of dust and sweat.

With the linen in her arms, she went out into the yard, where Mrs. Grierson filled a tub with water.

"It's warm," Mrs. Grierson said as Lucille dumped the sheets. Washing sheets and other things was a task she had done for herself, so she rolled her sleeves and scrubbed at the sheets with the bar of laundry soap Mrs. Grierson gave her. They worked in silence. It was demanding work, and there was perspiration on her brow, the sunshine growing hotter as their day wore on.

She straightened, back throbbing, as Mrs. Grierson hauled the washing out and dumped it in a basket. Lucille tipped the tub out, gasping at the strain on her arms, while Mrs. Grierson fetched a bucket.

Once the laundry was hanging on the line, Mrs. Grierson declared that they had completed the morning tasks. "You can go and rest for an hour. We'll make the lunch at around eleven o'clock."

Lucille's back was strained and sore, her arms tired. Her hands were raw from rubbing the laundry, and once she was in her bedroom, she rubbed the salve into her hot, reddened skin, grateful she'd brought it.

"Is this really why I am here?" she murmured, directing it to God as much as to herself. Leaning back on the bed, Lucille shut her eyes, exhausted. She didn't get that blank emptiness that greeted her prayers before; instead, she had a warmth in her heart. It was pleasant, and she was surprised when Mr. Barnes and his smile when he spoke to her that morning emerged in her mind.

There is some reason for my being here.

She smiled as she opened her eyes again. It seemed peculiar and impossible that she had gone from Pinewood to Oxplains. Then, instead of practicing as a physician—which had elated and terrified her—she worked as a housekeeper. It was a job for which she had no skills whatsoever. The fact that she'd be a better physician than a housekeeper was almost funny to her, or it would have been, had she not been so grateful for the job.

She sat up; she couldn't let herself fall asleep, or she might not wake in time to help with the lunch—a task she was determined to learn.

Learning how to be a housekeeper was as challenging as her first suture, and she grinned to herself, remembering how her father had been so proud of her then. He always said she liked tasks to be hard to feel satisfied when she achieved them. And he was right. She would learn to make the best fried eggs this side of the world—just see if she didn't. She stood, fresh warmth filling her, knowing that she would make this something to enjoy.

Chapter Ten

Nicholas's heart thumped as he scanned the ranch. There'd been a bandit sighting, but he couldn't spot them now. Luke rode beside him, and another young man, Chris, rode further behind.

"I can't see them." He jerked his head at Chris. A ranch hand by training, Chris expressed an interest in defending the town, so Nicholas fetched him from the Gable's ranch before coming out here if he needed backup. "Chris? You spot someone?"

"Clear up that end, sheriff," he called. Nicholas dismounted, joining the ranch owner and his wife, who remained by the house.

"You, Luke?"

"Nothing, sheriff," Luke answered, staring eastward, where the empty landscape stretched toward distant hills.

A tall, thin-faced youth, the ranch hand looked as if he expected a reprimand for sending them out so needlessly. "You did the right thing to send for me," Nicholas assured the young man who'd ridden into town to summon him.

"We saw them in the distance," the ranch owner said. He was an older man with white hair, face seamed and dark with exposure to the harsh light. "Over there, where that hillock stands. We were frightened they'd come raiding. They stole all the supplies from the Cranehill ranch."

"I know," Nicholas sighed. He'd already been out there to inspect the damage. Recalling his anger and the frustration of not being able to help, his shoulders tensed. A man had been injured there—struck a heavy blow with a stick when he tried to defend the supplies—and Nicholas wondered how he fared since there he could do so little to help the man. He was glad that the ranch hand had fetched him—better that he and Luke faced the dangers of the bandits than the townsfolk and ranchers. Though he had already seen the damage they could do, he didn't want to see more.

"We are glad you came out," the ranch owner's wife said gratefully. Her white hair was concealed under a headscarf, her face friendly and warm. Her wool dress was dark gray, and he couldn't help recalling that Miss Newbury also favored dark, plain colors—but then, she was still mourning.

"I am glad you informed me," Nicholas said, annoyed with himself for getting distracted from his work. Making a mental note of the terrain, he thought he'd ride over there with Luke and a few men tomorrow. He could borrow Alfred and Glen from the ranch since there wasn't much work on the ranch. If he was going to go anywhere near those fellows, he'd need backup. Two men on their own were no fit opponents for the group of bandits camping out there in the northwestern hills.

"Can we offer you dinner?" the wife offered.

Nicholas smiled. "Thanks, Mrs. Burwell. But I ought to get back to town. Chris? You want dinner?"

Chris grinned, nodding enthusiastically, and Mrs. Burwell chuckled. He looked gratefully at Nicholas and swung his leg down from the horse, dismounting with the ease of someone riding since they were a child.

"Thank you, sheriff!" Mr. Burwell called after Nicholas.

"Sure, Mr. Burwell. Send for me immediately if they come back," Nicholas called as he rode his horse to the gates, not wanting to tax the poor steed's strength. He might need to get away fast if the bandits were around. His chances against a group were small as one person riding alone. He allowed his thoughts to drift to Miss Newbury again on his ride back.

***

He arrived in the early afternoon, watering and feeding his horse before striding to the inn, his leg aching.

"Hey, sheriff," Mr. Elwood greeted him as he winced, sitting at the bar. "The usual?"

Nicholas nodded, knowing he should have felt hungry. After all, he'd not eaten any breakfast, but his stomach churned. This problem with the bandits was getting worse. This was the first time someone had reported them abroad in full daylight and this close to town. Mr. Burwell had reported five men, all with horses, which meant more men had joined them.

This is getting tricky.

The tragic thing was, part of his mind understood the bandits—desperate men with no experience outside of being soldiers, returning from the war—what else had life for them?

However, he blamed the situation. Young men, trained only in violence, embittered and fueled with resentment, were released into a world that didn't fit them. What other life was possible besides a life of thieving? Shutting his eyes briefly, he wished that God could send him answers.

"Hey, sheriff," a man behind him called. Nicholas's eyes opened as the barman set a plate of stew before him, spiced and with bread to match.

He recognized the man who spoke. "Hey, Mr. Canfield," he greeted. He was a relative of Lewis, Bert's friend.

"My nephew told me something interesting yesterday," the man began, "he told me that he'd seen you in the street with Bert, and a woman physician is practicing in Oxplains?" The man's eyes widened.

"Not right now," he explained hesitantly. "The office needs mending."

"Oh." The man leaned on the table, just close to where Nicholas sat. While his manner was relaxed enough, Nicholas was aware of his pistol by his side as he felt his muscles stiffen, ready to act. "Well, that relieves me. I thought you'd clean lost your wits." Mr. Canfield chuckled.

Nicholas frowned. In part, he would have sympathized, but now, it agitated him. It was no surprise that people would respond like this—he perceived it differently from how he would have just a day or two ago. He'd seen the young lady at her job, and really, she was capable.

"Anyone knows a lady isn't capable. It isn't right. We need a physician we can trust."

Nicholas struggled to hold back his irritation. His knee ached, and he shifted in the chair. His fingers were white where they pressed on the table, trying to rein in his temper.

"We'll be glad when you get a real doctor, but we're not taking this lady on," Mr. Canfield commented as he walked away. "You know the rest of the fellers agree with me on this."

Nicholas turned back to the barman, grinding his teeth. Mr. Canfield might appear to have no more power than any other rancher, but he was the most prosperous farmer in the area, and besides that, many of the others were related to him. The Canfield family was large and represented the only truly wealthy family in the district. What he said was not wrong—the other ranchers would follow his lead. And besides, they didn't need much persuading in that view.

A frown tightened his brow, and his stomach twisted. In addition to the stress about the bandits, he had additional pressure from the townsfolk refusing to recognize his authority. For now, he'd sidestepped the issue of a female physician, but how long could he continue to do so?

Nicholas ate his stew and bread without enjoyment, the chunks going down his throat without real relish. He barely spoke to anyone, his head too full of thoughts.

Once he returned to his office, he greeted his deputy as he limped to his desk. In the hallway, the young man was all fresh-washed skin and earnestness. As Luke followed him in, Nicholas noticed him shifting about awkwardly.

"Sheriff," Luke said, scratching his neck. "We had a report from the Cranehill ranch. Mr. Cranehill said he's repaired the damage."

"Good," Nicholas replied, slumping forward with relief. When he noticed Luke scratching under his collar again, he frowned. "You all right?"

Luke's face turned red. "Fine, sir."

"You don't seem all right."

Luke shrugged. "My skin's a bother, sir," he said, rubbing under his jacket. "Nothing, really. Just an itch that bothers me. Worse in severe weather, sir."

"Take a lie down if you need to," he sighed. He wished he could offer the young man reprieve, but there was no practicing physician in Oxplains right now, and his knowledge extended only to bandaging and a little to stitching wounds. He certainly knew nothing about a skin problem.

"Thank you, sheriff." Luke seemed pleased. "I won't be more than half an hour, sir. I'll nap out back in the yard if I may?"

"You do that, Luke," he nodded. "And look after that skin, hey?"

"Will do, sir!"

Exhausted, Nicholas leaned back in his chair. He'd been here only a few hours and already felt like he'd done a day's work. His feet hurt, his knee was like fire, and his hands were chafed with riding.

Resting for a moment, his eyes were half-closed as he wondered about Miss Newbury and how her work was going. *It must be tricky,* he thought with a grin, *for her to learn so many new skills.* He wondered how it was that she'd never cooked an egg before and was curious and interested. He'd not really had a chance to talk with her and hoped he could talk more. Recalling her tear-stained face that morning, his heart twisted. He would not have guessed how defeated she'd feel, tackling all these tasks that must be so new to her. If nothing else, he hoped she was getting along well.

By the end of the day, feeling weary but not as confused as he had, Nicholas was on horseback, riding to the ranch. It was just getting dusk when he arrived at the gate, the smell of dirt in his nostrils as he jumped down from the saddle, wincing at his sore leg.

The sunlight was still low on the horizon, the rich red glow of sunset streaking the cooling sky. Calm filled Nicholas when he opened the door and went inside.

As the two women looked up at him, he beamed. Mrs. Grierson and Miss Newbury were at the fire, making tea.

"Good evening, ladies," he lifted his hat. "Something smells good."

"Thank you, Mr. Barnes," Mrs. Grierson greeted.

"Thank you," Miss Newbury echoed wearily.

"What's for supper?" he asked, pausing to rinse the dust off his hands in the copper washbasin.

"Fresh bread and cheese," Mrs. Grierson answered. "And stew from lunchtime, if you want some."

Nicholas thanked them, actually quite hungry, and it felt good to have his appetite back. Once he sat at the table, he realized that the kitchen was cleaner. The stew Mrs. Grierson put in front of him tasted different, too—he couldn't quite say why, but it seemed more wholesome. The bread was a little stiff, and he wondered if she had left her helper in charge of cooking it. Other than that, the benefits of having a housekeeper and cook seemed appreciable.

Mrs. Grierson announced she was turning in for the night, bidding them a good evening. Nicholas glanced up from his bowl, noticing Miss Newbury was still there, the firelight playing over her skin, giving a new aspect to her face. Nicholas froze as Mrs. Grierson shut the door softly behind her, leaving him alone with Miss Newbury.

Though Miss Newbury's bowl was still half full, she wasn't eating. She was quite stunning, her profile soft, her face sweetly oval. In the darkness, with the livid orange lamplight, she seemed so young and defenseless. Overwhelmed, he cleared his throat.

"Sir," she said shyly. "Ought I to go?"

Nicholas frowned. She was so unlike the fiery young lady who'd fought to protect Bert. He wondered why she seemed reluctant.

"No, please," he responded quickly. "Stay. We both have as much place here as each other."

She nodded, her eyes wandering again.

"How did your first day go?" he asked. He coughed, his voice straining.

"It went well enough."

They sat in silence as they ate. Nicholas wished he could think of something to say, but nothing sprang to mind, and the chance to contribute any comment grew smaller with each second.

"What is it, miss?" he asked hesitantly, but she was about to leave the kitchen. It shocked him that he desperately didn't want to lose the chance to speak with her.

"Nothing." When she looked up at him, her lips were set in a line.

"If there's trouble with the fellers or anything bothering you," he continued humbly, "let me know."

"There's not any trouble."

Though he wished he could cut through the awkward silence, he didn't want to press her further. He could only watch as Lucille finished her stew, washed her dishes, and walked out. Miss Newbury's subdued nature was so out of character that it troubled him.

Nicholas went to the stairs, wincing at the pain in his knee. Her footfall was neat and quick as she moved about her room above, and he was reassured by her presence. His heart was filled with so many emotions—his interest in her, his curiosity, and his delight whenever he saw her. He had loved his parents and the Radfords, but life showed him that caring and affection were like a knife—if you chose to use them, they would cut deep. Early on, he had decided that he would rather stay aloof from painful, dangerous emotions like falling for someone.

Reminding himself of this, he retreated to his room and sighed after the arduous task of removing his shoes, leaning back. Just sitting down with his boots off was a wondrous rest.

Washing his face, he wondered if Mrs. Grierson had told Miss Newbury where the pump was and hoped she had. He'd ask her some time; no point worrying now about whether she had water. After undressing, he slipped a nightshirt over his head.

His glance fell on the bed as he recalled putting the sheets outside the door. The bed was neatly made, the starched sheets folded back at the corner. He gulped. Mrs. Grierson might have made it, but he would have recognized the style—she always left the pillow on top of the covers and tucked in the left and right sides to the top. This wasn't Mrs. Grierson's work. A strange sensation traveled down his back—a mix of embarrassment and delight that he couldn't name.

Miss Newbury had been up here; he was sure of it. He visualized her tucking in the bedsheet corners with the same focus and care as she treated sutures. Nicholas felt unexpectedly vulnerable, and he flushed.

Stop being such a fool. She made your bed. She is the housekeeper—that's going to happen every week as long as she works here.

Nicholas folded back the sheets, pushing away the vision of her slim, pale hand as he held it, patiently letting her cry. He couldn't let himself imagine anything about her.

As he lay in bed, his mind chased itself in circles. The bandits, the townsfolk, the upcoming meeting he needed to plan about the new physician... All the troubles refused to let him rest. Though he wanted to pray, he did not even know which issue to pray about. His mind was filled with things he needed to do, like the meeting with the ranch hands to discuss the pasturage. He had so much to do, but the trouble with the physician was uppermost in his mind. It was the one that had concerned him the most. How could God land so many problems on his head and then provide him with a solution he couldn't use?

Rolling onto his other side, he murmured a prayer. "God, grant me Your guidance. I need it."

He sighed. He was sure a better prayer or some verse would comfort him, but he couldn't think of them now. He fell asleep to memories of Bible studies at the ranch, Mrs. Radford sitting at the table in the parlor with the printed copy resting on the desk in front of her. In a dream, he imagined her beckoning to him, showing him something, but he couldn't make out what it was. His thoughts drifted to breakfast and Miss Newbury's newfound skills at the stove before falling fast asleep.

Chapter Eleven

Lucille scrubbed, polished, and washed the floor, her eyes barely focusing. The cleaning tasks were at least familiar to her, but the tiredness wasn't because of the work—she'd been awake for three hours already, and it was only eight o'clock. She stretched, her lower back a mess of pain. Taking a moment to rest, she leaned against the counter. Her mind was hazy with weariness, and she took stock. Mrs. Grierson swept the rest of the house, leaving Lucille to clean this room.

She replayed the morning in her head. Mr. Barnes had come down for breakfast once the bread was already freshly baked, and he'd eaten without much talk. She hoped he must have noticed that the bread was better than her first batch, though she hadn't risked glancing at him. Avoiding his eye, she'd busied herself fetching water from outside. He asked if she had slept, and she'd said yes, and asked him likewise, but they had not conversed further.

Tucking a strand of dark hair out of her eye—she had coiled her hair and pinned it back, but it had come undone while she cleaned the floor, and she hadn't stopped to redo it—she limped up the stairs to find Mrs. Grierson.

She'd had little chance to explore, peeking into the rooms as she headed to hers, but her curiosity was piqued. Mrs. Grierson swept the parlor, seemingly not noticing Lucille's presence. The pale wood floor was shining, and the walls were white and fine. A big window looked out onto the stony desert view, and a fireplace stood in one corner, faced with stone tiles. The furniture in the parlor was of the finest quality—a leather-covered chair facing the door, a rug, and a low table to her right. The painting on the wall caught her eye, and she couldn't help staring.

"Miss Newbury?" Mrs. Grierson asked, sweeping the dust from the top of a bookshelf.

Her cheeks flushed as if she'd been caught in some mischievous act. "I was wondering if you needed something."

Mrs. Grierson smiled. "No, I'm just tidying. I'll be done in a minute or two. You could straighten that rug, there? I'll make some tea for us. You can join me when you're ready."

After she helped Mrs. Grierson straighten things, Lucille hesitated, reluctant to go into the kitchen. Curiosity overwhelmed her.

The oil painting was a portrait of young people. The woman had delicate, golden-blonde curls, and the man had brown hair. He had a friendly face, kind and smiling cheerily, and Lucille instantly liked him. The woman appeared so kindly too, her blue eyes gentle, staring out with a wise, half-smile.

Lucille studied the faces. Gentle and soft, and sharp and pointy. Neither of them looked like Mr. Barnes. Were they relations of his? Mama and Papa? She realized how little she knew about him. The house always seemed prosperous, but seeing the furnishings in the parlor, she realized that Breakwater must have been very successful at some time in the recent past. The rugs, leather chairs, and paintings all indicated wealth and affluence.

Mr. Barnes was a mysterious man.

Glancing up at the people she presumed to be his parents, she wondered about her mother. The only image of her she had ever seen was a sketch drawn by a family friend on thick paper with a delicate pencil. It showed a woman with a soft face and big, soulful eyes. Lucille had asked Max to keep it for her and the only possession of her mother's—a little glass container for face cream, the glass prettily faceted, and the painted porcelain lid. They were some of her most precious possessions.

It was silent in the hallway, and her footsteps echoed on the stairs. How many years had this place been standing? Had Mr. Barnes grown up here, running up and down these stairs when he was younger? She imagined him as a small, cheeky-faced boy, those green eyes sparkling in earnest as he ran and played about the house. She smiled. It was all information she longed to have—the stories of his childhood, the tales of how he became who he was nowadays. The desire to get to know him was exciting, and she was bemused with herself.

The kitchen was as clean and bright as she'd left it that morning. Mrs. Grierson beckoned Lucille when she saw her. "Come and have some tea," she said in her low, melodious voice.

Lucille joined Mrs. Grierson at the table. The tea was flavorful, and the warmth soothed her. But even the sweet, sugary taste could not raise her spirits. Deep down, she was weary.

"I'm going to take a rest," Mrs. Grierson announced. "I'll come up to the kitchen at midday to cook. A man brought onions this morning. I have a mind to cook up a new stew flavor. I'll come up to the kitchen around midday to cook," she smiled.

Lucille nodded, touched to see the woman's pleasure in her work. When she had first met her two days ago, her physician's eye noticed the pain in her joints. She was glad that she could help. It was so quiet, the kitchen clean and warm, the smell of tea mixing with the scents of vegetables on the counter and the lingering aroma of carbolic soap.

While she couldn't imagine another day like this, she knew that she had no escape—this was the safe place God had brought her to, and she appreciated that fact. Here, she had food and a bed and work, which was all she'd really wanted. Despite her gratitude, she still felt uncertain about her purpose.

God was looking after her, but she was so frustrated that He'd offered her the chance of working as a physician, then snatched it from her.

Was He showing her that she was inadequate?

She wasn't inadequate, was she? She really had helped that man. It seemed unbelievable that the Lord would bring her all this way to show her she wasn't that good. And He had shown her she could do something—she'd had to do a complex task without Papa helping. Succeeding in stitching the man's leg all on her own had made her so proud of herself. Was that wrong?

Was she unable to practice because she had been arrogant?

Lucille went to the sink. It didn't feel right to her—she had been proud, but it was a good pride, that of a worker who knows they're skilled. There was no sin in recognizing talents—in fact, Christ had encouraged His followers to use all the Lord's gifts. It seemed hard to believe that God was reprimanding her for that.

"Lord," she whispered. "I wish to do Your will here. Please, I humbly ask that You show me what it is and guide me on that path."

Her words were the only sound in the silent kitchen—not even the hearth fire crackled. With a deep breath, a sense of peace washed over her. For the first time in a long while, she was sure her prayer was heard. After rinsing the remaining cups, she went up to her bed-chamber.

There was a long day ahead, and even if she felt clouded, tired, and unsure of what she had been brought here for, she would have to complete the tasks set out for her.

***

A week later—carrying out tasks, learning, and feeling slightly more competent—Lucille's spirits lifted, and she decided to take a walk outside.

It was still cool outdoors, and her steps drew her to a path she'd noticed earlier, curious about the ranch that bordered Breakwater. She judged it was at least a ten-minute walk but close enough for her to see a house from the very gentle slope on which Breakwater was built. Chickens were wandering near the house, and a woman emerged, a basket on one arm.

The path led down the slight slope and across the field, and as she neared, she lost sight of the neighboring ranch. When she rounded the bend, the woman was still there, hanging the washing outside the house. Lucille's cheeks reddened as the woman caught sight of her. Afraid of being accused of trespassing, she held her breath.

"Hey!" the older woman shouted. Her voice was strong, even though Lucille guessed from her white hair and gait that she must be older. But her tone was welcoming, not defensive. "Hey, miss!" The woman waved, her arm encased in the sleeve of her brown linen gown. "Good morning to you!"

"Good day," Lucille responded politely. She was tempted to return to Breakwater Ranch, not wanting to explain who she was, when the woman approached.

"Hey there," the woman greeted. She had a long, slim face, high cheekbones, a kind smile, and a friendly expression; her turquoise eyes were bright, bracketed with lines. "Sorry for disturbing you," the woman smiled. "I'm Mrs. McCauley. I live there."

"Hello," Lucille murmured shyly. "Sorry I was loitering—"

"Please! No need to bother yourself," she said warmly, offering a hand. "I'm pleased to meet you. Not many folks out here." She tilted her head. "So, you must forgive me for being so eager to meet you."

Lucille shook her hand, squeezing it in her own. Mrs. McCauley's fingers were cool, and her palm was soft yet thickened with years of work. Studying her face, joy at meeting someone so genuine welled up in Lucille's heart. "I'm Lucille Newbury," she said. "Pleased to meet you."

"Good to meet you, Lucille. Please, call me Matty," she chuckled. "I'd be glad to welcome you for tea. I baked a cake this morning and have nothing to do with it."

"Matty, I'd be delighted." Lucille's heart skipped at the idea of having afternoon tea for the first time in weeks. "I have work to do, but I'd be pleased to visit if I can. I keep house for the sheriff." She indicated the ranch with a gesture. Under any other circumstances, she would have been worried to mention that she worked for the sheriff—it was an awkward position for a young girl to be in, unchaperoned in a man's home. But she felt Matty would understand—something about her warm demeanor suggested she was not the sort to think such things.

"Of course! Mrs. Grierson's getting too worn out to look after such a big place. Good," Mrs. McCauley nodded. If she thought it was improper for Lucille to stay at the ranch, the thought didn't show. "Well, if you can call on me, I'd be delighted." She gestured to where the chickens were scratching the floor of a shallow-sided pen. "I should see what my chickens are about. The naughty creatures fly out when you turn your back."

Lucille laughed, her spirits lifting as the new friends went their separate ways. Her steps were lighter, as though she floated back to Breakwater Ranch.

***

After helping Mrs. Grierson to prepare for the evening meal—a task of baking more bread and cutting cheese and boiled eggs, Lucille mended and sewed while Mrs. Grierson ironed. When a clock chimed somewhere in the house, she realized it was already three o'clock. She needed to tidy herself up if she went to tea next door.

"When I'm done with my chores, I'm going next door to have tea with Mrs. McCauley," she told Mrs. Grierson, her throat catching. She wasn't sure how it would be received—as part of the staff at Breakwater, was it acceptable for her to pop out for a visit?

"That's good, miss," Mrs. Grierson said.

Lucille thanked her, and when the mending was done, a task she felt well equipped to do, she went upstairs to change. After choosing a brown dress she particularly liked, she combed her hair, coiling it into a neat bun.

I look presentable, at least.

She reckoned this dress was one of her best, thinking the oval neck was flattering and that the style was modern enough. Though she suspected that the older woman would not judge her from the richness of her clothes, she wanted to make a good impression on Matty.

She studied her reflection. Whether or not she was beautiful was something that had never preyed on her mind much. Living with Papa, doing the cleaning, nursing, and making calls with him to the neighbors had never led her to consider her appearance, other than to worry that she was clean, tidy, and presented an air of crisp confidence when assisting him. Now, she assessed her looks.

I do look pretty.

Flushing, she was unable to stop staring at herself. It felt as though she'd never confronted this aspect of herself. Turning in front of the mirror by her bed-chamber fireplace, she saw herself as a stranger might for the first time. She stared at the soft, gentle-eyed creature who stared back, awestruck by how they looked.

If the sketch was accurate, her mother's face was not too different from hers. She didn't recall the details all that clearly, but the softer lines of the face were like hers. Her eyes were not quite as soulful, though there was a similarity there.

What would her mother say, seeing her now? Lucille wished she had known her, that she was here to guide her.

The clock chimed again, and she hastened downstairs. It was half an hour past three, and if she wanted to be in time for tea—which she assumed was around four o'clock—she should hurry. The sunshine was baking now, the day hotter than the last few had been. Crossing the yard, feet hurting in her stiff boots, she headed toward the McCauley ranch.

"Good afternoon!" her neighbor greeted after a single knock. Lucille smiled. Mrs. McCauley had donned new clothes, a white blouse and a skirt, her gray hair framing her long face. They were both dressed for the occasion—likely because it was rare to see other women out on a ranch or have any chance for socializing.

"Good afternoon, Matty," Lucille smiled at her, using her name due to Matty's insistence.

Matty grinned. "Come in! It's so good to have a visitor. A woman gets so lonely out here on the ranch. You must have noticed that, surely." With Matty's friendly look on her face, Lucille's shoulders relaxed, and any hesitations washed away.

"I have."

She followed Matty through to the kitchen, the warm, wood-paneled house comfortable to her. It was much smaller than Breakwater, but it felt familiar and cozy to her. She breathed in the smell of sponge cake. The soft, buttery, sweet steam reminded her of when she was a girl, and a neighbor had brought cakes to share at teatime. Abruptly, tears welled, and the edges of her mouth tugged down.

"Sweetie!" Matty said as she noticed Lucille dabbing the corners of her eyes. "Why, my dear, you look quite sorrowful."

"Sorry," she sniffed. Matty set a slice of cake in front of Lucille, glowing with care. Talking with others was not something that came easily to her—she had become accustomed to herself and Papa being alone together; the only visitors from their town were Mrs. Powell and Mr. Longford. But at this moment, with all the familiar aroma and closeness of a friend, looking at her with such tenderness and understanding, she could no longer hold her secrets inside.

"I was just, well... It's been hard."

"Lucille, sweetie, whatever it is, you can tell me," Matty said gently, sitting beside Lucille, covering Lucille's hand with her own. "Sorrows are best shared."

Reaching into her pocket for a handkerchief, Lucille sniffled again. She wiped her face while Matty watched her with gentle blue eyes.

"Sorry," she sighed. "I...I lost my father a month ago. And the bank took our house. I missed simple things, like visits and having tea with someone." She knew it would sound odd to anyone who hadn't lived a similar experience.

Her neighbor, who was fast becoming a friend, nodded. "I understand. It was rare for me when I first moved here, too." Her smile was kind, but the first hint of sadness flickered across her face. "I was from Prescott, you know. A big town." She shook her head. "James was from here but left to work as a journalist in Prescott. He saved, borrowed, and bought this place." Her eyes flicked over the room as though memories were paying before her. Matty chuckled. "I was not the object of friendship among the local ladies. A woman from another town, marrying James?"

Lucille grinned, easily imagining what Matty had gone through. She already sensed the hostility and suspicion of strangers and wondered how long the village had been like that. It must have been so for the last thirty years. "You must have been lonely."

Matty nodded, reaching for a white, porcelain teapot. "Desperately so. I was isolated out here, and nobody wanted to talk to me." She sighed. "In the town, it was worse. The ladies ignored me. It took ages before people started to talk to me."

It was as if Matty's words healed Lucille's heart. The locals didn't accept her, and it had been deeply troubling, causing her to question herself. If she wasn't a physician, if she was different, maybe she would fit in. Matty was a lovely woman: kind, openhearted and warm, yet, she'd been isolated and pushed out of Oxplains. Just because she was new, the locals mistrusted her.

Tears subsiding, Lucille looked around the kitchen and its paneled walls, lit with bright sunshine pouring through the window. It was warm, close, and intimate, unlike the imposing, cold kitchen at Breakwater. Even the small stove was neat and tidy, and there was a pot with a design drawn on it that contained herbs for cooking.

They ate, drank, and talked about comfortable things such as the weather or Matty's garden. Lucille listened and contributed words occasionally, happy to listen. Though she didn't want to address it directly, she waited for something about Mr. Barnes to be mentioned. Somehow, it would feel better if Matty were to raise the topic.

"I say," Matty said contentedly as she reached for her cup. "It must be almost five. I should put supper on the stove."

Lucille agreed and stood, admiring the small, wise woman who walked her to the door. It had all been so quick, yet she knew they must have talked for a few hours. She wished she had asked Matty more questions and even told her about her role as a physician. But she'd been reluctant to raise it since she wasn't sure how Matty would respond or what she'd think about female physicians. Now, she felt anxious to mention it, in case her reaction was the same as the villagers.

"You must come and call again," Matty said warmly. "It was a lovely afternoon."

"Thank you," Lucille said sincerely. "It was good to talk with you."

"Not at all. My pleasure, truly. Please, call again. Perhaps we could go to Bible studies together on Friday?" the woman suggested. "I host it in my kitchen. It's very friendly—just a few ranch women talking about the Good Book."

Lucille swallowed. Friday was in three days. The thought crept up her spine—she was met with hostility in town and was hesitant to meet new people, regardless if they were from Oxplains. "Maybe."

"I'll ask closer to the time." Matty patted her hand sweetly. "But tomorrow, we could have tea again? There's still all that cake to eat, and it would be good to sit with company."

"Thank you. It would be fun," Lucille nodded. She meant it. Talking to Matty had lifted her spirits, and she hoped she'd have time to see her again. The discussion soothed some of the pain and fear inside her after being unable to work in the town.

"Good. Good. We'll see one another over tea and cake tomorrow."

Their plans to see each other were established and Lucille decided she would do her best to make time. As she strolled to Breakwater, she felt better than she had in a long while. It had been stimulating and just what she needed. Already, her emotions felt less muddled and painful.

Removing her boots outside the kitchen door, she breathed in the dry, earthy smell of the yard. The day had cooled off while she was at tea, the shadows growing. In an hour or two, it would be sunset.

Lucille beamed, thinking that Mr. Barnes would be back soon. She was amazed by how much she looked forward to his presence after their rocky beginnings. Even though she was uncertain about him, she still enjoyed having him there. Since they still needed to prepare the bread for tomorrow and fetch the laundry, she went upstairs to dress more simply. But she wished she could leave the brown dress on. Some part of her felt better being elegant and knowing she looked nice and hoped for another opportunity soon.

Chapter Twelve

Weary, Nicholas breathed in the scent of cool earth and water from the trough. It was a good smell, clean and earthy, and he waited a moment longer, savoring it and trying to find calm. It had been a long day.

His meetings with Miss Newbury were confusing. Miss Newbury changed a little more every day, shrinking into herself and losing some of that shine. It reminded him of the river pebbles he and some of the younger ranch hands and neighboring boys collected for their games—if left in the sunshine, they became dull and ordinary, but when wet and polished, they shone until glossy and smooth. Miss Newbury had lost that shine over the last week, and somehow, he believed it was his fault for bringing her to the ranch. He added it to the list of things that made him feel useless.

When he walked into the kitchen, the first thing that struck him was a woman giggling. The two women—Mrs. Grierson and Miss Newbury—looked up when he entered.

Mrs. Grierson stood, wincing at a pain in her back. "Evening, Mr. Barnes," she greeted him.

"Good evening," Nicholas said politely, eyeing Miss Newbury. It struck him that she was dressed in a gown prettier than the simple, unadorned gowns she typically wore. He stared into her lovely dark eyes.

"We were talking about stew recipes," Miss Newbury stated, her tone akin to keeping a secret.

"I am glad to hear it." Though curious why they were laughing, he didn't push the matter.

"Your food is on the table, sir," Mrs. Grierson said from where she stood at the stove. "Bread, cheese, and boiled eggs."

The thought of the eggs reminded Nicholas that he needed to speak to Grant—the chickens needed a new fence around their coop, or the predators would be getting in at night. "Thank you, Mrs. Grierson." Nicholas sat at the table, thinking boiled eggs with supper was a positive change. He glanced at Miss Newbury, who remained where she was.

Mrs. Grierson bid them goodnight, limping to the door that led to her room, a bit away from the ranch hand's dormitory.

"Goodnight," Miss Newbury called. Mrs. Grierson bestowed a smile on her, a bright grin that lit her dark eyes from within. Nicholas smiled too. Miss Newbury was a likable person—sweet, considerate, and compassionate. Though he might not have seen that side often, he had witnessed her care for Bert and his wife. He wished to convince her to trust and like him a bit, too. But she seemed so diffident and standoffish with him.

Chewing on some bread, he waited for her to say something. It was soft and a little moist—just as bread should be. If Miss Newbury had made it, she had acquired skills in a shorter time than he would think somebody might. He wished he could ask her if she had made it but was too shy to raise the topic, resolving to ask Mrs. Grierson later.

He cleared his throat. "Did you have an enjoyable day?"

Miss Newbury rose as though to leave. "Yes."

Nicholas raised a hand. "Hold on a minute," he said softly. "I didn't mean to chase you away."

She sat again, eyeing him. There was bread and a small slice of cheese on her plate—she hadn't eaten anything yet. He hoped she was eating enough, though her face was still gently softened, and he didn't think she had lost weight.

They watched each other, and he thought he noticed a brightness in her eyes, a relaxation in her pose that wasn't present in the earlier days. Emboldened, he smiled hesitantly. "You are settling in?"

She shrugged. "I guess."

Nicholas sighed. He'd hoped she would tell him what caused that change—what had made her seem happier today than before—but she didn't elaborate further.

"I know it can be hard here," he said gently. "It's pretty isolated." He gestured outside, just visible through the windows that showed the distant landscape beyond the yard.

"It's not too different from anyplace else," she shrugged. "Just fewer humans about."

He chuckled softly. "I reckon that's the most accurate description of ranch life I ever heard."

Brief humor sparkled in her eyes. Each smile felt like a victory. They sat quietly, but the silence was not taut and stretched.

"How was your day?" Her voice was bright, and the tone was uplifting.

He blinked, stunned that she returned the question. She hadn't ventured to ask him anything before.

"I guess about regular," he sighed. "Some fellows saw the bandits; another fellow believes someone moved a boundary stone. Took a while to convince him not to hit anyone with it." He chuckled.

Miss Newbury's smile widened. "I imagine he was fuming somewhat."

"A bit."

They both snickered, and Nicholas smiled at her. It felt so good to see her looking so alive, so beautiful. He couldn't express how that extra bit of happiness made her glow within and transformed her, like a candle inside a stained-glass sconce that made the colors glow. He wished he could tell her that; he wished he could relate to her how beautiful she was. But he was desperately shy when it came to Miss Newbury. Besides, all of that was emotional territory, which was dangerous territory.

"I hope it wasn't too demanding," she added, nibbling on a slice of cheese.

Nicholas shrugged. "Not bad, no. Better than in a while." Leaning back in his chair, he gazed at the ceiling. It had been a better day, almost relaxing by the standards of recent weeks.

"Good." She looked as if she wanted to ask him a question. He waited at length before she asked it. "What made you take a job?"

His brow rose. "You mean, what made me want to work besides being a rancher?" He tilted his head. When she nodded, he started slowly, "I guess I wanted to do something for someone besides myself. I could have sat out here and raised cattle and been prosperous. It's a thriving piece of land, a nice house. It's got a water source and everything." He gestured. "But it didn't feel like enough. It didn't satisfy me inside." Nicholas flushed when he realized he hadn't ever talked so openly to anyone. "Silly, huh?"

"Not silly at all," she murmured. Her dark eyes stared at him, lit from within. The flamelight danced between them both, painting inscrutable shadows on her face.

"When old Mr. Rowell, the former sheriff, was a few years off retirement, I chatted with him. We'd worked together—I used to ride out with him when he needed help—and he made me his deputy. I wanted to take on the task, and the villagers trusted me, so I did it." He smiled. It had been such a good feeling but also frightening. The responsibility of twenty families' well–being had settled on his shoulders, and it was a daunting feeling.

After a moment, she asked intensely, "It was your divine calling?"

He sighed. "I guess. I don't know—I guess I never really thought about it." When he accepted the job, he had just been regaining his faith. After his childhood struggles to come to terms with what happened and make sense of it, he'd taken a long time to return to any sense of belief.

She nodded slowly. "I guess one doesn't know." She fell quiet, and her head bent as she focused on her plate, as if his answer had somehow added to the burden on her shoulders.

He felt her pulling away from him across the table, growing distant and dark.

"What about you?" he swallowed. "I mean, you followed a different path. Not many women think about following in their father's footsteps."

"No," she replied. Her expression was haunted again. "No, I suppose they don't."

Nicholas drew a breath. He had hoped that she would share her story; tell him more about her extraordinary path. But remained silent, and he watched her posture closing in, shutting him out. She ate the bread and cheese, not seeming to enjoy it but simply eating because she had to.

"I'll see you tomorrow," she said, pushing her chair back.

Something inside him couldn't let her walk out yet. He rose and followed her to the hallway, pausing at the stairs.

"If I can do anything to help," he said caringly. "Anything at all, please tell me."

As she gazed into his eyes, her eyes seemed clearer and brighter, and his heart skipped.

"Thank you," she smiled softly.

Standing before her at the stairs, it was difficult not to take her hands, the sudden change making him want to comfort her. The lamplight was on her hair, making her eyes lucent pools in the darkness, and he ached to touch her. His entire arm had tingled for about an hour when he'd tried to wake her in the wagon. Though he longed for that sensation, he knew that if he did so, it would change everything.

"Goodnight," he murmured.

Something flashed in her eyes, a smile remaining at the corner of her mouth. "Goodnight," she replied, her voice gentle.

Without thinking about it, he rested his hand on her shoulder, just the briefest touch, but it made his heart race. When she didn't recoil, relief washed over him. She smiled, a sudden flash of warmth, before quickly ascending the stairs.

Almost forgetting to breathe, Nicholas's heart soared with feelings, mystified. After a deep breath, he returned to the kitchen, his smile mirroring hers.

Chapter Thirteen

Though it was barely light, Lucille rolled out of bed, accustomed to rising early. Her mind still raced with the thoughts of what had happened the day before.

He touched me.

The memory whirled at the forefront of her mind, filling her with too many emotions to name. While she felt hesitant and bewildered, his eyes had been caring. She could not help recalling Mr. Barnes' hand, resting just softly on her shoulder. She had never been touched like that—she had never imagined that a single touch could feel so different, so utterly unlike anything she'd felt before. Just the feel of his hand coursed through her body like fire, igniting her heart and making her soul want to sing. It was nothing she could put into words; she didn't feel like she knew how to describe it.

Lucille grinned. Before, she always believed those ideas were fiction—that a touch could ignite someone from within, or resting a hand could alight a heart. But now, she would not scorn poets because, for a moment, she had become one.

Now, that is silly. Lucille giggled, feeling lighter than a breeze.

It didn't feel silly, though. Something profound changed inside, and she didn't understand it. In the last week, her perception had altered. When she first met Mr. Barnes, she was determined to dislike him, perceiving him from the first as aloof and oppositional, not believing in her as a physician. But now, she saw so clearly that he had a good heart.

Getting dressed felt less arduous, as did rinsing her face and pinning her hair. Practically skipping downstairs, she felt ready to start her.

"Good morning, Mrs. Grierson," she greeted in a sing-song voice. Mrs. Grierson was already preparing the trays on which they would bake the daily bread. With a friendly smile, Lucille realized that she would never have known where to start without Mrs. Grierson instructing her.

"Morning, Miss Newbury," Mrs. Grierson replied politely. Even after over a week, they were not yet comfortable with first names. Lucille decided they had to do something about that.

Rolling up her sleeves, she mixed the flour and the fresh yeast from the pantry, where Mrs. Grierson kept it warm under a cover. They worked in companionable silence, and when Mr. Barnes came down for breakfast, the kitchen smelled deliciously of the first baked bread. Mrs. Grierson grinned at him, passing him a teacup as they exchanged pleasantries.

Lucille smiled at Mr. Barnes, her cheeks pink. She didn't understand her sudden shyness. "Good morning," she said softly.

He grinned warmly, and they stood for a moment, staring into each other's eyes. After yesterday, after their conversation and that brief touch, she felt intrigued about him and needed to assess him anew. Lucille assumed he felt the same since he held her gaze. Though Mrs. Grierson seemed focused intently on the tea, Lucille blushed deeply and glanced away upon remembering her presence.

"I'll get water," she murmured.

Embarrassed, she hurried outside, her body flooding with heat. She was still distracted, lost in their gaze, and filled the water on the force of habit. When she returned and placed it on the counter, Mr. Barnes and Mrs. Grierson sat at the table.

Lucille needed to keep thinking about something else, so she washed the dishes. If she turned to see Mr. Barnes, she'd be staring. And then Mrs. Grierson would notice and ask them what happened, and she'd be mortified.

"You can eat breakfast first," Mrs. Grierson said with slight amusement in her voice.

"Oh." She flushed, drying her hands and rushing to a vacant chair. "I quite forgot about breakfast." She hadn't expected to feel so flustered. Somehow, being near him was throwing her mind off its usual course. Acutely aware of Mr. Barnes, to her right at the head of the table, Lucille stared at the bread, neatly sliced on the wooden surface.

"Do you have to go shopping today?" Mr. Barnes asked her. "I wonder if I should take the wagon into town to work today."

"No," Lucille stammered, glancing at Mrs. Grierson. "I don't think we need anything."

"I'll go on Monday, sir," Mrs. Grierson said. "We have enough of everything to last until the weekend."

Lucille swallowed, looking down at her plate. Her eyes had drifted to him as he spoke casually with Mrs. Grierson, and the moment he glanced at her, she beamed without really understanding why. She watched him eating, casting furtive glances sideways, her cheeks hot.

"I'll be back at around seven o'clock, as usual," he announced as he rose from the table.

Lucille nodded. "That's good."

When he paused in the doorway, they locked eyes again, and a small smile lifted the corner of her lips. He waved to them both, and Lucille did the same, feeling childish.

Mrs. Grierson didn't notice, setting about her daily duties of wiping the table and sweeping the floor. "He's a nice man, Mr. Barnes," she said after a few moments.

"What?" Lucille choked before composing herself and nodding. "He is."

"Nice and kind," Grierson continued. "I guess you don't think so at first. At first, he's got teeth in his mouth and nothing else. He's so quiet! But he's a nice man. Friendly."

"He is a good man," she nodded.

Mrs. Grierson smiled. After they finished tidying, Mrs. Grierson limped to the door. If she had any insights about Barnes, she didn't share them, just removed her apron and left, dragging her sore feet.

As Lucille scrubbed the counter with soap, her heart raced, and her mind whirled.

What happened yesterday?

She went from being trapped in her worries and concerns as though her heart was bubbling with spring water. The change was so abrupt that even she couldn't follow it.

"God," she sighed contentedly. "I don't know what happened, but I am glad about it."

It had been a while since she had felt this warmth when she prayed. If anyone would understand this, God would. She certainly didn't understand it. For the first time in a long while, she felt more at peace with her faith, somehow closer to God.

By teatime, she was ready to call on her neighbor. Dressing for tea, she bounced over, heart flittering with joyfulness.

"My! You look energized," Matty chuckled as Lucille sat at the table.

"I am, Matty. I feel better."

"That's wonderful," Matty smiled warmly. "The Lord be praised."

"Quite so."

While they ate cake and drank tea, Lucille spoke openly with Matty, something she had thought she'd forgotten how to do. It had been so long since she'd had a friend, someone who would listen without judgment, and she poured out the concerns of her heart, telling Matty about her calling and how confused she was.

"You must remember Colossians," Matty reminded, taking a moment when Lucille quieted again to contemplate. "I don't recall the words, not exactly, but I know it says in Colossians, somewhere, that we must do whatever work we are given to do because it is work for Christ."

Lucille nodded. Bowing her head, she did remember that. "You are right." She paused to consider it. Though she still didn't quite know why Christ wanted her to be a housekeeper, if this was where God had brought her, she was ready to accept that He knew what He was doing. "The Lord has mysterious ways," she grinned, recalling her father quoting that.

Matty agreed, and they shared a smile, an unspoken bond intertwining them.

The conversation was delightful and freeing. Still, Lucille's mind drifted to Mr. Barnes, wondering what he was up to. She looked forward to seeing him again soon.

Thanks to Matty's gentle reminder to trust in God, Lucille considered the offer she made last time. A Bible study group would be a bit intimidating—so many new people and some who would resist her or be against her being the town physician—but, at the same time, her faith felt strong, and she wanted to explore it again.

Nervous, Lucille hesitated. "Matty...um...would it be possible for me to attend Bible studies with you on Friday?"

Matty beamed. "Of course!"

Lucille let out a breath she wasn't aware she held and leaned back in the chair, joy flooding her heart.

The excitement and joy in the new connection grew every moment, and after chatting with Matty a while longer, she hurried back to work again.

When Mr. Barnes arrived, Lucille was just cleaning up the plates. She smiled at him as he came in, and he returned the gesture before removing his hat and sitting at the table.

"That looks good," he said, taking a big whiff of the rich broth.

She thanked him, absentmindedly tucking her hair behind her ear, despite it being pinned back.

Mrs. Grierson eyed her with amusement before muttering something about being tired and leaving the kitchen. Lucille reddened as she sat to eat.

After supper, when the dishes were all in place and drying on the sideboard, Lucille became increasingly aware that she was alone with Mr. Barnes.

He seemed to be focused intently on the centerpiece candle, cheeks red. "Did you have an enjoyable day?" he asked.

"Yes. Thank you."

The fire popping on a wood knot in the grate was the only sound. The air felt tense, so she took a few deep breaths.

He shifted in his seat, seeming as uncertain and reluctant to break the awkward, intense quiet between them as she was. "You are certain you had a good day?"

Lucille nodded, a soft smirk at the corner of her lips. "Certainly." Her voice was tight, and she cleared her throat, thick with nerves. She sipped her tea, taking solace that he seemed equally uncomfortable. It seemed impolite to rush off, but at the same time, she didn't know how to talk to him. She felt desperate to stay longer but was unsure how to.

"Miss," he coughed awkwardly. "I hope you're well." He hesitated, rubbing his neck. "I mean, it's been a challenging time for you lately. Being in a new town, finding a new place, and being bereaved. I never told you how sorry I am for your loss."

She blinked, overwhelmed by his kindness and fighting the urge to cry.

"Sorry," he added quickly. "I didn't mean to upset you. You...you must miss him."

After a moment, she couldn't keep her feelings to herself—about Papa, the house, and more than anything, about her calling. She slowly shook her head. "It's not that. Well, it is. I mean, I cry for him too. But, well, it's not just my father I've lost. It's me. It's my sense of who I am. My place." She sniffed, feeling silly. From his silence, she thought perhaps he didn't understand what she meant.

"I understand," he sighed. The pain was evident on his face as though lost in aching memories. "When my parents died, I felt something like that, too. I guess."

Her heart throbbed at the connection sparking between them and their similar situations. "Your parents?"

Mr. Barnes nodded. "They passed away when I was a small child—it was an accident. A ridiculous accident with a coach. A storm blew in and scared the horses. The coachman fell off, and the coach ran into a rock outcrop." He stared at the table. There were so many emotions on his face: grief, fright, and anger.

She felt all of them burning in her chest. "That's horrible." Unsure what to say, she swallowed. "I am so sorry."

"It was so long ago now," he shrugged, a joyless twitch at the side of his mouth. Sniffing, his eyes remained locked on the table.

She shook her head, fighting the urge to touch his arm across the table. "It was long ago, yes. But things like that don't just disappear." She sighed. "I don't know when I'll ever really be able to think of Papa without it being this horrible."

"You will, eventually," he responded kindly. "It can take a long time, but it will get better. I promise."

She smiled. Mr. Barnes was handsome, but when he smiled back at her, it transformed his face, making it glow from within.

After a moment, she sat a little straighter. "I talked to a neighbor this afternoon."

"Oh?" he asked, brow slightly raised. "Which one? Mrs. McCauley?" He gestured through the window, pointing toward the farm to the right.

"They're the closest ones," she nodded. "Matty was friendly and invited me for tea."

The light returned to his eyes as he grinned, seeming pleased. "Good. I'm glad you're settling in."

"It was good," she admitted. "At least she is someone not so suspicious of me. At last, someone trusts me."

"I'm sure," he nodded. "You know, if you came into town with me, we could ask Glen—the big ranch hand—to take you home on the cart. I thought you might like to talk to Mr. Simmons since he used to be the physician in town."

"I might," she answered, stunned at his offer. "But why?" she added softly. "I can't practice there."

"Either way, it would be good to see him and talk about medical things."

Lucille's heart raced, realizing how much that would mean to her. It would be perfect, actually—the best thing she could imagine. Until he suggested it, she hadn't realized how much having to step away from it had hurt her.

"I thought you might," he beamed. "And I reckon you might like a change of scenery. You could stay at my office and chat when he comes in. It would be good if you could fetch the things from the trading store. Carrying the sugar, tea, and spice is heavy work for Mrs. Grierson."

"Oh," Lucille grinned, joy radiating through her. "Thank you. Thank you, Mr. Barnes." She didn't know how to express her gratitude—she didn't know how he'd thought of it, how he realized that this was precisely what she needed. His eyes glowed as they exchanged genuine smiles. His grin was as bright as anything she'd seen lighting his face.

"Well, then," he chuckled warmly. He eyed her brightly. "I will see you tomorrow."

Lucille thanked him again, and after a while of them only sipping tea without a word, he went to bed. After some light cleaning and setting the stale bread aside for the animals, she did the same. Before she got into bed, she prayed sincerely, with more hope and wonder and gratitude than she had in a long time. God had granted her a wish she didn't even know she had.

Chapter Fourteen

The cart rattled, and Lucille watched the landscape, the hills on the horizon giving way to a flat desert that stretched unchecked to the edge of Creation. She had expected to feel sick like the journey with Mr. Chaffee but was amazed by her clear sight and calm stomach. Smelling dry dust, she was thrilled to be going into town and seeing new things again.

They were on their way to Oxplains so she could talk with Mr. Simmons.

Her hands were folded on her lap, on top of the fabric of her nicest black skirt. Choosing a more professional outfit made her feel more like herself—not because she felt the need to convince Mr. Simmons of anything. She had almost forgotten who she was in the last week and a half, and it was important to remember. These clothes reminded her that she truly was who she claimed: a physician.

Lucille had decided she would focus on groceries, so if the townspeople were unkind or the physician refused to see her, she wouldn't feel hurt. She squeezed her basket's handle, ensuring it was still there. At the same time, the light had sparked inside her, and her sense of self returned. Maybe God wasn't trying to tell her that she was foolish to believe it was her calling. Maybe He wanted her to at least help assist someone.

"How much time does it usually take in the trading store?" she asked, hesitant to admit how she hated waiting in lines. After her experience in Pinewood, she was nervous about doing shopping of any kind. The thought of running into

Bert's friends didn't exactly appeal to her, either. They might have accepted her at the moment, but she knew how grudging it was, and she didn't want someone to be rude.

In the driving seat, Mr. Barnes shrugged, flicking the reins. "About half an hour, if it's full? Maybe take Glen with you." Without looking at her, he called over his shoulder. "Hey, Glen?"

"What?" the large blond man in the back of the cart turned, frowning.

"You could accompany Miss Newbury to the trading store. There's lots of time," Mr. Barnes instructed.

"Sure thing," Glen muttered.

If she were truthful, the ranch hands intimidated her with their rough ways—jostling and shoving each other playfully, eating with their hands—and their loud speech at mealtimes. She had barely interacted with them, keeping her gaze elsewhere during the dinnertimes she and Mrs. Grierson shared with them. She wasn't too comfortable about Glen escorting her to the store without Mr. Barnes being present. But if Mr. Barnes said it was safer that way, she would accept it.

"Thank you," she smiled sheepishly.

Mr. Barnes glanced at her. "It's better to be safe."

Glen shrugged and leaned back in the cart. Mr. Barnes tugged the reins, slowing the horses as they turned toward the town. It was close now.

Lucille watched Mr. Barnes from the corner of her eye as he drove the cart. His behavior last night astounded her. He had been so observant, noticing that she was downcast without her mentioning it. While he had shown compassion to her already by taking her to his ranch, this was the first time she'd thought he cared about more than just her surviving. Without question, she knew that he was concerned for her emotions.

His hands on the reins were solid. Mr. Barnes had long, fine fingers and wrists strong enough to make two of her own. Studying the strength of his shoulders, the broadness of his chest, she felt her cheeks flush with heat, her palms sweating.

He was an exceptionally handsome man.

Lucille smiled to herself when they reached the sheriff's office. The town was still new to her since she only saw it once before, and it took a moment for her to recall where the office and the inn were. Mr. Barnes stopped the horses, and Glen jumped firmly out of the back. Lucille flushed as Mr. Barnes offered a hand to her.

"Allow me to help you."

"Thank you," she said. Lucille felt they touched flame as his hand closed around hers, gently squeezing as she balanced on the cart's edge and hopped to the ground.

Mr. Barnes smiled, and she hesitated for a moment, peering up at him in this close proximity. His green eyes—like grass, like emeralds—stared down at her. A muscle twitched at his lip, suppressing his grin. She could not look away, her heart threatening to leap from her throat. His gaze drifted, his demeanor shy.

"Glen?" he called to the ranch hand, who took the horses to the stables around the back. "If you could come back in an hour? Miss Newbury will be going for the groceries around about then."

Glen shrugged his assent. Mr. Barnes hesitated outside the building, staring at her. After a moment, he coughed softly as if there was a lump in his throat. "Have a nice day, Miss Newbury." His eyes flickered to their surroundings like he was checking for others out and about.

"And you, Mr. Barnes." Flustered, she watched him as he went inside. He left the door open but didn't look back as he walked down the hallway to his office.

Was that care in his eyes? Affection?

His hand on hers left her skin tingling, an enchanting sensation rushing through her. She didn't understand, but she knew it felt good when he looked at her.

Lucille blinked on the doorstep, surprisingly unsure whether she could enter. Since Bert's operation, she hadn't been in the sheriff's office and felt reluctant to enter where Mr. Barnes worked. It would feel unfamiliar—this was his world even more than Breakwater.

With a sigh, she went inside. The hallway was silent. She tiptoed across the floor, and her eyes darted around, steps echoing loudly in the stillness.

"Good morning, Miss Newbury. Why, this is a surprise. Can I do something...?" She jumped as the young man spoke, emerging from around a corner. She recognized him as Mr. Barnes' deputy from when they had been briefly introduced a week earlier.

Briefly, her hand went to her chest from fright. Bemused, she explained, "Hello. Mr. Barnes said I could stay in here for about an hour." The respect Luke showed her was unexpected. All she could remember from when she helped the rancher was how cruel his friends were. She hadn't realized she'd impressed the sheriff's deputy so much.

"Oh! I see," Luke nodded. "Of course. Do you need anything? A chair? I'll get you the spare from the hallway." He disappeared to fetch it before she responded.

Lucille didn't know why he might be so kind and respectful when all the other townsfolk had seemed so reluctant and suspicious. She smiled as he returned, carrying a chair and putting it by the window.

"Please, sit," he offered politely. "If you need anything, just ask me, and I'll do my best to get it for you."

"Thank you," Lucille smiled, settling into the chair. Luke was young and friendly, and she understood why Mr. Barnes seemed to like him; he was eager to please and generous in spirit.

Leaning back in the chair, she tried to keep alert, but she still wasn't sure when to expect Mr. Simmons. Hunched over his desk, writing something, Luke scratched his neck.

Lucille frowned. He had flushed, pale skin and her mind listed the conditions he could have. He scratched his chest furtively, and when she tried to look away, he coughed politely.

"Miss Newbury," he said carefully. "Um, well…since you are here, I thought I might ask you something. Um, could you look at my skin?"

Lucille wanted to grin but maintained a professional demeanor. "By all means."

He reddened, itching his neck again. "Thank you. Sorry. It's so bad."

"I'd be glad to help."

The deputy closed the door and unbuttoned the top buttons of his starched shirt, flushing. Lucille drew a breath, examining his chest and neck's red, inflamed skin.

"This is dermatitis," she announced. Her brow lowered as she studied the skin. Luke was stiff with embarrassment, so uncomfortable he could barely stay still. Though she was fascinated, she wanted to give him some reprieve. She returned to her chair as he buttoned his shirt, clearly suffering from acute embarrassment as well.

"Is it itchy or hot?" she asked. "I mean, does it feel painful, or is it just annoying?"

"Itchy," he admitted as he sat. "So itchy. And when I scratch, and it gets raw, it burns," he said. "It's not everywhere—just my chest and neck," he added quickly, not meeting her gaze.

"Well," Lucille said, nodding. "Have you got a new housekeeper?" she asked, hit with inspiration. "Or has anyone been washing your shirts with something new?"

He frowned. "I don't rightly know, miss." He tilted his head. "This horrid rash started a few days ago. But it was when my shirts were washed."

Lucille's brow furrowed as she considered. "Do you have them done in the village?"

He nodded. "Yes. Mrs. Blackwood washes them."

"I see," Lucille said. "The best thing would be to ask Mrs. Blackwood what she uses. If I were to guess, I would say that she uses lye soap. You have sensitive skin, and I think that has caused its reaction."

"Oh!" He grinned. "Miss, I can't tell you how much of a relief that is. I reckoned I was sickening." He shook his head, and she saw tension drain from him.

She leaned back with a glimmer of satisfaction. Sometimes, her father had felt the same way, she knew. Some patients came in with some peculiar ailment, and he'd been stumped for a while, but he'd figured out the cause with careful questions. He'd been so proud of himself that they would go to the inn to celebrate.

"Well," she said, the memory making her throat hurt. "I'll prescribe a lotion that should ease the itching," she continued. "But I think you should take your shirts back and have them rinsed and insist that Mrs. Blackwood uses something less irritant for you.

"Thank you!" Luke grinned. He looked truly relieved, and, more than her pride, her delight at having helped someone lifted her heart.

"Not at all," she said fondly. "Now, I suppose I ought to wait for Mr. Simmons to arrive and then go and get the sugar and tea from the trading store."

"Of course, miss," he nodded. "Of course."

He settled to his work, his broad smile remaining. He still scratched, but Lucille thought he seemed much calmer. While she waited, she grabbed a sheet of paper to write what she needed for the lotion. She'd make it herself, at home. She had the white clay her father used to use for skin lotions—it was imported and rare, but for raw, itching skin, she knew little else was soothing. Adding rainwater and some black tea was also good for sore, raw skin.

"I'll send the lotion with the sheriff," she said. "I'll make it up tonight and get it to you tomorrow morning."

"Oh, thank you!" Luke exclaimed. "Thank you so much, miss. My, I'm glad you were here to have a look at it. I reckon there isn't anyone else who'd know as much as you about skin."

Lucille beamed with joy. "Thank you, Luke."

She tucked her list into her pocket, glad she had extra tea when she went to the store—it was always suitable for medicinal purposes, and it could soothe many skin conditions and have some use as a fabric dye.

She felt so much better after using her skills, and when Mr. Simmons arrived, she stood tall, confident in her God-given gifts.

Glen came to fetch her an hour later, and she was still smiling. "If you could escort me to the store, please?" she said.

"Yes, miss," Glen said, sounding awkward and nervous as if he'd never met anyone like herself before. She smiled, her understanding from earlier making her realize he was shy, not standoffish. However, she was still buzzing after healing Luke and meeting Mr. Simmons and felt far too uplifted for anything like that to bother her. She walked with him to the store and even felt emboldened standing in line with the other villagers.

Lucille was so glad to be in town that she couldn't wait to tell Mr. Barnes about her experience. The store smelled of tobacco and dust, and she thought about the ride back to the ranch and how she could tell Matty about her experiences when she saw her again.

Chapter Fifteen

It was another long day. An elderly couple had their outbuilding broken into, and Nicholas had no other suspicion than that it was the bandits. They'd taken the last supplies that the ranchers had stockpiled for winter—potatoes, corn, flour—and caused damage to property, including shattered windows. The fence was broken, and someone had trampled through the shrubs around the property.

"We didn't see anything," the old man said. "We just heard them in the middle of the night—we were fast asleep."

"Of course," he nodded. "I am so sorry this happened to you."

"We needed that food, sheriff," the elderly woman said. Her voice was raw. "It was all we had." Though it was springtime, it would be weeks before fresh stock could be gathered to replace what was stolen—months before the next potato harvest.

Nicholas swallowed. "I know," he said. "I will do my best to compensate you. And you can have part of the potato to stockpile at my ranch."

"You mean it?" the old man gaped. "Oh, sheriff! Thank you!"

"Thank you, Sheriff Barnes," the woman cried.

Nicholas sighed, seeing the relief in the set of their shoulders. The late afternoon sunshine was an intense orange, harsh on the lined faces. His guts churned. Those bandits had plenty of food for winter; they'd stolen food, valuable goods, and cash. How could they leave those poor old people so vulnerable?

He had assured the couple he'd do his best to provide for them. But, as he saddled his horse at the stables in town, he wasn't sure how he would fulfill that. He had potatoes, for sure, but he needed them himself—there were the ranch hands, himself, Mrs. Grierson, and Miss Newbury to feed. While he could buy more potatoes, he also needed supplies during winter for the cattle. And new equipment. And he'd been planning to repair the stable roof.

As Nicholas swung himself into his saddle, he wondered what Lucille had done during the visit to the village. Hopefully, she had enjoyed the meeting with Simmons. He also hoped the grocery shopping had gone well, and Glen had returned her safely to the ranch when he drove the cart back home. Nicholas wanted to know and wasn't sure he'd have enough time to ask her about it, as he had so much to do.

He would just have to do his best.

"God," he prayed as he rode home, the sunshine lengthening the shadows, the horizon glowing redly. "I guess You have a plan, but it sure is mysterious."

Sometimes, Nicholas wondered if he wasn't just being fanciful in his belief. The world seemed so full of hardship, so painful. And senseless things happened—these bandits, stealing and intimidating. Innocent families suffered. Innocent people cowered in their homes. None of it made any sense to him, and it seemed so hard to believe in good and light in such a dark, troubled world.

The other thing that bothered him was that he'd been hearing more comments about Miss Newbury. He'd heard people in the store when he quickly visited that morning to get some oil for his saddle, and his shoulders stiffened, anger and tension mixing with a need to keep her safe. He knew Bert's friends were behind this. They had felt foolish for being shouted down by Max and tried to get back at him indirectly by stirring people to complain about her.

"A woman doctor! Absurd," one woman scoffed.

Another woman laughed. "Unnatural. Like me wearing trousers or smoking a cigar!"

Nicholas's heart thudded. He had never felt so angry. He was glad he was at the shopfront, or he'd have walked out without the oil. He didn't want to stay there and hear the ridiculous slander about Miss Newbury.

He was still irritated as he rode home, hoping she hadn't heard anything like that when she was there. He should never have suggested she go anywhere. Maybe it would be best for her to stay on the ranch as his housekeeper. Given the state of her feet and hands, it would only be fair to find Mrs. Grierson another place to work, doing fewer physical tasks. But even the thought of letting Mrs. Grierson leave made his chest hurt.

Maybe he acted too hastily, bringing her here. Now, she knew someone at the ranch next door she'd find herself.

His eyes slanted in the early evening light. He knew what to do, and it was better than trying to make the villagers accept an idea that was out of their grasp. Blinking in the growing dark, he realized his horse's hooves were on the grit of the path, the familiar sound echoing in his tired head. He could almost see his ranch. Just around the bend, he'd finally have a chance to ask Miss Newbury about her day.

As he rode closer to the gate, his brows furrowed. It took his eyes a moment to make out the figure holding a lantern. Somebody was in the yard.

Nicholas's chest tightened, his heart thumping, pumping blood fast around his body, on full alert. He squinted; it was peculiar that the person had a lantern. If they were a bandit, they wouldn't want to make themselves stand out in the darkness. The figure wavered as though uncertain, standing not far from his boundary fence.

Mrs. McCauley? He frowned. The figure was coming from the McCauley ranch, and he had to admit that the figure's stride matched hers, but he could not be sure.

Nicholas urged his horse to the yard with a soft click of his tongue. When he dismounted at the stables, he confirmed it was Mrs. McCauley, fear haunting her face. His heart raced. *Something had happened.* His mind jumped to conclusions: She had been robbed, Miss Newbury was not back from the village as expected...

"Sheriff!" his neighbor shouted, running to him. The lantern showed her face clearly, distress tightening the corners of her eyes, her chest heaving. "Mr. Barnes! I need Lucille! Is she here?"

"Lucille?" His eyes widened. "I believe she's here, Mrs. McCauley. Why? What do you need her for?" His frown deepened as she drew a breath.

"She's a healer, isn't she? Mrs. Amberley is at my farm, and she needs help. It's her son, Keith. He's sick."

Nicholas nodded. "I'll get Miss Newbury."

He ran into the house, hoping she was here and praying that she could do something to help.

Chapter Sixteen

Mr. Barnes startled Lucille as he ran into the kitchen. Her heart jumped. His apparent struggle to be calm made her heart leap to her throat, her mind racing to imagine what might drain his face. She drew a breath, fear gripping her.

Somehow, his voice was steady as he spoke. "There's a child... He's extremely ill. He needs your help."

Without hesitation, Lucille grabbed her coat, shoving her feet into her boots. The fear had left her, absolute certainty settling on her as she joined him. "Where is he?"

Mr. Barnes's eyes widened with a beautiful sparkle, even though they knew the seriousness of the matter at hand.

"He's at Matty McCauley's," he answered. "And thank you."

Lucille smiled softly. "Of course. I must try."

Mr. Barnes led Lucille to Matty, a lamp in her hand, terror on her face. As Matty grabbed Lucille's hand, gripping it tightly, Lucille caught sight of Mr. Barnes returning to the stables, where his horse stood, still saddled and half-asleep.

"Lucille!" Matty gasped with relief. "Oh, God is good. I am so grateful you're here. Come quickly. It's Mrs. Amberley's son. He's so sick."

"It's all right," Lucille soothed with her father's unwavering strength. "We can help him. Where is he?"

"In my parlor. We'd best be quick. Heaven knows how long the poor child still has got."

An utter calm descended on Lucille. Her father always told her: *Where love is, there is no need for fear.* She would not allow fear to take hold. She would stay in her heart, where love was, and fear could not be.

"What sort of sick is he?" Lucille asked Matty as they hurried down the path that led to her house, the wavering flame lighting their way down the gravel path. "Was he coughing? Sneezing? Throwing up?" Her mind ran through all the possibilities as she made as many suggestions as possible. *Choking. Influenza. Infection.*

Matty's face was pale in the light of the lamps. "Gracie said he was coughing and vomiting earlier, but now, he's just lying there, like he can barely move. He's hardly able to do anything." Matty sniffed, clearly deeply affected.

Lucille breathed a steadying breath. "All right. So, he was vomiting. About an hour ago? A few hours?" If he was vomiting, he had at least got some toxic substances out of his body. But too much vomiting could dehydrate a person, particularly a child.

She coughed to ease her throat as they hustled. The landscape around them—the one she loved so well—was invisible in the darkness, the only light the pale glow of moonlight on the distant hills that seemed black against a dark blue sky. It was impossible to see the ground under her feet, but Lucille darted ahead, desperate to reach the house as fast as possible.

As they reached the house, Matty was only a few paces behind. "He's in the first room," Matty called as she joined Lucille.

Lucille paused in the parlor, taking in the scene.

A woman with pale hair sat on the long couch that ran along one side. Her face was drawn and tight, a picture of fear. On a padded chair lay a small boy about eight or nine. His skin was white, and his veins were blue at the temples. Though his eyes were open, he didn't respond as she approached.

"Keith?" Lucille said gently. "Keith? I'm here to help you."

He didn't respond, and his mother sniffled. "He can't talk. He can barely move. He's been like that for more than thirty minutes now."

Lucille exhaled slowly. Thirty minutes wasn't that long. *Thank Heaven they got here on time.* She squeezed the child's shoulder gently.

"Keith? Can you hear me?" Her heart thudded. If he was unconscious, she had to act quickly, doing what she could to revive him. But it would be guesswork since she didn't know if he was dehydrated or if it was another problem. It could be so many things—food infection, high fever, snakebite...all she could do was ask questions. "When did you see him vomiting? Where had he been? What more can you tell me?"

She sighed with relief as the child stirred.

"Uh..." he said.

His irises were deep brown, so Lucille couldn't see his pupils and how they reacted. The boy's gaze wavered. His arm jumped, a spasming motion before laying still.

"Keith was outside," his mother, Gracie Amberley, said, her brow furrowed in concentration. Exhaustion and terror were on her white, lined face. "He'd had the morning off from chores, and he was playing with a friend Ralph from the neighboring ranch at the corral. When he came in for dinner, he was walking oddly. I thought he had drunk something— spirits. He was weaving around like he was under the influence..." her voice was strained as though choked, "I was going to reprimand him, but he vomited, and there was no smell of spirits on him. Just fluid... And then he vomited again and again. And he couldn't get up and was shaking... He could speak at first, but then he stopped, just lying there, like this. Matthew isn't at home, and I didn't know what to do, so I carried him here."

Lucille drew a deep breath. "Did he vomit before then? Do you know?"

"I don't know," the woman shuddered, shaking her head. "I would have talked to Ralph's mother, Jessie, but she wasn't home."

Keith was breathing shallowly, the sound harsh and grating.

"Let me look at him," Lucille said, her hands moving over the child. Though he was skinny and lightweight, it was normal for a growing youth of about his age. Moving the lantern closer, she saw his eyes could still focus. His heart was beating slowly, so slowly.

Poisoning.

Lucille's heart raced. "He's eaten something. I think I know what." Relief flooded her. "Is there a tree at your neighbor's house? Or where he played? It'd be a small tree with slender branches. And blackberries. The berries are about the size of a raisin."

Gracie made a face, clearly lost in thought, before nodding. "Yes. Yes, I think so. Jessie has one like that she planted for the birds. It's quite pretty in summer but unusual."

"It's poisonous for humans," Lucille said. "I don't think he ate enough to kill him, but that is what's made him so sick. He needs to be kept warm." While her mind raced, her thoughts were clear as she listed what he needed. "And we need to make sure his heart keeps beating. Mrs. Amberley, fetch that blanket and cover him up. Matty, get water and some fat if you have some."

Matty hurried to the kitchen while Gracie covered him lovingly with a shawl. When Matty returned with lard, Lucille rubbed some on the child's chest to keep him warm and help massage over his heart. The toxins slowed his heart rate, and all she could do was keep it beating as best as she could. As long as it was still beating, that was enough.

"Should we make him vomit?" Matty asked.

"No," Lucille answered instantly. "He's already vomited, and in his uncoordinated state, he might choke. The best we can do is keep his heart beating and wait for him to wake. The toxins sap strength, so he will need food as soon as he wakes up. Squeezed fruit juice is good—anything that will give him energy fast."

Lucille rubbed his chest as he lay on his side, keeping his heart beating, as Matty went to the kitchen to check the larder. Keith's heartbeat below her fingers was steady. Her back was to the fireplace, where Matty stoked it, the roaring flames making her sweat. The child's skin was icy, so Gracie helped her move the chair nearer to the fireplace.

"He's still breathing, and his heart is still beating. So, I think that he will live through," she said. She was almost sure of that as she kept his heart stimulated. "When he wakes, he will be very tired. We need to feed him and keep him warm, make sure he coughs out whatever's settled on his lungs, and tell him not to eat those fruits or anything he finds in the garden without asking someone if it's poisonous."

"I will tell him." With her head bowed, Gracie whispered, "I should have."

"It's all right," Matty assured, sitting beside her, wrist in her firm hands. "It was not your fault—you didn't know. The Lord had His hand on him, and he will survive. The Lord also sent my friend, a skilled healer."

"Thank you," Gracie said to Lucille.

"I didn't do anything," she said softly.

After a while, Lucille showed Matty how to massage his chest and then Gracie. Lucille by the roaring fire, her eyes not really seeing. She was exhausted and didn't know what time it was. They could have been there for hours or just minutes; she had no idea. All she could hear were whispered prayers. Shutting her eyes, she sent a prayer up, silent and wordless. She had no energy for words.

***

It was gray outside, rather than black, when the boy stirred.

"He's waking!" Gracie cried out.

"Lord, be praised!" Matty exclaimed. She rose to her feet, wincing as she stood. "I'll make him breakfast."

As Matty went to the kitchen, Lucille knelt by Keith. His mother held his hand and sobbed, tears running down her cheeks.

"Keith," Lucille whispered. "Can you sit up?"

"Where am I?" the boy asked, his voice ragged and heavy with sleep. "Who are you?"

"You're at Auntie Matty's house. You were poisoned, and this woman—this *doctor*—saved you," Gracie said. "I was so worried about you! Oh, Keith! Lord be praised that you're alive."

His mother was crying tears of joy, laughing with relief. Lucille just smiled and said nothing. The boy shifted to sit up slowly. Gracie enfolded him in her arms, crying noisy tears as the boy held her, awkward and groggily trying to comfort her.

Dizzy from lack of sleep, Lucille clasped her hands together, forming a prayer. She had so much gratitude in her heart. The boy had lived; he was awake, and his mother's joy restored. It was the most beautiful thing she'd ever seen, and in her prayers, she thanked God for letting her be part of it.

It was her entire world.

Matty hobbled in, looking exhausted, her face pale, hair unbrushed. Her grin lit the room. "Breakfast's ready when you want it. Eggs, ham, and toast for us. I squeezed some orange juice for the boy. It's on the table when you're hungry."

At the mention of food, Lucille's stomach growled. She'd barely eaten supper, and she breathed in, detecting the smell of eggs. She watched Keith grin.

"Breakfast."

His mother chuckled. "Yes! Breakfast! Oh, Keith. I'm so happy."

Matty patted her shoulder, and Gracie lifted Keith from the chair. He was weak, his legs still a little uncoordinated. His mother picked him up as easily as if he weighed nothing.

"Lord be praised," Matty repeated as they sat at the table. The daylight was pale at the window, the firelight orange in the grate, and Lucille breathed in the strong smell of eggs, ham, and toast, almost collapsing now that she realized how exhausted and hungry she was.

Keith drank his orange juice slowly.

"Lord be praised! And thank the Lord for bringing you to us," Gracie added, grinning at Lucille.

"It was His work, not mine," Lucille nodded, but her heart glowed, and the pain of the last weeks fell away, replaced by the warmth of friendship and toast and tea in this enticing place.

Happiness flooded through her, lifting her heart as they ate a meal in the warm, comfortable kitchen.

Chapter Seventeen

The sun was still a thin line of gold on the horizon when Nicholas got up. He shrugged into his clothes, his head pounding. He'd barely slept that night. Though he had wanted to go next door every minute, something stopped him. He didn't want to interfere with Lucille and her work.

His entire heart wanted to be there, to keep her safe.

Part of him knew that she was highly skilled and that this was her calling. The rest of him—the larger part—just wanted to rush over to be sure that all was going well, that Lucille had slept a bit and that the Amberleys had received her help well. He didn't want to think of her being in trouble.

While he had lain awake for a long time that night, it occurred to him that Miss Newbury was meant to be the physician—or else, why would God be calling her to it, sending her cases and patients without her searching them out? It had been an odd thought as if a limb tingled that had long ago been paralyzed. He had not *really* thought about matters of faith in a while.

He tugged on his boots and limped downstairs, grabbing his coat by the door. Mrs. Grierson was starting the fire when he came in. He guessed it was exceedingly early as he greeted her.

"Morning, Mrs. Grierson," he said. "I'm going to fetch Lucille from the McCauley house."

"Good, sir." Mrs. Grierson nodded. She smiled at him from where she sat, holding kindling.

"I'll be back for breakfast soon," Nicholas promised, wanting to get there as fast as possible.

He hustled as briskly as he could, annoyed at how slow his leg made him. He tried to run, but it ached, and so he could only jog toward the house. The only sounds in the still air were his footsteps crunching on the small stones of the pathway and, in the distance, the first birds calling to one another in daylight.

Nicholas reached the door, gasping from running and lack of sleep, and was startled when it opened instantly.

Mrs. McCauley grinned at him. "Mr. Barnes! Why, sheriff! Come inside."

"Mrs. McCauley," he greeted her politely. He removed his coat at the door, wiping his boots on the step before entering. He felt perplexed by her smile; he hadn't expected that. Nicholas took several deep breaths, smelling frying and toast.

"We're having breakfast in the kitchen," Mrs. McCauley explained, leading him down the wooden-paneled hallway. The scene before him was astounding.

A woman with blonde curls and a soft face sat at the left of the table. A child sat beside her, hair blond and tousled. His eyes were enormous as they saw Nicholas. Across the table sat Miss Newbury, looking as if she'd started her day like this every morning since her girlhood. When she saw him, she smiled a weary grin, revealing the lines of gray exhaustion under her eyes and exposing how tired she really was.

"Mr. Barnes."

"Good morning," he said. His voice was soft, and when Miss Newbury smiled, he forgot everybody else.

"Would you like to join us?" Mrs. McCauley asked when the silence had stretched a moment. "There's enough bread for everyone, and I can get another egg for you."

Nicholas glanced at Miss Newbury, eating her breakfast slowly, seeming so tranquil and at ease. He shrugged. "I'll bring more eggs and bread over later, Mrs. McCauley."

"Now, you needn't, Mr. Barnes," she waved fondly, already cooking another egg.

Nicholas sat at the table in the empty seat across from Miss Newbury. Her cheeks tinted pink, and his heart suffused with an intense warmth that he couldn't explain.

"You aren't here to arrest me?" the child asked, his terror palpable.

Nicholas frowned. "Why would I do that?"

"Cause I ate berries that were in someone else's garden. I didn't mean to. I didn't mean to steal, sir."

The poor child was terrified, and Nicholas rested a gentle hand on his head with a light chuckle. The hair under his fingertips was silk floss. "Boy, you didn't do anything wrong. And I'm the neighbor. I'm not here to do anything except say good morning. I promise."

"Good. Thank you, sir," the child sighed with relief, his shoulders relaxing.

The child's mother watched him with some wariness mixed with respect. As Mrs. McCauley chuckled, her laughter eased the tension in the room. Soon, everybody laughed, even the child who grinned at Nicholas with fondness. The child respected him, which amazed Nicholas. Since all the trouble they'd been giving him about the new physician, he'd forgotten that the townsfolk still held him in high regard. Miss Newbury smiled at him as though confirming his thoughts.

"I see all went well," he said. His voice was soft, intended only to be heard by Miss Newbury.

She shrugged, helping herself to more bread. "The boy ate berries. Not much I could do. Just keep his heartbeat going and keep him warm until he slept it off."

"You knew that. You knew what to do. Never underestimate what you do, Miss Newbury."

She smiled. Nicholas's eyes held hers, and he utterly forgot that anyone else was present. He only remembered when the child's mother spoke again.

"Miss Newbury is a fine doctor. I am grateful to her."

Nicholas nodded, beaming in agreement. Miss Newbury looked as though she might try to refuse praise, but the smiles spread around the table with the affirmation of Miss Newbury until it felt like the kitchen glowed with it.

Miss Newbury looked down shyly at the table, and something shifted inside Nicholas's heart. It might genuinely be that she was brought here to be the physician. He had forgotten that the Lord worked in not always apparent ways.

The light settled in his heart. At this small community breakfast, he relaxed for the first time in a long while. These three people—Mrs. McCauley, Mrs. Amberley, and little Keith—clearly adored Miss Newbury. It was only a matter of time before the townsfolk followed suit. The horrible event of the child's poisoning would be used by the Lord for a good purpose. Nicholas leaned back and admired the happy scene in the kitchen, sure that soon Lucille would find her place and be contented again.

And if he was right, that this was the beginning of the townsfolk accepting Lucille, the town would have their physician.

Chapter Eighteen

A few days after the incident, Lucille gaped at Mr. Barnes in bewilderment as they stood in the kitchen. She couldn't understand what he had just said.

"The townspeople have been asking about you."

Lucille's heart raced as he repeated it. "They asked about me?"

"They want you to come to town. They want you as the town's physician."

"*What?*"

Lucille practically jumped upright. He chuckled, the grin tugging at the edge of his mouth, looking more handsome than she'd ever noticed.

"They asked me if you would return. Mrs. Amberley was industrious when it came to telling people about your help, and the whole town heard. And, combined with Bert's leg healing wonderfully, and Luke's rash, they are eager to have you work there. They want *you* as a physician."

Lucille stared at him. While the words were easy, the meaning was terrifying.

Wonderful, challenging, and terrifying.

"They want me to be a physician." Sheer wonderment outweighed the terror and the sense of disbelief for a moment, and she laughed, joy like a fountain in the desert welling up within. As they laughed and stared at each other, they glowed like they'd won a contest.

Mr. Barnes tilted his head, considering, trying—it seemed—to bring a note of seriousness. "Of course, the accommodation will need to be tidied up."

"And the office. Yes. You're right," Lucille said, recalling the reason for her living on the ranch, besides a need for employment. Frowning, she recalled that nobody had said yet they would help fund the repair of the old office and accommodation above it.

He raised a brow as though understanding the course of her thoughts. "I think the town councilors will agree to what you wish. Luke's uncle is on the council, and I'm sure he will be persuaded to provide whatever investment you need."

She remembered the deputy and smiled. "I am glad he's better. And I didn't know his uncle was on the town council."

Mr. Barnes nodded. "I know. Nobody thinks you fixed his rash self-servingly, just to get the council to like you, Miss Newbury." He smiled at her. "*I* know you wouldn't do that."

She teased. "Thank you for your faith in me."

They shared a chuckle. "I was wrong, miss. You know, it's hard for me to say it, but I was wrong about you. When it comes to being a physician, I know I doubted in the beginning that a woman could really do it...but seeing you in that house after saving that boy, I realized something."

"Oh, Mr. Barnes..." she began, but the look in his merry eyes stopped her.

"I find it hard enough to say that, so don't make me take it back. Let me admit it."

It felt as though the kitchen was filled with light.

***

Lucille and Mr. Barnes had the day off. Of course, there was a stream of chores to be done about the ranch and the household, but since the major duties halted on Sundays, there was time for contemplation and prayer.

Since attending the Bible study afternoon with Matty, and given the events of the previous day, Lucille wanted more time with the Lord. That morning, she had spent an hour on Bible study in her room, and still felt the warmth within her, the contentment and closeness that time with His Word always used to give her. It was a special, peaceful place deep within her that she had not visited for months. It felt good.

Mr. Barnes returned from the village church, and so the rest of the afternoon could be used for lighter tasks like sewing, or simply relaxing for a few hours. Lucille had a few items to fix—a sock with a hole in it, a glove and a blouse that had torn—so she worked at the table, the weight of an awkward silence growing between herself and the man at the end of the table, reading a book.

Lucille caught Mr. Barnes watching her, and she blushed.

"You know," he said carefully. "I fancy a walk. Would you join me, Miss Newbury?"

Her heart fluttered. "I would like that, Mr. Barnes."

His face tensed as he stood, and she recalled his knee that she still hadn't had a chance to ask him about. Mr. Barnes shrugged on his coat as she fetched her cloak, which smelled fresh and pleasant after she'd washed it.

Mr. Barnes stood back with his gestured down the steps. "After you."

Her cheeks flushed as she led the way with a murmured, "Thank you."

Lucille strolled beside Mr. Barnes as he limped from the house, walking toward the corrals and pastures where cattle grazed. At the sight of the distant, shaggy forms of the cattle in a far-flung corral, her heart lifted. She had become fond of them, as she was of the chickens that clucked in the pen by the back door.

Neither of them seemed inclined to speak at first, and they ambled along silently, pausing beside the last of the outbuildings before reaching the wide expanse of the ranch. Lucille scanned the wide landscape. The land was a mix of white and gold sand, the horizon a series of hills. There was scrubby grass here and there, a tree, and cactuses near what she guessed must be a water source. She loved the landscape, pitiless and harsh as it was. The vast, open space was inspiring to her. Since coming to Breakwater, she had learned to love the land even more than she had in her childhood.

"It's hot weather," she breathed.

Mr. Barnes chuckled. "It is. Must be hotter when you're wearing a dress." He eyed her gray wool dress sideways.

Her cheeks warmed as she giggled. Though the dress had a high neckline, covered her boots, and sleeves covered her arms, it was breathable material. "It's not actually," she admitted. "Why would it be hotter than trousers and shirt?"

"I guess it likely isn't," he said after a moment. "Just looks like it is, that's all."

"It's difficult to say," she teased. "I have never worn any different."

He tilted his head. "How do you ride? I mean, I know ladies ride in skirts, but sidesaddle." He chuckled awkwardly. "We don't have things like that out here."

She shrugged at his odd question. "I haven't ridden, sir."

Mr. Barnes gaped at her. "You haven't ever ridden? You must have *had* a horse, though?"

Lucille shook her head. "No, I didn't," she chortled, surprised that he was astounded. "You don't really need one, when you live in town. And besides, Papa had one, and if the patients needed both of us, we went in the cart. I had no call to learn how to ride."

He blinked at her in astonishment. "Well," he said, "We must do something. You can't stay out here and not ride, miss."

She frowned. If he was going to have the rooms cleaned up above the doctor's office, why was he talking about teaching her how to ride? She would live in the town, where she could get anything she needed, so there was no need.

"It might take a while to get the office fixed, miss." He rubbed the back of his neck as if reading her thoughts.

"I suppose," she sighed.

They walked along in silence for a while, content to be in their own thoughts. Lucille imagined living in town, warm with delight. She would miss the ranch, with its wide-open spaces, and Mrs. Grierson and the ranch hands, and Matty. She would miss the landscape, the horses, cattle, and chickens. And she'd miss Mr. Barnes. Her heart twisted.

The shade from the stables provided some protection from the heat as they slowed.

"If you like, I'll show you the basics," he offered. "You could ride my horse. He's easygoing."

She stared at him, amazement filling her heart. "You want to teach me... to ride?" she asked slowly.

He chuckled. "Yes." The shadows around his eyes were deep in shade. "Why should I not do so?"

"No reason at all, sir. Just that, well...it's nice of you to offer to teach me something." She blushed. *It would be nice,* she thought, *to spend time with him.* It surprised her how much she wanted to be in his company. She would love to spend time with him, learning something different. "Thank you for offering."

"It's no trouble. Now, if you want, you can try and find something that you can sit in comfortably, and I can see how my horse is doing. We should wait until it's cooler, mind. Shall we say four o'clock?" He squinted at the horizon.

She grinned, her heart thudding. "You mean it? You mean today?"

"In a few hours," he nodded. "And, of course, I mean it. I would be pleased to teach you."

Delight flooded her senses. "In a few hours, I'll be ready to get my first lesson. Right here."

She returned to the house with him, sweat on her brow from the heat. It felt so wonderful and uplifting to be here with him. She had received so much exciting news in one afternoon, complete with the offer of riding lessons. Her palms grew sticky with nerves and excitement.

"Thank you," she repeated.

He gave her a friendly look. "No need to thank me, miss."

She grinned back and hurried upstairs, heart racing. The thought of riding a horse made her nervous—they were big, and the idea of being on one was scary. At the same time, riding a horse would give her independence in a way she'd never dreamed before. She wouldn't have to rely on her patients to send a cart for her. She wouldn't need to ask someone to escort her to remote locations. She could take herself there, on horseback. It was such a wonderful thought.

Searching through her wardrobe, she selected a dress with a wide skirt. Her brown dress was the only one she had that would work. Though she hesitated to use it—it was her favorite dress, and if she fell or it snagged, she would risk ruining the skirt—she had nothing else wide enough for her to sit astride without it tearing. And without her boots sticking out.

It was quite unheard-of for women to ride astride. *But then,* she thought with a grin, *not many women were practicing as physicians, either.* And in a few weeks, when they cleaned up the office, she would be practicing as the first woman in Oxplains to have a doctor's office.

Lucille closed her eyes, hands clasped together. "God, thank you," she prayed softly. "I have doubted, I have lost faith. But You never left me." She swallowed hard, the thought moving her to tears. "You were always there. Your love never falters. Your hand is always strong on my shoulder, guiding and protecting me."

She blinked, tears in her eyes as she whispered the words. *Love beyond understanding.* That was what her father had always said: The Lord's love was beyond understanding.

Letting the memory of that fill her heart, the knowledge lifting her soul, she went to the mirror to pin back her hair.

She was going for a riding lesson.

***

At four o'clock, she passed the stables, her brown dress rustling in the slight breeze as she headed to the corral. When Mr. Barnes saw her, he gave her an admiring smile.

"You're exactly on time. I saddled Starburst for you," he announced, gesturing to the black horse with a white mark on his forehead that looked quite like a star in shape.

"Thank you, Mr. Barnes." Lucille swallowed; her throat tight. The large horse snorted when she approached, tossing his head. Her muscles stiffened. "Why is he doing that?"

Mr. Barnes chuckled. "It's all right. He's just greeting you. Weren't you, old fellow?" He stroked the horse's nose. The horse snorted and gently lipped his palm.

Lucille relaxed, reassured by the horse's unthreatening gesture.

"Come inside," Mr. Barnes said, scratching Starburst in the hollow between cheek and neck. "He's quite safe. I promise. I won't let him hurt you."

Lucille swallowed nervously but walked into the pen. The horse tensed when he saw her, but as she approached to stand beside Mr. Barnes, the horse relaxed.

"Hey, boy. This is Miss Newbury. She's a nice lady; you'll like her. Are you going to let her sit on your back? Of course, you are." He grinned at the horse, who snorted in return.

Lucille's mouth went dry, palms damp, as Mr. Barnes offered his hand.

"I'll help you," he said quietly. "It's best if you climb onto that block, there. See? It'll make it easier to mount up."

Lucille nodded, her mouth too dry for speech. She stood where he instructed, taking a deep breath. She knew what she was supposed to do—she'd seen people mount up into a saddle every day of her life. But she had no idea how to do it.

"Put your foot into the stirrup, there," Mr. Barnes directed gently by her side. "Hold onto the saddle horn."

Lucille paused, grateful when Mr. Barnes gestured to the projection on the front of the saddle. Though she'd seen saddles and horses all her life, she'd never thought about the various parts of a saddle. When she put her damp, sweaty hand on the horn, the horse lurched forward. She tried to slide her foot into the stirrup, but the horse was moving, and she could almost have cried she was so scared.

"Good," he soothed. With a pat on Starburst's neck and a soft pull on the horse's rein, the horse stilled. "Now, just like sitting on a fence, swing your leg over. Nice and carefully. There."

Terrified, Lucille shut her eyes. She didn't know if she could do this. After a deep breath, she put her weight on her left foot, and swung her right up as she pulled herself up, almost giggling in a mix of fear and amazement as she perched on the saddle.

"Good! Now, hold tight onto the horn while you get both feet nicely in the stirrup. Ankles down." She did exactly as he said, hands shaking slightly. "There you are! You did it!"

Mr. Barnes beamed up at her. For a moment, Lucille was too frightened to look away from where her hands gripped the horn, but she did.

Lucille sighed. She was quite high up. Her heart raced, like it had the first time her father let her help him do a stitch in a patient. She had been every bit as terrified now as she had been then. Her breathing became slow and deep. Then she smiled, fizzing with delight.

"I did it!"

Mr. Barnes laughed. "Absolutely. Now, if you like, I'll take the reins and lead you a bit. Just around the yard. Just so you feel how it feels and you can figure out how you balance there. Now, don't worry, I have the reins. Are you ready?"

She nodded, and once he clicked his tongue, the horse stepped forward. As Mr. Barnes had said, Starburst was a patient horse. He walked slowly, each step taking its own slow time. All the same, Lucille rocked and pitched with each step, and gasped, sliding sideways as her foot slipped from the stirrup.

"Whoops! Easy, there." Mr. Barnes gripped her leg. "Easy. You're all right. I have you."

Lucille gasped. He cheeks flooded with warmth, his hand remaining on her calf. Once he realized that, his cheeks reddened too, and he released her.

He glanced at the ground, and she smiled, heart thudding, body fluttering. Her leg tingled, the warmth of his touch spreading into her face.

She held onto the saddle as he led the horse. After a few circles, Mr. Barnes stopped, turning to look up at her. "There. Your first twenty feet of riding."

She giggled. "Well, then!" Her soul soared, sweat pouring down her brow and making her feet and hands slippery. "That wasn't too bad."

"You did so well. Now, if you do that every day, you'll be riding in a week. I promise."

"Every day?" she gaped. She couldn't do that by herself; he would have to walk with her. She couldn't even lead the horse out by herself, never mind saddle or mount him without someone holding him steady at the mounting block.

He shrugged. "I can help you when I get back from work," he suggested. "Or Glen or Alfred can help, but I don't know if you know them very well—"

"I would prefer you to help," she stated firmly.

He grinned. "Very well."

It felt odd to be sitting so much higher above him, her head a foot or so over his. His hair was not as black as she thought—one or two strands of white wove through. Her heart melted seeing them.

"Well, I guess I'll get that saddle off. You want to get down?" he asked.

"I suppose." She shifted in her seat.

He chuckled. "Well, we can't have you sitting there all night. Starburst will get tired, not to mention your back. Let me help you get down."

Giggling as he led the horse to the mounting block, she followed his instructions to dismount. She threw her leg over and slid off, landing in front of him. He caught her hands to steady her, and she hoped he didn't notice how sweaty they were. "Thank you," she said.

He gazed down at her, green eyes crinkled in the corners. "It was an honor, Miss Newbury."

As they stared at each other, Lucille's heart thudded. It was as intimate as anything she could imagine. She had never felt like this about anyone and, suddenly, she realized that she knew what this feeling was—this joy that welled inside her whenever he was near, this need to be close to him.

She was falling in love with him.

It should have been obvious for so long, but the knowledge was new and fresh and exciting and a little bit scary. A blush rose to her cheeks and he looked away, stepping toward the house.

"I guess I should go and rest, eh?"

Lucille was still affected by his gaze, still longing to stare into his eyes, but also partly glad that he had broken the contact, relieved to be in safer waters. "Yes, you should. Doctor's orders."

He grinned. "Yes, ma'am."

Her heart filled with warmth. She couldn't quite believe she'd sat on a horse and had ridden twenty feet in the yard. She was alight inside, lifted both by the wonder of her new achievement and by the strange, wonderful connection with Mr. Barnes. Recalling his green eyes staring into hers, a grin stretched her lips.

It was love. She knew it was.

Lucille went to her room and sat on her bed, overwhelmed by the day's joy. In addition to the lesson with Mr. Barnes, she'd received good news. She wondered when Mr. Barnes would have the opportunity to talk to the town councilors about the doctor's office, and the renovations. Practicing as a physician would mean so much to her, and she hoped it would be soon. And the sheriff's office was not too far from the house. Smiling to herself, she thought that was at least a small compensation for having to live above the office.

She would see Mr. Barnes as often as she did now.

Lucille didn't know what to do about this new, strange, and wonderful realization growing inside her. She looked out the window at the landscape, her faith strong within her.

"God," she prayed. "If this is love, please, send me a sign. I am so confused, and I don't know what to do about it. If it is, I pray you send me a sign so I know."

With that, she was comforted and she washed her face. After her long day, she was tired with all the things she had learned. Drying her hands, she gazed out the window at the distant hills, wondering about tomorrow and all the excitement of readying the new office.

Chapter Nineteen

The sunshine poured in through the white-edged paned windows onto the scuffed floor of his office. Nicholas sighed, still processing what he'd just heard an hour or so ago.

When the town councilors met, the meeting reached an almost-unanimous agreement. The councilors, except for Canfield, voted for Miss Newbury to be the physician. And—having come to that decision—they also agreed that the doctor's office needed repairing.

It was a miracle.

Nicholas stared out of the window. He had not expected that. It had seemed—given the attitudes of so many of the villagers—that there was no likelihood of them accepting her. But they had. The time she'd intervened for little Keith had made a huge impression. Mrs. Amberley and her husband—who had connections all over town—had wasted no time in telling everyone about how Miss Newbury saved him. That had swayed the villagers, he thought, plus her success with Bert's leg and Luke's rash.

All those incidents together had swayed them and changed their outlook. It was a real miracle.

He had almost stopped believing in miracles, but each day, his faith returned, and with it, his happiness.

Nicholas's heart was full of gratitude and joy. Soon, he was sure, the town would have its physician installed in her office.

The only difficulty was the money.

The town didn't have the money to refurbish the rooms and repair the cracks and other damage in the doctor's rooms, and he'd come to agree with Lucille that it would be impossible to work there before the building was repaired.

Nicholas sighed. Considering the other difficulties— acceptance, endorsement, the goodwill of the councilors—this seemed simple. He knew it would cost a fair amount, but he was somehow certain they would solve that problem. Leaning back in his chair, he took another deep breath, the weight that had been on his shoulders for the last months eased another fraction.

Soon, the trouble of the town physician might be finally off his shoulders. He wouldn't have to mend all the injuries himself with only Mr. Simmons to assist him. It was quite wonderful.

He shifted in his seat, wanting to go home, to tell Miss Newbury the news at once. He grinned, wondering how her riding practice was going. They had done three days of riding—seizing the half-hour of almost-daylight when he got home—and he wondered if she would soon feel as though she could manage by herself. Recalling taking her hand to steady her once or twice, and the time his hand had touched her calf, he blushed. He could not get that feeling from his mind.

It took effort to push the thought away. She was the town physician, and soon, she would be moving into the rooms above the office. He should not feel like that about her. Though he was sure she felt the same when their eyes met, he had no idea how she felt about him, and he did not want to presume on her good nature.

It was all things he shouldn't consider.

Luke hurried past the doorway, pausing when he caught sight of Nicholas. He didn't itch anymore, which was good, and Nicholas thought his shirts looked even cleaner than usual, startlingly clean and crisp.

"Good day, sir?" Luke asked.

Nicholas nodded. It was a fine day. He'd met the councilors to receive their good news, had a fine lunch, and been called out once to look at damage on a ranch—the nature of the damage ambiguous as to whether the bandits had done it, since nothing was stolen. A positive change.

"Indeed," he agreed. "How are you?"

"Good, sir," Luke said happily. "Absolutely fine. Couldn't be better."

Nicholas smirked as Luke bounced on the balls of his feet, eyes darting down the hall. "Are you meeting someone?"

Luke blushed. "No, sir," he said quickly, though Nicholas strongly suspected he was hiding a fact. "Why do you ask?"

"No reason," Nicholas chuckled. He leaned back in the chair, recognizing the look in Luke's eye and the eager way he rushed off. He felt that way himself.

He reddened as he realized what he admitted to himself. His feelings were not just fondness or protectiveness for Miss Newbury.

The realization snuck up on him slowly; he had never considered the likelihood before that moment. The fact that he, Nicholas Stuart Barnes, might be falling in love was a possibility that had not occurred to him before. Seeing Luke rushing off, his eyes bright and sparkling, was the only thing that had made him consider it. But he knew how he felt as sure as he saw it in Luke.

He must be feeling the same way for Miss Newbury as Luke felt for whomever he visited.

The sensation of fear, a coldness, ran through him. Could he really risk falling for her? Was he really, or was he just impressed by her? She *was* a remarkable woman—brave, talented, amusing—and it was admiration. It must be that. That was it.

No need to entertain any other dangerous ideas.

Nicholas Stuart Barnes did not—absolutely not—fall in love. He had loved his parents, and they had been taken from him. He had thought he had fallen for Gertie Radford, Mrs. Radford's niece, but she had rushed off to marry a wealthy mining-magnate and he had heard no more of her. He'd come to dismiss that as youthful calf-love, but he still was sure that any form of falling for anyone was too painful and he wasn't ready for it.

He just admired Miss Newbury, that was all.

It was just another half an hour or so before he could go home, but he was eager to get there. He told himself it was to find out how Miss Newbury fared and to share his news, but he knew that wasn't entirely true. She meant a great deal to him and her smile lit him up.

Reaching for the book about boundary disputes, he tried to distract from his own troubling ideas.

***

It was already dusk when he rode back to the ranch and dismounted. Miss Newbury was waiting at the door, wearing the brown dress she wore as her riding attire. He had to admit that she looked beautiful. He couldn't help noticing the paleness of her neck and admiring it, too.

Stop it.

As he went to the corral, she hurried over. "Just a quick walk, miss," Nicholas greeted as she took the reins, her confidence amazing him. It had developed so quickly. He had to admit, she was an extremely talented pupil.

"Yes, Mr. Barnes."

Using the mounting block, she mounted Starburst, and he barely had to help—just stand close by in case the horse wandered off.

She squeezed with her knees, setting the horse moving forward one pace at a time as he walked beside them. He didn't take the reins anymore, just followed as she gently guided Starburst around the yard. Nicholas was sure that soon, she'd want to walk around the ranch, or trot. He wasn't sure which she would decide to do first.

"There." Miss Newbury led the horse to the mounting block and slipped off. Her dismounts were becoming incredibly graceful. Nicholas couldn't help admiring her—in some ways, she might even be a better rider than himself now, even with riding in a full dress.

"That was good," he smiled.

"Thank you, Mr. Barnes." She beamed up at him, eyes bright.

She artlessly tucked a strand of hair behind one ear. She was so beautiful, her big dark eyes like pools, her skin so pale, even after their afternoons of riding. *How gentle she seems... how strong.*

When she frowned, he realized he was staring into her eyes, their dark depths compelling. He glanced at the kitchen, where Mrs. Grierson was setting bowls out for the evening meal.

"You had a busy day?" he asked Miss Newbury, trying to distract from his awkward staring. He was sure she must think he was very strange.

She shrugged. "No more than usual. The chickens got loose, so we had to run to catch them. It was quite funny."

He chuckled, imagining the pair scurrying after rattled poultry. "And you caught them all?"

"I caught three. Matty caught the rest."

He smiled. She rode, was a physician, and could catch chickens. "Remarkable."

"Not really," she insisted with a blush.

He laughed. She peered up at him, and again, he felt as though he was drowning, falling into the dark depths of her eyes.

They walked inside and sat at the table. Mrs. Grierson came to join them with a pot of leftover stew. "Stew with carrots and onions. It's just boiled," she warned as he sat poised to take a mouthful.

"Thank you for warning me."

They all laughed. Nicholas waited for the stew to cool a bit before trying it. He decided he would rather wait until later to tell Lucille about the council. Since she didn't know they had met, it would be quite a surprise. He knew it was selfish, but he wanted a chance to tell her without Mrs. Grierson there. He wanted to keep her reaction for himself.

Eventually, after they ate their stew and bread, making small talk about their days, Mrs. Grierson stood, her back clearly hurting as she straightened. Mrs. Grierson smiled at them both, wished them good nights, and slowly walked out. Nicholas watched her, wondering if she suspected that he felt something for Miss Newbury. If she did, he reckoned she had guessed long before he was aware of it. He smiled.

Miss Newbury was still eating, and he poured them some tea, not wanting to rush her. He waited until she was sipping her tea, the bowls in the copper basin before he shared the news.

"The council met today," he started. He couldn't help the grin that lit up his face. "And the decision was almost unanimous," he paused. "They want you to practice. And they agree to oversee the repairs of the office and rooms for you."

"What!" she squealed. She was grinning, and he was surprised as she covered her face with her hands. "Mr. Barnes! No! They did?" She was laughing, and his heart skipped a beat. He wanted to stare at her, to enjoy the delighted laugh that shook her body and made him want to chuckle too.

"They certainly have," he confirmed. "Unfortunately, they say there isn't enough money for the repairs, but they said it should be easy enough to find. We just need to use our imaginations and figure out where we can get eighty dollars."

"Eighty dollars?" Miss Newbury stared, open-mouthed with eyes wide. She leaned back in the chair, seeming to be thinking about something. As she poured more tea, her eyes focused on some reality that he couldn't see.

He wanted to ask her what she was thinking about; what wheels were turning in that head of hers. After a moment or two, she gazed over at him with bright eyes.

"I remember when our church needed its roof mended— there was a storm and the roof got damaged. The pastor organized a cake sale. We helped—I helped—sell cakes. Some of the town ladies donated cakes, and we all had a tea-party in his garden and the proceeds from selling the cake went to the church. We did that three times and he had enough for the repairs. We could do something along that line." She tilted her head, eyeing him hesitantly.

Nicholas's brow raised in consideration. It was an idea; it certainly was something he wouldn't have thought of by himself. When he thought about it, he had to agree she was right. The village could get together and have a sale like that. Most of the villagers were poor, especially given the recent raids by the bandits, but would they want to sell things to raise money for the doctor's office? They were all keen on Miss Newbury staying, and she was gaining popularity with the village folks. It had just taken them time to get used to something so modern.

"You're right. We could have a cake sale," he suggested. "I think the village ladies would like that. Or a jumble sale," he added. There was a lot of old furniture he could do with selling himself.

"I know!" Her face brightened "We could host a barn dance! Like for when you build a barn or do the harvest, except that now it's for building the office. And we could charge people to attend, like a town ball. Only not as much, of course." She looked wistful. "Not that I ever attended one, but Mrs. Powell's daughter went to Prescott, and she said there were such things there."

"A dance where you charge people to attend?" He frowned; he hadn't heard of such a thing himself—people invited the neighbors and they turned up. Sometimes they brought food and cake, but mostly they just arrived, and they danced and celebrated after some work they had helped with, like a barn or the harvest. "People pay for attending dances?"

"In towns and cities, they do," she laughed. "You buy a pass, like getting a ticket for a train. It's like in London," she explained, though, of course, that was hearsay.

"I see," he said with his head tilted. "Do you think people would do that?"

Lucille shrugged. "We could ask."

He grinned. He had never met someone as full of enthusiasm and joy and it made him feel delighted just seeing it. "We could," he agreed.

Nicholas couldn't help thinking that it would be good to plan something like that with her. Everyone would enjoy it, and he had no doubt that she could make it a success. He looked forward to the day when they would host it.

Chapter Twenty

The drawing-room was quiet, the still, afternoon air scented with dust and the only sound the slow tick of the clock. Lucille sat with her hand on the table. Even though she was the housekeeper and not strictly permitted to use the upper rooms of the house for her own free time, Mr. Barnes had invited her to do so, and she'd brought her medical books and the Bible to study both. For the first time in weeks, she felt like studying. She felt like herself.

She was going to be a physician for the townsfolk.

Lucille grinned. "Papa," she said into the still air. "You would be so excited for me. I know you would." A warm sense of joy and achievement filled her, and she knew that he would have been proud.

Peace settled inside her, and her lips lifted in a grin. If Papa were near, somewhere, he would have laid his hand on her shoulder, the way he always did when he wanted to show his pride in her. Lucille swallowed hard, her throat tight with love and sadness and pride all mixed.

She leaned back, thinking. Was this the sign she'd asked the Lord to send her? Since that prayer, she had not thought too much about her feelings for Mr. Barnes, resolving to hide that question somewhere in the recesses of her mind, filling the rest of it with studying. She still felt uncertain, not knowing, what the sign was or whether she would recognize it. Glancing at the textbook, she chose to push the thought away and focus on her work.

The medical textbook was turned to a diagram of the spine. She studied it, her finger running down the illustration, the sunshine painting the page in gold and black. It wouldn't be long before she'd go downstairs to help Mrs. Grierson with the evening meal. And tomorrow, they'd be planning the barn dance.

It was a wonderful, slightly crazy plan, but in the last week, they had sold thirty tickets. She hadn't expected that, and the sheriff was even more surprised than herself. The ticket sales had accumulated enough money to pay for plaster for the walls, replacing the windows, and a craftsman to do some of the skilled work. The remaining labor would fall to Glen and the other ranch-hands to accomplish, but that was not too bad—they had expressed their willingness to work for a noble cause.

Shutting her eyes a moment, gratitude filled her heart. During this week, she had accompanied Mr. Barnes to the sheriff's office three times to discuss the plan and organize it, and each time, she had been amazed by the kind way she'd been supported. In the meetings with the town council—where Mr. Canfield had fortunately not been present—she had been well-received and complimented. And in the street, people had stopped to talk to her and share their views on the new doctor's office and their excitement. She'd heard people speaking well of her for the first time in weeks.

Everyone had heard the story of the boy and how she'd saved him. Their doubts had been turned to a clamoring desire for her to treat their ills. Everyone in town, it seemed, had some sort of ailment, from rheumatic aches to sinusitis, and they all had been waiting for a new physician to move in. It would have been amusing, or even daunting, but she was too happy to be able to help to mind.

"Miss Newbury?" Mrs. Grierson called up the stairs.

As Mrs. Grierson entered, Lucille said, "Please, call me Lucille." The set of her mouth and her posture made it clear that her feet were sore from standing. Some of her delight evaporated, replaced with concern for the woman who stood before her.

"Lucille," Mrs. Grierson said hesitantly as though a little uncomfortable with using her first name. They'd known each other for a month now, and Lucille had insisted she called her by name, as formality seemed so unnecessary. "A letter for you."

"A letter?" Lucille frowned. "Thank you." *Who could it be from?* Her heart skipped. The only names that sprang to mind were the banker and lawyer, and she felt sick, thinking that they might have written her. When she took the parchment from Mrs. Grierson, excited relief steadied her.

It was from Mr. Chaffee!

Standing by the window, she let the sunshine illuminate the page so she could read it clearly.

Dear Lucille, she read. *I wanted to find out how you're getting on, but I had to go to Tucson for a shipment of wool. I'm in Prescott and I should be back next week. I trust that you are well. I heard in the village before I left that you're at Breakwater, and I am sorry to hear the townsfolk have not been treating you as they ought. I shall have words with Nicholas Barnes, the sheriff, if you want. I am sure your papa would be proud of you. Take care and write me for anything. If I can't help you with it, my farmhand Reese will be there, and he would be more than glad to assist you. With my fond regards, Max Chaffee.*

Lucille blinked, tears in her eyes making the writing blur before her. He was so kind—and the mention of her father made her heart ache. "Thank you," she whispered. She didn't know who she was thanking—the Lord, Mr. Chaffee, or Mrs. Grierson for bringing the letter. She was grateful to all.

"I'll put the kettle on if you like, Lucille." Mrs. Grierson smiled. "We can have some tea."

"Thank you," Lucille repeated. "I'd be glad of some tea."

***

She woke early the following day, jittery with excitement to prepare for the barn dance. Mrs. Grierson was already making bread when she went down to the kitchen, and Mr. Barnes was there unusually early.

"Morning, Miss Newbury," he greeted her. He was leaning back in the chair, a small smile on his lips. "You're looking happy this morning."

"I am happy, Mr. Barnes," she giggled. "Happy and a little tense. We're going to have a lot of work to do this morning."

Mr. Barnes nodded. "I've asked the lads to help." He jerked his head in the direction of the outbuildings, where the ranch-hands lived on the ranch. "I will also try to be early from the office. I reckon I'll be here at around five o'clock to help with setting up."

"Oh!" Lucille grinned. "Thank you, Mr. Barnes. That would be good."

He shrugged. "I can't expect you ladies to move all that furniture by yourselves."

Seeing the sparkle in his eye, Lucille's smile deepened. She knew he expected her to retort, saying they were perfectly strong, thank you. But she didn't—she just tilted her head and looked at him untroubled, and he laughed.

"I'll see you ladies at five o'clock, then."

Lucille fetched bread and eggs for them. Matty had taught her the secret to fried eggs, which was to make the pan hot—but not too hot—and leave the lid over them so that they cooked evenly.

Mr. Barnes smiled in genuine enjoyment as he ate. He didn't say anything—Lucille appreciated that he didn't mention them in comparison to her former skills—but she could see he enjoyed it. He donned his hat and coat before leaving for work.

The moment he was out of the door, they immediately rushed to get the kitchen tasks out of the way. There was so much to get done this morning.

"We need to get the benches to the barn," Lucille commented as she carried the laundry outside. "And then set up in there."

"The boys are already working there, Lucille," Mrs. Grierson said, scrubbing the counter firmly.

Matty came to help, and a few hours later, Grace and Jessie came too from the nearby ranches. Their team of five set up the barn, cleaned the yard, carried tables—along with the ranch hands—and got the premises ready for the dance that evening.

After a late lunch and when they felt utterly exhausted, the musicians arrived.

The group of youths in the doorway were eager with bright faces, and Lucille felt joy just seeing them. It was such a fine day, and she said a small, inward prayer of thanks. She hadn't felt this uplifted and excited in a long time.

"Good evening," Mrs. Grierson greeted them. "If you'd like, you can set your things up in the barn? That's where the dance is being held."

"Sure, Auntie Rachel."

Lucille glanced at Mrs. Grierson. Her lined, strong face was calm as she instructed the young men—one of whom was related to her—about where to go. Lucille thought the name Rachel didn't really suit her. She wondered what her real tribal name was and made up her mind that—if she had a chance—she would find out. Until now, she had felt a little shy of the older woman, whose calm dignity made her difficult to approach. She decided she had to try to reach out to her.

She was distracted as the men carried their instruments into the barn: A guitar, a flute, and a drum. Another boy with glossy dark hair and high cheekbones carried a fiddle.

"It's going to be beautiful music," she murmured.

"I love a dance," Matty said with a grin. "It's going to be good fun."

Lucille nodded, her heart fluttering with excitement. She hadn't felt like this about anything for years. It wasn't just the entertainment and socializing, the chance to wear pretty clothes, or hearing music. It was the thought that Mr. Barnes would be there.

She reddened just thinking about it. He'd see her in her brown dress. While he'd already seen her in it before, that couldn't be helped. It was the only suitable dress she had.

"What are you wearing, dear?" Matty asked.

Lucille frowned. "My brown dress, I think."

Matty gasped. "You can't wear that all the time! Come over and let's see if I have something that'll fit you. We're of a similar height, and our figures weren't too different when I was young."

"Oh! Matty..." Lucille's heart danced. "Are you sure? I mean—"

Matty chuckled. "Of course, I'm sure! What am I going to do with my old clothes? I can't wear them, and I don't have anyone to give them to. Come on! It's going to be good fun."

Lucille swallowed hard, relief filling her. "You're so kind, Matty. Exceedingly kind."

A small grin was on Matty's lips. "Not too kind, my dear. You can make me more of that salve for my hand if it'll help...it worked good for the aches in the morning."

Lucille laughed. "Of course, Matty. I'd be pleased to."

She helped Mrs. Grierson carry some cushions out to the benches and then excused herself to follow Matty to the ranch.

"Here you are," Matty said, as she opened her closet in her bedchamber. It was a tall wooden one, a little taller than Lucille. It was as wide as when she stretched her arms out to the sides, and dresses and skirts filled it. "The ones over here are the ones that I had when I was about your age." She gestured to her left, where four or five dresses hung. A white one with a pattern caught her eye.

"I love it!"

"Try it on," Matty said, grinning. "It looks as though it'll fit you. If it's not long enough, you can wear a long petticoat under it to make up the length."

"Oh, Matty..." Lucille held up the gown. Made of printed cotton, with little flowers decorating it in pale red, the dress had a "v" shaped waist, wide skirts, and a low neckline, trimmed in red ribbon. It had puffed sleeves and frills about the skirt, and it was the prettiest dress she'd seen.

"There, my dear. Let me help you into it. It's never easy by yourself."

Lucille stood still while Matty helped her out of her own, easy-to-button dress, and into the other, which was more elaborate and harder to put on without help. When she had it on, she checked her reflection in the mirror and gaped.

"I look beautiful."

Matty nodded with fondness. "You do."

The woman in the mirror had chocolate-colored curls in disarray about her pale face. Her eyes were big, the color of the patterns on the gown making them seem large and mysterious. Her skin was shown to advantage by the low-necked gown, which clung in all the right places. Lucille thought that she had never seen herself look so good.

"Is that really what I look like?"

Matty chuckled. "You know that better than anyone. You can tell me how a mirror works, I'm sure."

Lucille giggled. Though she vaguely recollected her father showing her a diagram with light rays, she couldn't recall it clearly now. Lightheaded with excitement, her heart thudded in her chest.

"Matty, you really are sure?" she asked her friend.

"My dear, of course. You're my dearest friend. I want you to use it. Please, use my things when you want to. It makes me happy to see you get some use from them." She was blinking, blue eyes damp with tears.

Lucille hugged her, emotional too. "You're my best friend too, Matty." She cleared her throat, the words low. "I didn't have friends in Pinewood, not really, and now I realize what a lack that was. I'm so glad I came here."

Matty beamed. "I'm glad to hear it, my dear. So glad to hear it. Now, will you have a cloak to wear with it? It's cold in the evenings."

"I do. Thank you, Matty!" Lucille said, heart racing. "Thank you so much."

Once she put her cloak on, she followed her friend into the yard, almost unable to keep still. It was cooler outside, though it was fast approaching summertime and the days were scorching. She shivered, though she wasn't cold. Now she was excited about the dance and about seeing the sheriff.

She paused. Was this the sign she'd asked for? Her face lit up with a smile. The bubbling joy in her heart at the merest thought of looking pretty in front of him—it was quite a compelling sign that she loved him.

God, she prayed with her head turned heavenward. *If this is the sign, I thank You for it.*

It was a beautiful, gentle reminder. Assuming it was the sign she requested, how should she pursue the fact that she was falling in love with Mr. Barnes? Nevertheless, she was confident that, with the new knowledge, she would be guided in whatever else to do. Grinning, her heart full of warmth, she bowed her head a moment in appreciation, the evening sunshine casting shadows on the sand.

She hurried down the path, back to the ranch.

When she reached the kitchen, it was a flurry of activity, with Jessie and Gracie busy pitching in to help, and their daughters, the eldest of whom Lucille judged to be around ten, running around the house.

"Can I help?" she asked, taking care not to let the soup from the vast pot Mrs. Grierson stirred splash onto her clothing.

"It's all being done," Mrs. Grierson said with a tolerant grin as the four little girls cut bread for sandwiches at the table, squabbling among themselves. "You go up and get ready."

"Thank you."

Lucille hurried upstairs. She arranged her hair in a bun before hustling back out to the kitchen to check if there were any last-minute issues to clear up. Mrs. Grierson passed her a cloth for the table, and she agreed to bring it to the barn to give it to whoever was organizing the tables.

"Miss Newbury!" An exclamation from behind her made her turn around.

She recognized that voice—her toes tingled just hearing it. "Mr. Barnes!"

Mr. Barnes was standing by the kitchen door, grinning at her, eyes afire as he saw her new dress. She clutched her cloak shyly.

"Let me take that down to the barn," he said, taking the cloth she was carrying. "You wait inside. It's almost time for the dancing to start." His eyes twinkled, voice low.

"Yes, Mr. Barnes."

He grinned and her heart thudded as he gazed into her eyes. It was a look such as he'd given her once before—a tender look that nonetheless sent her blood fizzing to her head. She looked away, heart pattering.

Lucille wondered if he was going to change into some other clothing too—he was travel-stained and dusty, and she guessed he'd at least want to wash his hair. She went to her bedroom to wait.

The sky was pale gray, the horizon glowing with pink as the sun slowly set. Lucille glanced at her reflection in the mirror, her stomach a knot of excitement. Some of her hair had tumbled down, framing her face. She didn't tuck it back into the bun but left the loose curls where they fell. She was amazed at how she looked.

She looked happy and alive, eyes sparkling and bright.

At the door of the kitchen, she stopped when she saw Mr. Barnes. He had washed his hair and changed from the tan-and-white checked shirt to one with a smaller design in blue and green. It made his eyes seem even more intense as he grinned at her.

"Miss Newbury." He lifted his hat, admiration in his eyes, drinking her in. "You look stunning."

Lucille's face went hot. Her stomach tied itself into tighter knots. She peered into his admiring gaze and grinned. "Thank you, sir. You look nice."

It delighted her to see a grin of pure joy on his face, hastily hidden, though it lingered about his mouth, tugging at the edges of it. "Thank you, miss."

He escorted her to the barn, where music poured out of the doors as the band practiced. The interior was full of light. The benches were to the one side, while the vast area had been cleared, forming a dancefloor. The musicians were at the other side near the wall, their sweet, rhythmic music flooding through Lucille's soul. Her foot tapped and she looked at Mr. Barnes, eager to dance.

They stood together in the doorway and Lucille's heart soared as she waited for their guests to arrive.

Chapter Twenty-One

As Nicholas stood next to Lucille, he could smell the clean scent of her hair, and a faint lavender aroma that clung to her skin. He felt intoxicated. She looked so beautiful; it made his head spin. Glancing sideways, he saw how her pale skin shone in the lamplight, the gown exposing her shoulders. He had never seen her in such a beautiful dress, one that fitted her so perfectly. Her waist was narrow, hips generous. She had the loveliest figure he could imagine, and he went red just thinking it.

Stop it, he told himself firmly.

However, this was a dance, and he was finally allowed to notice and admire how beautiful she was. She was the loveliest being he'd ever seen.

Outside, it was just getting dark, the sky going from a molten orange sunset to cool blue with dusk. People were laughing and talking as he stood in the doorway, welcoming them.

"Mrs. McCauley!" He smiled, seeing their neighbor. She was wearing white and blue, a bonnet over her hair that he would never have guessed she owned, since she never bothered with anything as formal as a bonnet on everyday occasions. Mrs. McCauley grinned, her lips thin and showing white teeth.

"Nicholas. Good to see you. Look at you!" She looked at him, then covered her mouth with her hand. "Why, Lucille! Look at you, my dear! You're stunning."

Nicholas continued greeting guests.

"This place looks terrific," Mr. Burwell greeted, admiring the barn.

Nicholas shrugged. "Didn't do it myself—the ladies did it all." He gestured to Mrs. McCauley and Miss Newbury, where they stood giggling together. "And the ranch-hands did the heavy work," he added, waving at Glen, sitting at one of the benches, a mug of ale in his hand.

"I see. Well, it looks good," Mr. Burwell commented from the entrance. "And well-lit and everything."

"Should be, for the next couple hours," Nicholas chuckled. The lamps and candles would eventually run out, after about three hours, indicating the guests should depart.

Nicholas did his best to greet every guest with a nod or by shaking their hand. He recognized some of the townsfolk— they must have come in by wagon. Mrs. Grierson came to hover by the door for a bit, going back to serving the beer. Miss Newbury stood with him, but appeared a bit uncomfortable greeting the guests with him.

"I should help her," she said, gesturing to Mrs. Grierson.

"The barn dance is to raise funds for the office," Nicholas reminded. "It's right that you greet the attendees with me."

She shifted back and forth on her feet, eyes low. Nicholas frowned. He had never realized before how shy Miss Newbury was. She had such an air of confidence when he first met her, though he had discovered how easily hurt she could be.

"You should be up here," he said. "This dance is also a welcome for you."

"What do you mean?" Miss Newbury asked, eyes widening.

He nodded. "You're very much talked of in town. Everyone wanted to meet you. I think it's the main reason we sold so many tickets to people."

"Mr. Barnes!" She sounded cross, but from the big grin on her face, he knew she wasn't really offended.

His smile grew as he tilted his head to one side. "You're not mad at me?"

"Maybe not," she chuckled. "Of course, I'm not." In the midst of their guests, she looked into his eyes as though they were the only two in the room. "It would be impossible to be mad with you right now."

Nicholas didn't know how long he stared at her—it could've been a moment; it could've been an hour. He entirely lost track of the time, everything ceasing to hold his attention except her face.

"Sheriff! Good to see you. This way, girls."

Nicholas blinked back to reality, greeting Jessie, Stuart, and their children—two daughters and a small son. The children were dressed in their Sunday clothes, the girls with plaits and big smiles, giggling with excitement, the boy looking a little less impressed in his starched collar and shoes.

"Good evening, everyone."

The girls broke out into fits of giggles, and the family walked to where food was accumulating on the table. Each partygoer had brought something with them to add to the meal Mrs. Grierson and Miss Newbury cooked. The barn smelled of a delicious mix of hay and savory steam—the bread, stew, cake, cheese, and pie making the air smell headily good.

"How are you feeling?" he asked Miss Newbury when they had a moment to talk.

"Good," she breathed, sniffing the air.

"It's making me hungry," he confessed, chuckling.

She smirked playfully. "We'll only be here for another half hour at the longest."

"Half an hour?" He made a face, and she laughed even more.

"It can't be that bad," she teased.

Nicholas chuckled. Leaning back on the door, he scanned the room, his heart full of a new contentment as his barn filled with folk. He hadn't hosted a party here in years. The last party at the ranch had been when he was eighteen and Mrs. Radford was still alive, and many of her family had attended. Since Mrs. Radford passed, Nicholas had no desire to host parties and the ranch had become silent and unfriendly. Now, with the laughing faces all around him, the sound of chatter and excited talk rich on the air, he wished he had done so a lot earlier.

Miss Newbury had changed a lot of things around here.

"Miss Newbury!" Gracie Amberley greeted with her husband, Matthew. Keith and her daughter were with her, the little boy looking at Miss Newbury with puzzlement. He didn't seem to know how to approach her.

"Gracie." Lucille embraced the woman who clung to her, arms tight around her form.

Nicholas shook Matthew's hand and they chatted for a while as the children ran around the room, going at once to the table. Nicholas grinned, thinking that Keith looked perfectly fine—he was well enough to eat a massive slice of pie, and seemed healthy as anyone else there.

"Mr. Barnes!" Luke called excitedly behind him.

"Luke!" He grinned, shaking his deputy's hand. Though the young man was fresh-washed and looking proud in a new suit, he also looked extremely awkward. Beside him, her hand in his, was a beautiful girl with pale hair, a round, snub-nosed face, and big eyes. Nicholas thought she might be related to Mr. and Mrs. Burwell—he dimly remembered a niece who'd gone to school in Prescott. Maybe this was her? She looked like Mrs. Burwell's sister, Ruthie, who had been a town beauty.

"This is Daisie."

Nicholas grinned. He would have guessed she was the reason for Luke's distractedness for the last week. He inclined his head in a bow. "Glad to meet you."

"I'm delighted to meet you, sir."

Nicholas eyed his deputy, who was radiating pride. He thought of himself at that age and felt a wistful twist in his heart. Luke was so much younger than he'd ever been. Nicholas had seemed old and embittered when he was eighteen, but Luke glowed with innocent love.

As happy as he was for him, he was sad for himself. He had never been like that.

He glanced sideways at Miss Newbury. She wasn't much older than Luke, but she too was not like him. She seemed more serious, and, though she was often lighthearted and playful, when he compared her to Luke and Daisie, he saw the fear and sorrow she had lived through.

He smiled at her as their guests walked past. Miss Newbury watched at them wistfully. When she realized he was staring, she smiled.

"Now I know where my deputy's good sense has gone for the last while," Nicholas whispered.

They were both still chuckling as the musicians tuned up.

Nicholas swallowed hard. Miss Newbury looked so beautiful as she went to the table, her cheeks flushed, a big smile on her face. Chatting with Matty, she settled on the bench beside her as Matty passed her a slice of pie. Nicholas watched them, his heart aching. He wished he had the courage to ask her to dance.

Fool, just ask her.

His throat tightened as though he could never get the words out. Miss Newbury was his housekeeper. As it was, he'd pushed every boundary just lately, from teaching her to ride to touching her hand. He had fallen for her weeks ago and he couldn't hide it from himself anymore.

He just hoped he could hide it from everybody else.

If everyone saw, then he would have to let her stay in the physician's house as it would no longer be seemly for her to stay under his roof, and he wasn't sure he wanted to risk that. He liked having her under his roof.

His heart thudded. He was scared, he recognized—scared of feeling love. He had loved his parents and that had only caused pain. He had loved Mrs. Radford, and he'd lost both the Radfords, too. If he loved, he knew where it led: It led to a pain in his heart that was as big and as empty as the desert. It led to sorrow, and he'd already had more than he wanted.

He reached for some ale and heard a kind, familiar voice at his elbow.

"Sir, go talk to her."

He blinked, startled at first, and then as he focused on Mrs. Grierson, he sighed. "She's happy talking to her friend." It was true, at least—Miss Newbury looked perfectly comfortable where she was. He flushed, self-conscious. Was it so obvious how he felt?

Mrs. Grierson looked away. "Burying your heart isn't going to keep it fresh."

Nicholas opened his mouth to respond, but she had already stood, and he didn't want to chase her across the room. He wasn't sure if he'd heard right, but the more he thought about the comment, the more it made sense.

He had been burying his heart. And it hadn't done it much good; she was right.

With a deep breath, he shifted on his coat, watching the dancers. The music had started, and Miss Newbury was on her feet, dancing with Mr. Simmons.

Mr. Simmons and Lucille had become friends. On Lucille's visits into town, they had met on two occasions and discussed how they would divide the duties in the town. It seemed to Nicholas that Mr. Simmons was more than grateful for an opportunity to retire. Of all the people in the town, Mr. Simmons had never doubted Lucille's skill—he had said he'd seen the expert way she stitched Bert's leg, and that had been enough to convince him. Nicholas was glad they had settled matters in a way that benefited them both.

The old fellow laughed as they clapped, stamping their feet, and linking arms. It was lively, simple dancing, and Nicholas tapped his foot, unable to keep still with the lively music that flowed around the barn. The musicians were excellent—he was so glad he'd managed to find a group with such aptitude. Everyone was on their feet, even the children, who capered in a circle watching their parents and elders dancing.

The firelight was bright on their faces, the sound of whoops and yells as bright as the lamps. He clapped, laughed, and felt again that strange, new feeling like water flooding his heart.

The dancers cheered each other as the musicians transitioned to an even livelier tune. Everyone was on their feet with rhythmic clapping, stamping, and dancing.

Nicholas stayed seated, shy. He'd never been one for dancing, even as a youth. His ranch hands Glen and Alfred were dancing to the music, a pretty girl, hand in hand with Alfred. He recognized Mr. Elwood from the bar, and his wife, and was surprised that the barman—who he always thought of as extremely dignified—was whooping and dancing along with the rest.

There were so many folks he recognized—he spotted Chris the ranch hand, and the Burwells chatting with Glen. Rebecca, Bert's wife, sat with Mrs. Amberley. Bert made his way over to join her, a plate of sandwiches in his hand. Bert walked without a limp toward the table, grinning at Nicholas, who waved.

Though Bert appeared to anticipate that Nicholas would join them, something held him in his seat. It wasn't because his friends were there—they had all repented in their anger toward Nicholas and Miss Newbury, except for Mr. Canfield, who notably was absent. And it wasn't because he felt unwelcome—he knew they would be pleased to have him join them in their eating, drinking and lively bantering.

Somehow, he felt as if he didn't belong there. Though it was his barn, Nicholas didn't feel part of the circle of happy, playful people.

Nicholas sipped his ale. Restless, he headed into the night outside for some fresh air. Walking around the front, he leaned on the wall of the barn, the stone feeling cool through the fabric of his shirt.

The desert stretched out around him, gray under a black sky. The stars, huge and shining, hung suspended over the landscape like jewels on black velvet. Nicholas gazed up at them, awed by their beauty. The stars had always confused him—when he looked up there, he sometimes couldn't help feeling so alone, as if that big black cavern studded with glimmering lights mocked him with its questions. Was there a God? Or was he truly all alone?

"It's beautiful," Miss Newbury spoke faintly just beside him.

His heart thudded. "Yes," he said tenderly. "Yes, it is."

They looked out over the silent landscape. The sounds from the barn just behind them were strained, the notes of the violin high and thin like the wavering flame-light that spilled through the doors and onto the path. Time ceased to have meaning. If it hadn't been for the intermittent sounds from the barn—sounds of music, cheering, and gales of laughter—he would have thought they were the only people in a still, cold landscape.

"It's quiet."

Miss Newbury stared at the stars, her dark eyes wide. The starlight was bright, made brighter by the pools of her eyes. The light touched her skin, making it glow.

"The stars are so beautiful," she said softly. "I remember admiring them when I first came here."

"You did?" he asked, surprised. He had thought her so angry that night—and not unjustified, either, in that anger. He blushed and smiled sheepishly.

"That one up there? That's the North Star. And the Crown, just close by." She pointed to a group of stars; one Nicholas didn't think he'd recognize.

"Is it?" he asked. His lip lifted in the corner. "You know a lot about stars."

She smiled. Her eyes were focused on the sky, her head tilted wistfully. "Papa taught me."

"Oh." Sometimes, looking at the sky, Nicholas thought that his parents were there, somewhere, beyond the star–studded blanket, in the realm of the angels. Did they sometimes look down? He had no idea.

"Somehow, the sky seems so cold and distant," Miss Newbury sighed.

Her thoughts, it seemed, were not that dissimilar to his. "It does," he nodded. "The stars are so beautiful, but they are strange. Like ice. I remember holding a piece of ice, once. It melted a little in my hand. It was so white it seemed almost silver, like the stars, and it shone in the light."

"They are cold," she said. "They don't feel happy to me sometimes."

He nodded. "Me, too. I feel like they are all together up there, so distant, unaware of me watching." He wasn't just talking of the stars now.

After a moment, she murmured, "You miss your parents?"

"Yes." He almost whispered it. He had never actually told someone that. Even the Radfords—even though they had taken him in so soon after his parents' death—he had never told. He'd been so angry at first, so lost and afraid and mad with his parents for leaving him, and then he'd simply been unsure of how to voice his grief as it grew and changed within. He'd been older then, and sure that boys did not show their emotions.

Miss Newbury peered into his face. "I feel like that, too. But then I know that Papa knows what I do, and that he's proud of me. Love is like water—you can't hold it in one place, I know that it flows down from the heights like rain and falls on me."

Hearing the tears in her voice, he swallowed, moved to weep.

"Thank you," Nicholas whispered. He had never thought about that. He had never thought about the fact that his parents' love was always there for him and would always be there, as close as rain, as close as the tears on his cheek. "Thank you."

A sense of peace filled him as he stared at the starlit sky. He had often looked up there and felt alone and forgotten. Now, he had a sense of the Creator who brought it forth, its glory just a glimmer of His own. He also had a sense of his parents, up there somewhere, in the realm of angels, smiling down at him.

They stood without saying anything.

After a moment, she smiled. "You have a lovely way of speaking, sir."

"Nicholas," he said distractedly. "Please, call me by my name." He reddened as the words left his lips. His heart thudded—he'd had no idea what would happen if he crossed that line, and now, without thinking, he'd stepped across it like stepping down a stair. He held his breath.

As she smiled, the feeling in his heart went from fear to wonder. She didn't hate him for his familiarity.

"Nicholas," she repeated softly. "It's a fine name."

"Thank you." His throat was tight, and he swallowed. "And you?"

A small, confused look settled about her eyes. "What about me?"

"What shall I call you?" he asked softly.

"Lucille," she answered.

He knew her name—he'd heard it before. But he had never heard her say it, not except the first time she'd introduced herself, and, until now, he had never imagined it on his lips. "Lucille."

Lucille smiled, and the brightness in her eyes made his heart leap. Nicholas wanted to say it again, just to see her look at him like that again. Her cheeks grew red, while his cheeks throbbed with warmth. He was doing and saying things he had never imagined, yet he could not make the excuse that it was the ale talking. He'd drunk one glass, and the chilly wind sobered him even from that. This was his heart.

"Are you cold?" he asked gently.

She shrugged. "Not too cold."

The desert was dark, and the night was chilly through the thin fabric of his shirtsleeves. The heat of the day was still warming the rocks and sand, but within an hour, it would be icy out there. He smiled at her. "Shall we go inside?"

She tilted her head, eyes darting to the doors before nodding. "Let's go."

As she went inside, he followed, his heart racing. His head was thumping, and his body heated, and they rejoined the others—to celebrate *Lucille*.

Chapter Twenty-Two

Lucille leaned back against the cool wall, her eyes heavy. While she wasn't confident in guessing the time during the day, she was too exhausted to attempt it at night. She didn't need to know what hour it was to know that she was half-asleep.

Opposite her, Nicholas grinned. For the last few hours, they'd eaten, drank, and chatted at the table; the evening was the most enjoyable Lucille could remember. Her mind still raced with the delight that was thinking of him by name and recalling their quiet talk in the yard. It was the most beautiful thing she could imagine, and she knew she would always remember it.

Nicholas.

She knew now that she was in love. If she had asked for a sign, she had received it—more than once. Though she still had no idea what to do about it, after that moment in the darkness, she knew unshakably how she felt. Her heart tingled as she peeked shyly at Nicholas before looking away.

Down the table, Matty sat with her husband, conversing with neighbors and townsfolk. Gracie and Jessie—the only other women Lucille knew even a little, besides Matty and Mrs. Grierson—had already gone home, taking their weary children with them.

"Candles are almost out," Nicholas commented.

Lucille, straining to hear him through a yawn, nodded. "True."

The candles and lanterns that illuminated the barn flickered low. Lucille stifled a yawn and estimated that in under half an hour, the light would have gone. They ought to get people moving while they could still see to find the entrance.

"Matty?" she murmured, nudging her friend. She could help gently persuade the sleepy townsfolk to get back to their homes. Of course, for all those who felt safer, they could offer accommodation either in the barn or in the house. Lucille knew some of the neighbors from further-afield ranches were going to be staying with Matty tonight. "Maybe we should start suggesting people settle down for the night."

Her friend nodded. "Of course." Matty was most likely tired too—her eyes were always deep-set, but they were surrounded by dark rings and her expression was weary. Lucille got to her feet, sliding her leg over the bench.

"What is it?" Nicholas asked, voice soft.

"I'm just going to suggest people start heading to town," Lucille replied.

Nicholas made a face, etched with worry. They both knew it was dangerous for people to take the road back, especially at night. After a brief hesitation, Nicholas nodded. "Let me help." He shifted on the seat, swinging a leg over the bench to stand.

At another table, a few farmers and townsfolk sat, mostly half-asleep. The ranch hands dozed on a table—Glen's bright curls rested on the table, his big form slumped as he snored.

"Glen?" she murmured, gently shaking him awake. "Glen...?"

He stirred and snorted, moving his head to the side, slowly waking up. Nicholas was gently shaking a farmer who had fallen asleep at the table.

As they got the last of the guests to their feet, gently guiding them to the back of the barn, where a warm corner had been prepared, Lucille tensed.

The steady drumming of hoofbeats echoed through the night, faintly at first, but getting louder.

She wanted to go to Nicholas, but her body rooted to the spot, as though every part of her listened for the sounds of whatever was out there. Nicholas went stiff as well, eyes narrowed. He'd heard it too. His hand rested on the table, another hand at his side, gripping his pistol loosely. Her heart thudded. Clearly, he thought that the horsemen were not their friends.

Without warning, glass shattering echoed around the room, and a gunshot.

"Get down!" Nicholas yelled, vaulting to the doors. Lucille, heart thumping, ran after him. "Lucille, stay here," Nicholas commanded as she reached him at the door, eyes pleading. "Please. It's the bandits. Stay safe."

Lucille nodded. Her heart flooded fear, shock, and terror for Nicholas's safety. He bolted into the yard, and she froze, fright making her stiff with nerves.

After another shot and a shout, she flattened herself against the wall, some instinct making her get out of the line of the door. Desperate, she wasn't sure if she was more afraid for herself or for Nicholas, out there facing the bandits. A third shot rang out, and a tear ran down her cheek, pure panic making her weep. Men were shouting outside now, and she could hear horses. It sounded like at least six riders were out there, and Nicholas was *not* on a horse.

Before she could breathe, Luke darted after him. She hadn't even noticed that Luke and Daisie were still there. The pretty young woman with Luke huddled up on the floor beside the bench, staying out of the line of fire.

Lucille's mind was moving impossibly slowly, while another part of it was racing, trying to think. Her head felt full of wool. Then, there was silence. She managed, finally, to move her feet toward the table where Glen and the others jolted awake.

Of all the remaining men—Glen, Alfred, the big farmhand from the Burwell ranch—she didn't know or trust any of them as much as she did Glen. If she could get more men to help Nicholas...

"Lucille!" Matty grabbed her arm, pulling her into a relieved hug. "Are you all right?"

Relief washed over her as she recognized the older woman's gaunt, calm face. "Matty, it's so dangerous out there. I need to get the other men to go with him..." she explained, but Matty tilted her head, looking up at Lucille gravely.

"He's always armed, and so is Luke. The ranch-hands are in no condition to help."

"But Matty..." Lucille's stomach twisted. She was right, Lucille knew that—but at the same time, she couldn't bear to leave Nicholas out there by himself.

Matty shook her head. The sounds of hooves had stopped, but there was still the pops of gunfire, and through the open door, there was the flare of a pistol shot. The bandits were close.

"Matty..." Lucille whimpered.

What if the bandits came into the barn? They were all trapped here. There were no children, fortunately, but there were men and women. The townsfolk—their friends. At the sound of gunfire, a woman staggered to her feet, fear in her eyes.

Lucille knew she should go to her, but she was too afraid. At another shot, she pressed against the wall, eyes shut, terror making it hard to breathe. The men were out there, and if they came closer, if they came inside...

"There aren't as many guns out there as you'd think," Matty murmured, squeezing her shoulder.

"Maybe not," Lucille gasped. She was sure there were at least six bandits, if the rumble of hooves they'd heard earlier was an indication of number, but Matty was right. They couldn't all be armed. The noise of firing was too intermittent for that. Matty's fingers curled around her own.

As they stood there, too scared to move, a man ran toward the door. Lucille wanted to scream in alarm as he ran, sure he would come in. She couldn't see if he was armed or not, but he looked like he was heading their way.

"No!" she cried.

As a shot rang out, he ducked, falling to the ground. Lucille thought he'd been shot, but he crawled, zigzagging from his position as though avoiding being hit by keeping on the ground. She only watched while he got away.

"They have already ridden off. Listen," Matty soothed. Lucille listened, but she could hear only silence outside. "The bandits came for the cash; I'm sure of it."

"The cash?" Lucille's brow furrowed. For a moment, she didn't know what Matty meant, but then she recalled that the money they'd made—the proceeds from the tickets for the barn-dance—was in the kitchen in a strong-box. Nicholas had brought the money back with him from the town today for safe keeping.

Matty sighed, "Why else would they come out here? They've never attacked this far out."

Lucille didn't want it to be true, but she trusted Matty. After all, she'd lived in Oxplains much longer.

Someone running toward the doors distracted her from her thoughts.

As her hands balled into fists, Nicholas came in with Luke. Nicholas paused in the doorway, gesturing to him, and then came toward her and Matty. The expression in his eyes was marred with sorrow.

"Lucille," he uttered faintly as he approached, "It's not safe out there—best if you get the guests to sleep here."

"What happened?" she gasped. The physician part of her wanted to check him for injury, but it was so overwhelmed by her shock of being near danger, that she froze where she stood.

He swallowed hard. "They took it."

Lucille gaped at him. There was a hollowness in her chest, utter disbelief seizing her mind. *They couldn't have! How could they have even known where it was? How had they come all this way out here, just to steal it?* Her head reeled.

At that moment, Luke reentered, panting from scouting the area. "I couldn't see them, sir," Luke said. "The cash box is gone. They must have it."

Lucille's chest tightened. All their arduous work! The bandits waited until they were distracted and walked in to seize it.

While felt sick, she oddly didn't feel as downcast as she would have expected. Rather, in the place where sorrow and horror had settled, there was a new fullness, a new sense of purpose and trust.

"God will find another way," she murmured, the hearts pouring from her racing heart. "He meant us all to come together behind this goal, and if we are meant to repair the office, He will send another way to us."

Beside her, Matty bowed her head. First, Nicholas looked defeated, but then a small, flicker of hope appeared.

"I sure hope that's true," he stared at the ground.

They stood there, downcast. Lucille took a deep breath, but then Nicholas cleared his throat.

"Shall we pray?"

Speechless, Lucille nodded, and they bowed their heads. Nicholas led the prayer, saying the paternoster in his low, resonant voice. Lucille heard the familiar, soothing words, and as she said them with him, their meaning slowly sank into her bones. *Thy Will be done.*

This was God's Will, too. Dark as it seemed, this terrible event might have some good in it.

She didn't know where this new belief had come from, but she was convinced it was so. If the doctor's rooms were meant to be mended, they would be mended. They didn't need the money to make it happen. The barn dance had been meant for something else entirely—the villagers just needed to relax and have fun and celebrate their humanness.

If God wished the rooms to be fixed, another way would turn up.

Nicholas's eyes were gentle, and he was smiling. "Maybe that's true."

She grinned. "I think it is." They held one another's gaze, and in that moment, it wasn't altogether so important that the money had just been carried off to the hideout in the eastern slopes. It was more important that they were here, now, and that she saw him smile.

Luke sat heavily on the bench, looking defeated.

"Come on...it's not that bad," Nicholas said, resting a hand on his shoulder. He didn't sound all that sure, a small smile at the edge of his mouth, but she felt reassured too. "You can stay the night with me. Both of you. All of you," Nicholas added, gesturing to Matty and her husband and the remaining townsfolk. Mrs. Grierson's mouth was set in a line.

"Mrs. Grierson, if you could help people find their way to the house?" he asked her. The candles flickered, the last light in the barn wavering. Lucille was glad Nicholas was close by—she was scared.

Mrs. Grierson nodded. "Yes. My nephew and the boys can stay with me." She gestured at the cottage where she slept.

"Of course," Nicholas agreed. "Matty? Will you stay with us? I don't advise anyone to go wandering back to their home now."

Matty shrugged. "They came to steal, Nicholas. They have the cash, and lots of it—what good would it do them to stay here and attack anyone?"

Lucille swallowed hard. Matty had a way of speaking logically that cut through the fog of her emotions. Nicholas spoke to the ranch hands, Glen's eyes widening in alarm before calm settled on his features as Nicholas explained.

"It's true, what you said," Matty murmured. "God will show you a way."

"I know," Lucille agreed. She felt that without any doubt. Strength flowed through her as she locked eyes with Nicholas. His eyes were bright with flamelight, and she knew that whatever had happened, she would not forget their talk under the starlit night.

"Come on, miss," Mrs. Grierson said, laying a gentle hand on her shoulder. "Let's get back to the house. I'll help the others settle in the kitchen. Miss Wellford is to sleep upstairs with you."

"Oh." Lucille nodded, as the earnest, pretty woman approached. "Of course." She could hardly be expected to sleep in the kitchen with the other men.

Lucille was acutely conscious of Nicholas as he led them across the yard, the candle in his hand casting tall, wavering shadows across the stony path.

"Miss Newbury?" Daisie said sheepishly as Lucille led her upstairs.

"Yes?"

"How did you learn to be a doctor?"

Lucille smiled. It was a question she hadn't expected. The villagers might have disbelieved in women doctors, but none of them had thought to ask her how and where she had acquired her knowledge. Daisie peered at her, blue eyes filled with some expression Lucille couldn't recognize.

"I learned from my father," Lucille explained. As they reached her bedroom, she paused to light a candle, setting it on the mantel by the mirror. The light flooded into the room and Lucille caught sight of her face. She looked pale and weary, long hair loose about her thin, chalk-pale face.

"Your father was a physician?" Daisie asked. She rinsed her face in the bowl on the nightstand, unbuttoning the buttons at the back of her gown unselfconsciously. Her eyes were round as she gawked at Lucille.

Lucille made a small sound of agreement. "He was."

"Oh! How amazing." Daisie gasped, beaming at Lucille as if she had said something remarkable.

"Well, he was," Lucille reiterated, a little off-guard. Why was the girl acting as if that was so remarkable? Did she not believe her? She realized, as she shrugged off her dress and slipped her nightshirt on over her shift, that it really was more unusual than she let herself believe.

"That's wonderful," Daisie sighed, settling under the covers. Lucille slid in under the cover as well, an arm's width of space between them. "You know," Daisie murmured as Lucille's thoughts drifted further into sleep, "I wish I could do what you did."

Lucille murmured something she hoped sounded uplifting—she was so drained that she could barely think. As she lay there, the thought dropped into her mind through its jumble of imagery and weariness, that she could teach Daisie, like Papa taught her. It took only a second or two more for her thoughts to drift and for her to fall into a deep, dreamless sleep.

Chapter Twenty-Three

Nicholas rolled out of bed early, and he was exhausted. While it was his day off, there was a lot to do, and he considered riding out to the bandit's hideout. He had to try and recover the cash. At the same time, though, Lucille's words made a strange sort of sense to him, and another part of his mind felt it was best to wait.

"Maybe she's right," he murmured.

The Lord would show them another way, a way that would ensure the doctor's rooms could be mended without them needing the cash. He had brought Lucille there, and, even though he had always been aware of the injuries from bandits and at work, he had not been aware many of the elderly townsfolk were ill and needed help if they were to make it through the winter.

He brought Lucille here—He will find a way for her to help the folk.

He didn't doubt that. His faith might waver where he was concerned, but somehow, he knew God would take care of Lucille—such a tender, innocent soul—even where He might turn away from Nicholas.

He splashed his face in the bowl on the table and shrugged into a fresh set of clothes. After tugging on his boots, he wandered downstairs to breakfast. "Morning, Mrs. Grierson. Morning, Lucille."

Lucille blushed as he used her name. The kitchen was full of townsfolk and ranchers—mostly awake, some still sitting against the wall, slumped and half-asleep. Mrs. Grierson and Lucille had clearly been up early cooking for them. Nicholas felt guilty as he sat on the other side of Luke; the two women had not had any more sleep than he had. She had already cooked bread and was helping Mrs. Grierson fry a dozen eggs.

Luke sat with Daisie opposite him, as more townsfolk and farmers joined them at the table.

"Should we go and see what we can do?" Luke asked Nicholas. "I mean, take some men, and go riding out there and see if we can ambush them somehow?" His eyes were bright and earnest.

Nicholas shook his head, cautious compared to Luke's hopefulness. "We'd need a lot of men. You know there are a lot of bandits out there."

Luke nodded, his bright enthusiasm cooling, and Nicholas's own spirits lowered.

That was the trouble; it was evident as he looked around the table. None of the fellows looked in the state to be riding anywhere. He was exhausted, and, though he'd slept, he didn't really trust himself to go riding around in the desert after bandits.

They had to do *something*.

Riding after them wasn't the right approach. He glanced across at Lucille, sitting across from him, beside Daisie. She was eating fresh bread and cheese, a puzzled frown on her face. His heart raced as he looked at her. After the previous night, he couldn't stop himself from blushing when he thought of her.

She was so beautiful.

He noticed her watching him during the meal, and, as soon as Luke and Daisie were involved in a conversation, he leaned forward.

"I'm considering riding out to see if we can spot them," Nicholas told her. He didn't know why, but he felt the need to confide in her. He wanted her opinion.

A small furrow creased her brow. "Are you sure that's safe?" she said. "We can manage without the money; I know we can. It is not worth risking injury." She pleaded at him with those eyes so big and dark that he felt like his heart might melt.

"I want to see if I can spot their hideout," he stated.

"Of course," Lucille said softly. "But please, be careful. Injuries are a lot harder to fix than missing cash."

Her tone was not serious, but he knew she meant it and he nodded. "Yes. You're right."

"I know."

They shared a chuckle. It was the expression on her face and in her words that made him laugh—she reprimanded him playfully and it was a welcome change. He was used to townsfolk treating him with some amount of deference, though the ranch hands tended to tease him occasionally. Being teased by Lucille, especially now when he felt so low-spirited, was a delight.

When he realized that people were watching, he stared at the tabletop a moment, self-conscious. The graying wood was scrubbed, stains faint shadows on the surface. "I will take Luke and two or three other men and ride there now," he resigned, glancing around.

Some of the men had clearly taken the merrymaking as a good reason to enjoy his good ale, with pained expressions on more than a few faces. If he could find three other men who could sit astride a horse without the motion making them throw up their breakfast, he'd count it as his biggest achievement of the morning.

"Keep safe," Lucille said briskly. As she flushed, he realized she was worried for him. Having someone concerned for him was an experience he hadn't had in a long time, strange and precious to him. His pulse thumped.

Heading to the door, Nicholas gestured to Luke. "Shall we ride?"

Luke rose to his feet smartly. Nicholas's heart twisted as his deputy went to Daisie, took her hand, pressing it to his lips. While Nicholas didn't watch them, stunned by Luke's boldness to do so in a kitchen full of townsfolk, his heart was filled with warmth, and he felt he understood. He felt the same way now.

Clearing his throat, he realized that it had been a long time since he'd ridden out with the same reluctance that he did now. He didn't think he'd ever felt that way before. Nobody relished the thought of being shot at, but now, he wanted to stay alive for more than simply surviving. He wanted to come home and see Lucille there in the kitchen and take her hand and see more night skies with her. He wanted to laugh and see her dark eyes watching him and share her special smile.

"Come on, men," he announced, and two more fellows got to their feet. Chris was there with a man from the same ranch. The men stumbled to the door, getting their hats, and going out into the yard.

Before Nicholas went to fetch his horse, he paused at the door, looking back at the kitchen. He stared in, wanting to drink in the sight of Lucille at the counter. Chris stumbled across the view, leading his horse, and Nicholas had to move over to let the others pass.

Once the other three men were ready, Nicholas swung up into the saddle and they rode off.

***

"We'll head through to the town and then east, right?" Luke called.

Nicholas nodded, wondering how well Luke had slept in the kitchen, and he grinned, sure that the fellow had spent a hard night on the benches or on the floor. He had at least had the privilege of sleeping in a bed, and he rode ahead of three men who hung onto the reins, some of them looking more than a little regretful of the night's indulging.

They rode down the dry, cool road path to the road. The horse's hooves lifted the dust, white and fine in the early morning. Though it was still not particularly hot, in an hour, the road would shimmer, and the sweat would trickle down their brows. Right now, it was pleasantly warm, and Nicholas was not sorry for his long shirtsleeves and leather trousers.

"Sir?" Luke called, riding alongside him.

Nicholas frowned, slowing so that they could talk comfortably as they went forward at a trot.

"Will we try to get the money back,?"

Nicholas shrugged. "I don't know if we can, Luke." He glanced pointedly at the men who rode with them, Chris, pale as the distant sand, fingers white on the reins, and Ed, who looked as though he would throw up his breakfast any minute.

Luke nodded. "Should I scout ahead and see if they left the main road, sir?"

"If you want, Luke," he said. He didn't think there would be a trail to follow—the desert sand hadn't been stirred up by the wind, but he still reckoned that there wouldn't be a lot to see.

As they passed the first houses in town, he called to the men, "We'll stop by the sheriff's office a moment, then carry on."

It was early, but the curtains were open on most of the houses, though nobody ventured onto the street yet. The townsfolk preferred not to go about in the open alone, especially the older folks, who were scared—justifiably so—of being accosted by the bandits. The town was quiet and still, the sunshine touching the house roofs and shining on the tiles.

The men brought their horses to a trough to ready them for the journey ahead. Nicholas dismounted at the office, handing Luke the reins, and walked to the long, low terrace around the back. He stared out, sure that the men were wondering what on Earth he was up to, he tried to see if there were any hiding places from which the bandits might observe him at the office.

Squinting, he wasn't sure what to look for. A concealed space, an abandoned building that overlooked the office, perhaps. He couldn't see anything. He did the same at the front, scanning across the street to the inn and the other buildings along it.

He sighed. If the bandits were keeping a watch on the office, they were doing so by some other means than spying on the building. They must have been keeping watch from within the town. Someone in the town might be assisting or informing them.

He swore under his breath.

"Sir?" Luke asked as Nicholas limped back toward his horse. "Should we ride?"

"Yes, Luke," he nodded. "Let's see if we can find their hideout."

He swung up into the saddle and they rode down the main road out of the town.

The desert was already hot by the time they rode toward the cave system. The road shimmered and the heat made it hard to breathe. Nicholas patted his horse's neck reassuringly.

"Not much longer out here," he reassured Starburst as they rode slowly onward.

The caves dotted the distant cliff and Nicholas gripped the reins. There was little chance of them being able to confront anyone there—the bandits could hide all over and shoot at them without warning.

He shivered. He had so often felt as though these bandits were a curse or a plague on the town. His faith shifted and diminished every year since the death of his parents; he'd never stopped to wonder why God might have brought the bandits here. Although Lucille rekindled his hope, he still didn't have an answer. Pushing the question away, he deemed it too complex to consider.

As they rode closer, Nicholas could have sworn he caught sight of the glint of metal among the cliffs. He tensed when he saw it shift and move.

"Down!" he shouted, flattening himself on Starburst's back.

He heard the shot after he saw it, the bright glint of the gun firing so brief on the hill, followed by the crack. When he risked sitting up, the men were all slowly, nervously, straightening too. The horses were agitated, ears perked high as they snorted, eyes wide.

"Let's get back a bit, men," Nicholas called. He did his best to ensure he sounded calm, though he didn't feel it. "We can see them up there—no point getting in close range." Pointing in the direction where he had seen the shine of gunmetal, nothing showed there among the rocks now. Whoever fired did their best to hide the weapon. He could imagine the fellow lying flat on the ground, the gun hidden behind a rock to conceal it from their sight.

The men rode back a few paces out of range. As it was, the shot had been careless, its only target was to prove how confident they were.

Anger roiled inside him, but Nicholas pushed it down. That kind of egotistical response made people do stupid things. Flaunting their presence on the ridge wasn't meant to insult him, and even if it was, he'd not do himself or his man any service by letting that insult goad him.

Glaring at the rocks, Nicholas to think.

There was no way they would get them up there. The cave they must be using was virtually unreachable, perched by a ledge of rock accessed by a narrow path. If his men tried to ride up that path, the bandits could lie up there and pick them off as they came up toward them. No, trying to reach their hideout was not going to make sense. He'd have to think of another plan.

Nicholas waved for his men to ride with him, deciding to return to town. It was a long, hot ride back to the town, and the sooner they could get the horses there and give them more water, the more content he'd feel.

When they arrived, the sunshine was pouring onto the street, and he guessed it must be around eleven o'clock in the morning already. The ride out there to the caves had taken about three hours. His stomach grumbled. They watered the horses at the pump at the back of the office before heading to the ranch.

Chris and Ed headed home as they reached their land, and Nicholas and Luke rode back together toward Breakwater Ranch, subdued.

He'd felt confident enough about riding to the bandit's cave that morning, but, since having done so, there was quiet anger inside him—the product of his own feeling of helplessness, he was quite sure. There were too many of them, and the cave was too well-placed. If he assembled a group of men and rode up there, he would be risking all their lives.

Nicholas had wanted to dislodge those bandits for the past year, but he'd never felt quite this motivation to do so. Was it arrogance, that he wanted to repay them for thwarting their plans to raise money? Or was it just because he knew the townsfolk had enough?

Though he didn't know the answers, God did. He could only pray and hope that they'd be revealed to him. He focused on the road, the sound of the hooves were the only noise in the dry, still air.

***

The ranch was quiet when they arrived. Glen and the men were tidying up the barn, and Nicholas led his horse to the stables, wondering why it was so still. When he removed his boots in the doorway, Mrs. Grierson greeted him.

"Afternoon, sheriff."

"Good afternoon, Mrs. Grierson."

The kitchen was spotless and clean, the air smelling of bread. Their guests had departed, leaving behind a muted stillness. Lucille and Daisie came into the kitchen carrying a basket of laundry, talking quietly with each other.

He inclined his head in a bow. "Good afternoon, ladies."

"Sheriff," Lucille greeted him. Her gaze held his and his heart soared. "You are all back safely?"

"Good afternoon, sheriff," Daisie interjected politely, a fear in her eyes.

"Luke is fine," he reassured. "He's on his way up here to fetch you. All the men are fine. It went well enough."

"Good! Good." Daisie sighed with relief.

Nicholas gave her a kind, supportive look before returning his gaze to Lucille. She was smiling, seeming pleased to see him, which delighted him. He didn't mind too much about the money that had been stolen—she was right, there would be a way to proceed without it. His faith was starting, slowly—so slowly—to break through the surface of his heart like grass on a prairie after winter.

All that mattered to him was that she was here, looking at him, and he couldn't look anywhere else.

Mrs. Grierson laid out some food on the table—some bread and cheese. There was soup on the stove, the savory scent filling the kitchen. Lucille moved so daintily, her eyes on his as she took the seat across from him.

"Potatoes, sir?" Mrs. Grierson asked.

Nicholas flushed, embarrassed when it took him longer than it should've to respond. "Yes. Thank you, Mrs. Grierson."

As she fetched the potatoes, Lucille and Daisie chatted and laughed together.

"You really think we could?" Daisie asked.

Lucille shrugged. "Of course. I'm sure we could."

As if they became aware of him watching them, and they looked up, Daisie flushing bright red.

"Here's some soup, and there's potatoes to go with it," Mrs. Grierson said, thumping a plate down in front of him.

Nicholas nodded his thanks as Mrs. Grierson settled in her chair. He had the feeling that the three occupants of his house were keeping some secret from him, but with Lucille looking flushed and happy, and Daisie giggling shyly, he couldn't feel anything but gratitude.

Chapter Twenty-Four

The following day, Nicholas rode into town, surprisingly energized for all that he usually lacked some enthusiasm for the week of work. A new energy filled him, and he was looking forward to the day.

He dismounted outside the office, thinking that it was quiet in the streets—but then, Monday mornings were never particularly lively. The townsfolk were cleaning up after breakfast and beginning their daily chores. Around midday, the streets would become busy as people came in from the nearby ranches and fields for lunch.

"Morning, sir," Luke greeted, as he came into the office. He looked tired and pale, his brow furrowed.

"Morning, Luke," he smiled. "Something on your mind?"

Luke shrugged. "Not really, sir." He paused, clearing his throat. "Sir...what's your opinion about Miss Newbury? Really, I mean?"

Nicholas was astonished. "Why, you know I admire her. Surely, you know that, or why would I have endorsed her to be the physician?"

"I know, sir. But do you think doctoring is, well, something ladies ought to do? It's brutal sometimes." Luke rubbed his neck in uncertainty.

Nicholas nodded. "It's exactly that. Makes me want to pass out sometimes, all the blood. But Miss Newbury...why, she seems not to notice." He chuckled, recalling how comfortable she had been when stitching Bert that day that seemed so long ago now.

Luke shifted from foot to foot. "I know," he said. "But, well, Miss Newbury has a strong stomach. I was thinking that, well, it's not for all ladies. Not someone softer, like, say, well...Daisie. Miss Wellford, I mean."

Nicholas raised a brow. "I couldn't tell if it would be something for her or not. I don't know her that well, Luke."

"Well, I can't really imagine it," Luke sighed. "Miss Wellford's so gentle and sweet, she doesn't even like squishing flies. I can't see her as a nurse or anything like that."

"We can't say that without asking. And besides, a nurse ought to be gentle. Isn't that what you might expect from a nurse?"

Luke inclined his head. "Well, maybe, sir, when you say that..." He paused. "Well, you see...it's awkward, but..."

Nicholas knew the younger man and how he disliked expressing anything even vaguely controversial. Patiently, he asked, "What is it, Luke?"

Luke coughed. "Sir, Daisie—Miss Wellford—and Miss Newbury were talking and, well, Miss Wellford said she always wanted to be a nurse and Miss Newbury invited her to work at the new practice. When it's opened."

Nicholas gaped at him, but he was delighted. One of the things that worried Lucille, and which had worried him as well, was that there was nobody there to assist her. Operations like stitching—particularly when it was a large wound that needed several stitches—required more than one lot of hands to accomplish. He had worked with Simmons when a severe injury had come up, passing him sutures and helping to tidy up. But he had wondered who could help Lucille since he was so much busier now that the bandits were settled in.

"Daisie would be a major help," he reassured Luke. "She's sweet and clever—at least, that was what I thought about her—and she is already friends with Miss Newbury."

"I suppose you're right, sir," Luke said, awkwardly. "But I just, well...I don't know what I think. Miss Wellford told me when I came to fetch her at the ranch yesterday, and I guess the idea just troubled me."

"Let her try," Nicholas said. He understood Luke, since he had also believed much the same just a few days ago—but his ideas had been changed since he met Lucille, and he was sure his would be likewise changed.

Luke looked uncomfortably down at his feet. "I suppose, sir."

Nicholas grinned as Luke walked to the door. *Miss Newbury didn't let anything get her down long, did she?*

How she was planning to start the practice, he had no idea. She still didn't have an office or a place to stay, despite their best efforts so far. But already, she had found an assistant.

She seemed to have such strong faith, and, slowly, it was inspiring him as well.

Leaning back, his eyes drifted to the window. Out of sight around the corner were the distant hills where the bandits lurked. The confrontation yesterday had been troubling.

They are getting too cozy up there.

He shivered. *How many of them were up there now?* With the number of men returning from the war and unable to find proper employment, the numbers were certainly growing. There were already twice as many men up there as he could summon to oppose them.

That made things much harder.

His stomach rumbling brought him back to the present. The church bell was ringing, and it must be midday. An early lunch was in order.

Nicholas went to the door, donning a hat before heading out. The weather was warm, and the street smelled of dust and heat, the distant hills too bright to look at. Not wanting a hot meal on such a sweltering day, he turned toward the bakery. As he got there, he frowned.

The street was busy with people.

A few people active on the street at lunchtime would be normal, though a little odd since it was so hot. So many people milling about at midday seemed strange. About eight people were in the street near the bakery, and, as he approached, more people came out, carrying bread and other food, joining the other group.

Odd, he thought. Mr. Collingwood and Mrs. Newman and so many others were active—the whole village, as far as he could see.

He walked on, brow lowering in a frown. *What had made them all come out now?* If it was a Sunday, it would have a reasonable explanation—they would be on their way from church. But now?

"Morning, Fred," he greeted a man on his way down the road. "What's happening?"

Fred looked surprised. "It's the work party."

"Work party?"

"Yes," he continued. "For the doctor's office. We all heard about the money, and it was a shame. We all got together and decided we were going to pitch in. It won't be the best materials or the best labor, but it's so much better than nothing." He shrugged, a shy grin on his face. "Stuart has paint, and Mr. Collingwood's ranch hands came down with some plaster and buckets and we're all working together. Might not be experts or anything, not like some craftsman from Prescott, but we can do our best."

"*What?*" Nicholas gaped at him. He could hear his words, but he could barely understand what he was saying. The entire village was repairing the office. His heart thumped.

"Sorry, sheriff," Fred scratched his head awkwardly. "Should we have said something? We ain't breaking the law?"

Nicholas shook his head. "Sorry, Fred. No, not at all. I was just surprised. No, you are all doing remarkable things. Truly," he added, and the fellow look relieved.

"Good. Want to come along?" he asked. "We're just busy upstairs right now. We'll move downstairs when

Collingwood's fellers have finished with the plastering and painting."

Nicholas nodded. "I'd be glad to."

He followed Fred down the road, noticing villagers walking in the other direction, heading away from where they worked at the doctor's office and toward the inn and bakery. Work was stopping for lunch, clearly.

When he reached the doctor's office, he gawked. The villagers were busy working—a group was washing the windows, while another group mixed plaster in the yard. In the center, helping to direct the men who were carrying the buckets, stood Lucille. Her hair was tied back, she wore a dark gray dress; a tall, calm presence in all the rush and fuss around her.

He smiled as she waved in delight to see him. "Nicholas!" she exclaimed.

"Lucille," he greeted her with a grin. "What's going on? What are all these people doing here?"

Lucille was glowing. "They came to help us! Isn't it wonderful? This is the Lord's work."

Nicholas nodded. He knew she was right, and there was a strange sensation in his stomach, as though all the depression and sorrow that had settled and soured his world was shifting, replaced by hope.

"I can't argue with that," he laughed.

She giggled. "Quite so!" She gestured at the building. They were standing on the sidewalk beside the yard, watching people busily going about their tasks. Mr. Collingwood and his ranch hands were going in and coming out, plastering tools in hand, and a woman shook a rug in the yard.

"It's so wonderful," he murmured in awe.

"It is," Lucille sighed dreamily. "The Lord's work is truly wonderful."

They stood there for a long moment, and then, self-conscious, he realized that he was standing close to her, his hand almost touching hers. He rubbed the back of his neck, and stepped back, throat tight.

"I guess I should get going. You have something to eat for the midday meal?"

"I brought a sandwich," she said shyly. "Mrs. Grierson said I ought to."

"Good," he laughed. "A sandwich isn't exactly a proper meal, though."

Lucille raised a brow. "I am a physician, and I absolutely agree with you."

They both chuckled. Nicholas's heart soared.

"Well," he said with a small grin. "Should you, our most esteemed physician, want more lunch, I'd be delighted to buy you something."

She peered into his eyes, and he blushed. He had not actually offered to buy her anything before. He was offering her accommodation and paying her a small wage for her housekeeping, but he'd never actually given her anything as a gift.

Lucille tilted her head, eyes bright. "Thank you, Nicholas. But I assure you, I can manage with a sandwich. I'll have more to eat at the ranch this evening."

"Good." He inclined his head shyly. "I guess I should go on my way. If you need any help—any men to do any lifting—please come by the office. Luke and I would be happy to be useful."

"I will. Thank you."

"Good." He lifted his hat and went the way he came, glancing back at the old doctor's residence and the work being carried out. The townsfolk were still going about their tasks, and Lucille stood where with her back turned to him as she supervised the work.

She's remarkable.

The whole experience was remarkable. The Lord worked in mysterious ways, like Max had said. He wouldn't have believed it a few days ago, but now, he did. He knew that there was something profound and impossible to understand at work here, and all he could do was feel gratitude.

He walked on his way to the bakery, like springtime had awoken in his heart.

Chapter Twenty-Five

The doctor's office was clean: that was the first, overwhelming thing Lucille noticed. The floor was freshly sanded, the dust brushed away, and the wooden floor bright golden yellow. The walls smelled of fresh lime-wash, and the stairs were sparkling. Warm sunshine shone in through windows that were no longer cracked, but gleamed and let in light to sparkle on the spotlessly swept floor.

"It's beautiful."

Lucille's words echoed around in the room. She felt a flood of joy, pride, wonder and delight. It was such a gift, to have the space ready. And the way in which it had been achieved, through the good heartedness and love of the community, was a true miracle.

She paused, sending a silent prayer of thanks to the Lord, who she knew had made it all possible.

Lifting her head, she noticed Daisie standing uncertainly in the doorway. "Come in."

Daisie stepped hesitantly over the threshold. Her footsteps echoed on the sanded floor, filling the silent space. "Miss Newbury, it's just wonderful."

"It is," Lucille agreed. She sounded pleased, even to her own ears. "Please, call me Lucille."

"Yes, Lucille," Daisie replied quietly.

They had met intermittently over the last week or two, but there was still a shyness between them. Lucille guessed herself to be no more than two or three years older than Daisie, but her experiences and training made a gulf that Daisie seemed to find challenging to overcome, and Lucille was not sure how to speak across it.

Lucille went through another door that led into the small space where she would prepare medicines. Her shoes echoed as she walked over the freshly planed wood of the floor, the smell of varnish and paint in her nose.

"Thank you," she whispered.

She was grateful—both to the Divine and to the shade of her father, who she somehow felt sure was here, somewhere, looking down from the realm beyond life, smiling at her.

Daisie stood nervously in the doorway.

"There's a lot to show you," Lucille said, inviting her in with a wave of her hand. "I brought my bag with me. We can unpack. Of course, I'll need to send an order for some supplies—there's oil and other ingredients for the medicines that I'll need to order from Prescott." A frown creased her brow, instantly chased off by a big smile. *This was exciting!*

"Can I see?" Daisie asked shyly, as Lucille unpacked her bags. She had a stethoscope in her hand, and she set it on the table.

"Of course," Lucille said. "I'll show you how it works. Put it in your ears, like this..." She passed her the flattened sections and watching as she did as Lucille instructed. The hollow metal end hung loose, and Lucille placed it carefully on her chest, just over the bone. Her father had ordered the stethoscope from a craftsman in California, and it was one of the few that had real earpieces. Many doctors still used the flat ended post that they would simply rest on the patient's chest; the design requiring that the head was practically resting on the patient. Her father had preferred the most recent, earpiece-equipped design, thinking it more decent.

"What's that?" Daisie asked carefully. "Is that your heartbeat?"

Lucille grinned. She had the same reaction when her father had let her listen. The new piece of equipment arrived when she was ten, and he'd let her try it. She recalled, blindingly, how exciting it had been, and how she'd not stopped thinking of it for days. Seeing the delight on Daisie's face reminded her of herself at that time. She realized she was in the position, for the first time, of her father; a teacher of her art.

"Yes," she said, taking a deep breath. "It's my heartbeat. Now, listen carefully to what happens when I hold my breath…"

She repeated the lesson her father had given her, holding her breath to make her heart rate increase and having Daisie listen to hear the changes. Her student's eyes widened. She grinned, sharing her delight.

"It's faster! I can hear it!"

"Whew." Lucille let go the breath she'd been holding, and they laughed. Daisie passed her the stethoscope shyly, and Lucille opened her bag, unpacking the remainder of the objects therein. She found places for them—in this room and the other—and left some in the bag, the stethoscope included, because she might need them if she was called out to a ranch.

They spent the morning organizing the rooms; deciding how to make use of the space, moving in some linen that Lucille had brought from the ranch. Mrs. Grierson had shared with her the sheets, cushions, and soft furnishings that were not used in the house, since they were too old. In time, Lucille would buy new things for the office, but for now, they would do quite well.

Lucille sighed, scanning the room. She straightened her back. They were in *her* office, where she would see to the patients, and the bench on which they would sit, or lie, was covered in white sheeting and cushions, two chairs padded and upholstered with spare curtains from the ranch. Lucille flexed her fingers, which were sore from using a hammer to drive in thumbtacks.

"Looking rather nice," she commented.

Daisie laughed. "I sure never thought a doctor could upholster chairs, Lucille."

Lucille had to smile. "My papa used to do all that sort of thing," she said. "He was so handy. He repaired the cart all the time—sometimes, we didn't have time to get the cart up to the house before he had to hurry off." She blinked, recalling how proud he had been when he managed to fix major damage to the harnesses. His big, happy grin was a beacon in her mind.

"You must feel his loss," Daisie said softly.

Lucille nodded. "I do." She'd cried when she spoke to Matty—the pain of her new circumstances had been foremost in her thoughts. Now, standing in a doctor's office that could have been Papa's, she felt his loss. Tears were in her eyes for him.

"It's all right," Daisie murmured awkwardly as Lucille sniffled. She reached into her pocket.

"Thank you," Lucille said. She accepted a handkerchief and dabbed at her cheeks. The midday sunshine slanted in low, and she became aware that her stomach was sore. She pressed a hand to it, and Daisie must have noticed her do so.

"Shall we eat dinner? A cousin of my ma works at the inn. She'd be right glad to see you."

"Oh," Lucille grinned. "Thank you. That was very observant of you. You see, we'll make a physician of you yet. Noticing the discomfort of others is a fine trait."

"Oh." Daisie blushed shyly, looking at her feet. "Why, thank you." When she looked up, her eyes were bright.

Lucille chuckled. "Nothing to thank. And your diagnosis is sound. Yes, I could do with some food. Let's go and have dinner."

She walked with her new apprentice down the street toward the inn.

Chapter Twenty-Six

The kitchen was quiet except for the crackle of the fire and the sound of Mrs. Grierson eating her stew. Nicholas was lost in thought, not paying much attention to the sounds and space around him. He'd seen Lucille in the town briefly, and he couldn't stop thinking about how delighted she seemed by the newly refurbished rooms. Miss Wellford, too, seemed enraptured by them, and a small smile showed at the corner of Nicholas' mouth just thinking about it.

She's so pleased. It's so good to see her so contented.

Seeing her so full of joy lifted his spirits.

"Have a nice evening, sir," Mrs. Grierson said as she stood from where she drank tea opposite him at the table.

"Evening, Mrs. Grierson," Nicholas replied. He smiled at her as she rinsed out her cup and shuffled to the kitchen door.

Alone at the table, the kitchen darkened around him.

It felt strange, not having Lucille there. That was the one thing he was going to find hard about the fact that she'd moved into the doctor's rooms. He hadn't realized how much he enjoyed having her around.

She's a free person. How must I even know if she likes me?

He grinned to himself. He suspected—without really knowing why—that she liked him. Some moments they had shared recently—notably at the dance, and then, later, when she learned to ride—had suggested to him that she enjoyed his presence.

And I know I enjoy being around her.

His grin widened. He knew it was more than that. If he was honest—truly honest—with himself, he knew that he was in love with her after years spent reluctant to give his heart to anyone.

You have to sometime, he reminded himself.

What would be the point of living life without loving? He imagined his whole life at the ranch, by himself, getting older and more withdrawn. That was no life. Mrs. Radford had always said the most important thing in life was one's loved ones. He was starting to understand that she was right.

But to love like that took courage. He still wasn't sure if he was brave enough.

He stretched his legs out under the table, leaning back and staring at the ceiling. The kitchen was exactly as he recalled from his childhood. He hadn't eaten in the kitchen then—he'd taken meals in the parlor with Mr. and Mrs. Radford. It was only after their passing that he'd decided it made little sense to eat up there on his own and come down to the kitchen for mealtimes with the ranch hands or Mrs. Grierson—since they 'd usually eaten before he came back from work.

It had been horrid taking meals up there alone.

Stifling a yawn, he decided he really ought to get to bed—it was a workday tomorrow.

He stretched and limped upstairs to his bed-chamber.

The following morning, he woke to the sound of men's voices in the yard.

"That's odd," he muttered groggily to himself. It wasn't odd in itself—it could be Glen and Alfred talking—but they sounded strained, almost angry. He washed his face and got dressed before heading downstairs.

Nicholas listened for the voices at the kitchen door, but they were faint. Just as he stepped outside, Glen ran up.

"Mr. Barnes!" he called. "Chris is here. He said he had urgent news. I said I couldn't just wake you, but, as you're the sheriff and all, we said—"

"I am, and it would be right to wake me."

Chris came over eagerly, clearly distressed. "I know it's early, but I came across something on the road, and you have to come with me. There's people who need your help urgently."

"Show me." Nicholas hurried across the yard to saddle his horse.

Nicholas rode beside Glen, his ranch hand's big bulky form seeming to slow Hearthfire—his bright bay—as they raced toward the village.

A little ahead of them, Chris rode another horse from Nicholas' stables. He'd worn his own horse out on the ride to the ranch and it was resting in the yard. Nicholas gripped the reins, stomach in his throat, his mind worrying over the trouble ahead.

"It's not too far ahead, sir," Chris called as Nicholas rode up behind him. "I don't know if there are any bandits still around."

"I'll scout ahead," Nicholas replied. He trotted ahead, then slowed, wanting to save Starburst's strength in case they needed to race back in a hurry.

Chris had ridden to bring them news of a bandit sighting near the Burwell ranch. Chris had thought, at first, that the bandits would leave the ranch alone, since they had been quite far in the distance. He'd set off at a leisurely pace but then, on the road, he'd come across an ambushed wagon.

It was this wagon—and the survivors of the bandits' violence—that they rode to assist right now.

"How many did you say there were, Chris?" Nicholas asked. He had ridden ahead but saw nothing of the bandits.

"Just three," Chris said. "Can't say how many were armed," he added, with a worried frown.

Nicholas didn't comment as he was sure that they were all armed. The influx of soldiers—who brought their own weapons—to the ranks of the bandits would ensure that. He gripped the reins tighter.

"Almost there," Chris cautioned. Nicholas slowed, then let out a shout of pure rage, seeing the wagon ahead of them.

A woman was lying on the ground, her gray hair loose around her shoulders. He thought he saw blood on her shoulder, and she seemed unconscious. Fury possessed him, uncontrollable and mindless, and he rode forward, heedless of the men beside him warning him.

He leaped off his horse and ran to the woman. He didn't recognize her, and he assumed that the wagon drivers were from out of town, probably heading toward Pinewood or one of the larger towns nearby. She was awake, and when she saw him coming, she screamed.

"No! Please! Leave me in peace!"

"I'm the sheriff," Nicholas reassured as he bent to lift her. The wound in her shoulder had soaked her white dress with blood and her face was as pale as the cloth. Once he got her in his arms, he straightened. She was around seventy, he guessed, and her thin body weighed almost nothing. He walked back toward where Glen held his horse by the reins. "I won't hurt you," he repeated, as the woman seemed too terrified for words.

"Tom," she murmured. "Where is he?" She seemed dazed, perhaps concussed.

Nicholas looked around, seeing no sign of another person. He gestured to Chris, who was already walking over. "Go and look," he told the man softly. "And get the wagon up and fixed, if you can."

Chris nodded and went to the wagon. Nicholas passed the woman gently to Glen, who laid her beside in the shade of a nearby tree.

"Stay with her," he instructed Glen. "I'll see if I can find Tom."

He prayed that Tom was not dead, though he couldn't see how he could not be—the wagon had been turned over and the contents raided, and he doubted if the man who'd been driving it had been armed. And even if he had been, if their prey set up any kind of resistance, the bandits would shoot without warning.

The road narrowed here, a rock bluff on one side providing the perfect cover for ambush while, on the other, a tree grew. The wagon had fallen a few paces away from the rock, suggesting the bandits had shot on it from the vantage point beside it.

Wicked. They're wickedness itself to launch an attack on these people.

He still felt sick at the metallic smell of the blood from the woman's wounded shoulder, though it looked like a graze from a glancing bullet rather than a shot wound. All the same, he'd be glad to get her to Lucille.

"Here, sir! Over here!"

Nicholas tensed, and ran around the outcrop of rocks. He gasped at the scene before them.

An old man was on the ground, his hat beside him, beige trousers stained dark with blood. He was not moving, but he was shouting angry curses. Nicholas would have laughed at the volume of colorful swearwords the man was exuding, except for the fact that the scene was shocking. Glen walked over, the old woman with him, seeming more concerned with finding her husband than resting.

At the sight of the man, she shouted. "Tom! My Tom! You're alive!"

"Margery!"

Nicholas' heart ached in empathy as the old man—clearly severely injured—faced them. A grin lit his face and he struggled to haul himself up, and Glen ran to help him.

"I'll help him to the cart, sir," Glen said.

Chris yelled, "Sir! There's another man here—among the rocks."

"There is?" Nicholas frowned.

"That..." The old man began, launching into curses that were every bit as colorful as they had been earlier. Nicholas thought the woman, Margery, might be shocked, but she was laughing, her eyes bright.

"Tom! My Tom," she repeated, shaking her head. "Look at you."

Nicholas helped support her on her feet. "Help her to the wagon too," Nicholas told Glen. Whatever creatures—oxen or horses—had pulled their wagon before had been stolen. He glanced at the vehicle, which had been somehow righted by Chris.

"Yes, sir. The wagon could be mended, sir. Wheels are fine. Just the shaft is broken."

"Good." Nicholas said. The two travelers were critically injured and needed seeing to.

As he went to the spot where they had found the old man, he realized that a second man was indeed lying among the rocks. Nicholas would have thought he was dead at first, but that when he approached, the man was still breathing. A wound in his arm was bleeding and there was more on his hand. His arm had been badly hurt—whether through gunshot or a fall, Nicholas couldn't tell. And his leg must be damaged too, judging from how still he lay and how he didn't attempt to get up. As Nicholas approached, one of his eyes opened. It was pale blue, and it glared at Nicholas with hate.

"You..." the man hissed, swearing at Nicholas in a whisper. "Shoot me, then! Shoot me when I can't fight."

Nicholas tensed. This, then, was one of the bandits. He considered, briefly, doing just that—diminishing their numbers by even one seemed tempting—but he knew he could not. He couldn't shoot a defenseless man. Killing in self-defense was one thing, but to kill someone for no reason, in cold blood—even a bandit—seemed shockingly wrong. It was one of the worst sins he could imagine.

"I won't shoot you," Nicholas snapped harshly. "But you're coming with us, back to town." He knew there was a rope on Glen's saddle. They should tie the man up and put him in the back of the cart—if they could repair it, that was—and take him into town. They could jail him until such time as a trial could be arranged for him.

He went to get the rope—there was no point standing guard over the man, who clearly couldn't move—and tied him up, carrying him back to the cart. There was no real fight left in the man—he was too badly injured. He kicked out at Nicholas, but aside from that—and the force of his tongue—there was little resistance. Nicholas would have felt bad overpowering an injured man, but he felt little compassion for the bandits. When he got to the cart, Glen was gently helping the injured wagon-drivers into the back, while Chris did his best to repair the front so that the horses could be reined to it.

"What have you got there, sheriff?" Glen yelled.

"A bandit," Nicholas said, without much emphasis. He carried the man to the back of the wagon, his arms and legs trussed, and dumped him in. The fellow rolled toward Tom, grunting with pain as Nicholas let him land none too softly, and Tom swore in earnest.

"All right, old feller," Chris said good-naturedly. "No point making our ears ring with all those curses."

Nicholas would have laughed, but he was too tense to see the humor in the situation. He went to help Glen, who was leading the horses over, and together they yoked them to the wagon.

Slowly, they began the journey back into the town.

"They ambushed us," Tom said angrily. For a heavily injured man, he had a lot of fight still in him.

Nicholas stared grimly ahead, trying to ignore the talk in the back of the wagon as they rolled back toward the town.

"Those..." Tom paused to let out a string of curses. "They were hiding behind the rocks there. About six of them, I'd say. Didn't get the chance to count. They opened fire on us." He paused. "If it weren't for Margery here, I'd be dead."

"It's nothing, Tom," Margery said, voice tight. "Nothing."

"She pushed me down," Tom continued. "I would have got a bullet straight in me if she hadn't. Instead, it hit my arm and grazed her, there." He must have gestured at her shoulder. Nicholas' stomach clenched. Now he understood why Tom was furious. If it was Lucille, and she'd been hurt by someone because she'd defended him, he would be full of hate and anger for whoever hurt her. And full of guilt.

"You said six men?" Glen interjected. "How many armed?"

"All of them, I'd say," the old man spat. "Had a gun with me, praise the Lord," he continued. "Hit him here." He must have gestured at the bandit, because a string of oaths came from the man, none of them quite meeting the force and intensity of Tom's swearing.

"All right, fellers," Glen said, trying to keep the peace. "Let's all save our energy 'til we get to town."

Nicholas nodded to himself. He was glad of the silence—he hadn't realized how the talk had been making his head hurt. He focused on the reins in his hands as the wagon, groaning but staying together, got them into town.

They pulled up in the town after an hour on the cart, hurrying as much as they could until they came to the sheriff's office.

"Sir?" Luke called as he ran down the steps with shock on his face. "Sir! What happened?"

"Wagon was ambushed. About two miles out of town. Those folks were attacked. One in the back's a bandit," Nicholas explained briefly. He gestured to the cart, where the three injured people lay. Of them all, the bandit was the only one who had the energy to look up, and the hate still burned in his gaze.

He jumped down to unfasten the horses from the traces, worried for them. They were not carthorses and they had done a wonderful thing, transporting the heavy wagon this far into town. The strain on them was apparent, so he led them to the water, leaving Chris and Glen to guard the cart. When he returned from the stables around the back, Luke was standing beside the cart.

"We need to get them to the physician." Nicholas wanted to smile, thinking that finally, Lucille was their physician.

"Yes, sir."

Luke went to the inn, borrowing their ox to pull the cart the few hundred feet down the street toward the office.

"Nicholas!" Lucille grinned as they reached the office. Her eyes were wide, delight on her face. Then, gaze narrowed, she noticed the oxcart and the people in the back of it. "What happened? Are they injured?"

"Yes," Nicholas said. "These two were ambushed. This one's a bandit," he added, gesturing harshly to the man tied up at the back of the cart. "I'll take him back to the jail."

"Not yet," Lucille said, brow lowered. "We need to get the patients out of the cart and into the office."

"Of course," Nicholas said. He hopped down, glad Glen had come with him. He helped Margery down from the cart, walking with her into the office and helping her onto the bed. Someone ran up the short hallway and Nicholas looked up, startled.

"Luke?" he said when his deputy appeared, looking tensely at Nicholas.

"Sir, we need you at the office," Luke said quickly. "There's something that needs seeing to."

Nicholas' stomach twisted. He had enough to see to right here, without another problem. He was sure that it was a raid, too—those bandits would be riding around the local ranches by now, certainly. He was sure they were already out causing trouble for ranchers.

"I'll come right now," he said, hurrying to the door. When he saw Lucille, he lifted his hat. "And I wish you a good day." He winked as he hurried back to the edge of the town to his office.

Chapter Twenty-Seven

Lucille stood in the doorway of the doctor's office. The sunshine poured in onto the polished floor, and for a moment, despite the rapid movement and activity all around her, Lucille could only think of Nicholas. She was still glowing, stunned by the wink. She couldn't think about it, and so she pushed it aside, to consider later.

"Help him on the bench," she instructed Glen, who, big and strong as ever, was supporting a strong, healthy older man. She glanced over to where the older woman waited in the office. Nodding, she said, "Good. And him?" she gestured out at the cart outside the office.

Chris glanced at Glen. When his friend didn't speak, Chris replied. "Sorry, miss. But that's a bandit. We'll take him directly to jail."

"He's wounded!" Lucille gasped. She pleaded at the two men with her eyes. After a moment, Glen looked away.

"I'll bring him in, miss," he grumbled. He didn't meet her eye as he went to the door. "Where'd you like me to put him?"

Lucille drew a breath. "In my chair," she said. "Put him in the dispensing room. I'll deal with these two patients first. He looks like he can wait for half an hour or so."

"I'll stay and keep an eye on him, miss," Glen offered.

Lucille drew in a breath to object. She was going to need some help, but Glen and Chris standing around in her small office, with the three patients, would get in her way.

"He can't do much as he is, Glen," Lucille reassured. "His leg is damaged, and he can't use his right arm. By all means, stay awhile and help, but there's no need to guard him."

Glen nodded. Without any further convincing, he went out to the cart. Lucille turned away, focusing on her patients.

"This gunshot wound is nasty," Lucille commented to the older man. "I'm going to try and get the bullet out. Your wife might like to wait outside...?" She glanced at the older woman, whose shoulder needed attention as well. The woman shook her head.

"No, miss. I'll stay by my Tom. Are you the nurse?" The older woman scrutinized her with a frowning.

Lucille shook her head. "I'm the physician." She was too focused on Tom's arm to care much what the woman's response would be. These two must be from out of town, so they hadn't heard about her and adapted to the idea. She expected censure, but she was too busy to allow that to bother her.

She reached for a leather strap for Tom to bite on, and her scalpel, which lay in its small box. "Now, Tom," she said gently. "I need to remove this bullet, or the wound will fester, and you have a risk of blood poisoning. It's going to hurt. I can give you brandy for the pain?"

"Yes," Tom said.

Lucille got the bottle. She winced as she poured it—she had been lectured by her father about the evils of drink, and she strongly believed him, but she didn't have any other substance with which to dull his pain, though she recalled her father mentioning that chloroform was being used in the big hospitals in the north.

When Chris came in from outside, she beckoned to him. "Hold him down for me, will you, Chris?" She wished Daisie was here, but her assistant had gone to her parents' ranch and would only be back later that day. It would have been good to have her help—but the big ranch hand was even more useful at this point, for holding down the strong older man was going to be a tough job, best suited for the muscle of Chris.

"Yes, miss."

The big ranch-hand didn't show any expression on his face, but Lucille knew he was terrified and sick—he'd gone white, and his mouth was set.

After a second or two, she forgot about him, her vision narrowing to the point of the surgical knife she held. She had used a scalpel once or twice. She knew the feeling of the blade and how much pressure she'd need to cut without cutting too deeply. She sighed, said a prayer deep inside, and, once she had cut away a square of his shirt, carefully lifting the fabric from the crusting around the wound, she cut very carefully across the entry wound to widen it.

"Shh..." she murmured as Tom winced and his body jumped, jarring her hand. She knew Chris was holding him as steady as he could, and she couldn't afford to think what she was making him suffer. She could only focus on the scalpel in her hand and the wound she cut.

The blood welled up, dark and steady, around the edge of the wound she had just made. She held her breath. It was going to be hard to get the bullet out, since she couldn't see it under the fresh blood that was filling the wound. She reached for her forceps and focused on the task at hand.

Tom convulsed, and she soothed him as best as she could. Chris was pressing on the fellow's chest, holding him as steady as he could. She heard Margery speaking from behind her.

"Hush, Tom. It's all well."

The calm voice steadied her, repeating its assurance in a low, even tone. She pushed her awareness of the surroundings down, focusing only on the bullet and the cut.

"There..." she muttered, the forceps close on the object. It was small—no longer than her smallest fingernail—but the metal jarring in her hand made it seem big. She pushed hard on the forceps, glad that they were not too stiff for her smaller hands. Gripping the bullet, she pulled.

Pull slowly. Muscle is hard and it will pull back. Keep up a slow, even pressure. Easy now.

She could almost hear her father's words as he instructed her. She'd never removed a bullet herself before, but she'd watched him do it half a dozen times during her life and each time he'd said the same thing when he instructed her.

Muscle is strong.

The wound pulled back on the bullet, fighting her as she gripped and pulled. She held her breath. She could smell blood now, but she was used to that—the metal scent had nauseated her once, but now she was accustomed to it and she barely noticed, taking it only as an indication that the wound was bleeding well. Not too fast, not so slowly that it might be rotting.

"There!"

The wonderful moment the bullet started to be pushed out by the force of the muscles and slippery blood on it, she almost gave a cry of elation when it came out, gripped in the tool.

"Well done, Tom!" the older woman shouted with delight. Lucille stepped back, dizzy with relief, to put the bullet into the little tin where surgical waste went. She reached for a roll of bandages—hastily discovered in her bag—and pressed them to the wound. Though blood was on her hands, she was used to that feeling. She didn't mind—all she cared about was that the bleeding stopped.

"That was the worst bit," she reassured him, grinning. She was floating, delight and relief fizzing in her brain, making her feel lighthearted. After a stitch in the wound and a bandage, she'd let the poor man get some rest. He'd have to rest in the dispensing room, as she had no other space for him. Jessie from the inn would let him rest there later.

When Tom was ready to rest, she went to inspect his wife. She bandaged the wound and sprayed it with the only thing she had to keep it clean—carbolic spray.

Since Margery was able to stand and walk, she went to join Tom in the dispensing room, where Glen and Chris had borrowed a comfortable chair from the inn and propped him in it. She just had one more patient to see to.

The man who had been locked in the dispensing room had reddish hair and his eyes were startling—a flint-cold blue color that scalded her.

"Your arm is broken," Lucille informed him.

The man nodded, indifferent to the news.

"I think something has happened to your knee, as well," Lucille said carefully. "It might need to be splinted until you can walk properly." She hesitated to think too hard—if the kneecap was shattered, the poor man might lose the use of it altogether. Breaks there were complex and almost impossible to heal. She sucked in a deep breath and bent to examine the wound.

She rested a hand on the tattered cloth of his trousers. It was thin leather, the knee worn through on this side, fabric dirty.

"It's whole," she informed him, relieved. She had been afraid it wasn't. "I'll see if I can move it back into place." That would be tricky—she hadn't been able to move it when he was freshly wounded, and to push against his muscle now would need more strength than she might possess. Asking Chris or Glen for help was out of the question since they had no training. It'd be up to her.

Drawing on her courage, she moved the knee back into place. It wasn't easy—gripping the kneecap felt horribly uncomfortable and she was aware, constantly, of the unmoving expression of the patient. She couldn't tell if he hated her, was indifferent, or just focused on something other.

She gripped, pushed, and turned. The patient's gasp was followed by a click and Lucille sat back, panting, relief flooding her as the knee straightened.

"I think it's good."

The man grunt in response as she stood. She peeked into his eyes. He seemed amused by her relief as if he knew she hadn't been sure of what she did.

Lucille stared back at him, and his gaze held hers and for a moment, she thought she saw understanding there, and knowing, and some strange acknowledgment that, in its own way, was a thank you.

Turning hastily away, shaking her head, she washed her hands in the copper bowl that served as a sink before examining his arm.

"It's not as bad as I thought it was." She straightened. "It doesn't need to be pulled into place. It's not that sort of break. If I bandage and splint it, I believe it will heal straight."

The man didn't answer her, but she had that strange sense of understanding again. She set to her work, and finished half an hour later.

"Good," she sighed. "That's good. Now, I'll just go to tip away this water, then bandage that wound you have there."

Lifting the basin, she walked out into the yard, holding the bowl. She filled the bowl at the pump, wishing that she'd thought to bring the pitcher too—she was parched. Water was something she tended to forget about until she was thirsty enough to remember.

When she returned, the chair was empty.

"Hey?" she called, nervous. Glancing around the office, she could not see the man. She gasped and called again, heart thumping. "Hey, mister?"

Where is he?

She had no idea what his name was, and fear rose in her. He was a prisoner, and she'd left him in here. She'd only been gone a minute, but what was to stop him from running out into the road?

You're a fool.

She ran to the door. As she did so, a shout rang out from the street. Glen was down the road from the office, and the man was with him. She stopped dead. In the street across from him, face pale and expression angry, was Nicholas, glaring at her.

Chapter Twenty-Eight

Nicholas froze, struggling for breath. He had sent Glen off with the prisoner, but he forgot about all that. Instead, he focused on Lucille standing before him. He was in the street, the dusty air dry around him, and she stood in the doorway, the doctor's office with its harsh carbolic smell behind her. He couldn't think. Betrayal was the strongest thing he felt, mixed with horror and some strange lightheadedness he couldn't name.

"Lucille...what *happened?*"

Lucille gaped at him. There was fear in her eyes, and he hated himself for that, but he was also angry. He had never felt as angry as he did right now. It was only luck that had led to him and Glen finding and recapturing the prisoner. Glen was taking him back to jail, but he had been so close to escape.

And she had given the fellow the chance to do so.

Lucille spoke in a quiet voice, but it was forceful for all its quietness. He could tell the fear she had to conquer by speaking so—her face was white, voice wavery. But she spoke, all the same, and he listened. "He was wounded. I treated him as I would all patients."

"He's a bandit!" Nicholas shouted angrily. "How could you?"

He hadn't meant for that to come out laden with such bitterness, such anger, but he couldn't help it. That man was the only member of the group whom they'd ever managed to capture. He could have told them so much! And here she was, letting him escape. He'd come over at just the right moment. While he had meant to check on the patients, all that had left his mind. All he wanted now was to express his anger that she'd let his most important captive go.

Lucille blinked. "We are all wrongdoers. Christ would not have turned him away."

Nicholas swore but stopped himself, seeing her about to cry. She was close to tears, her eyes glossy. Instantly, he took back his words, shocked at himself. He knew she was right. He couldn't argue with that. He paused, realizing he'd sworn at her and almost sworn at God Himself. He lifted his hands to his brow, a prayerful gesture. "Sorry," he said, though whether he meant to God or to Lucille, he wasn't entirely sure. Ashamed, he needed forgiveness from the Lord too.

"I did wrong," Lucille said, but she was crying now, tears running down her face. "But I did what my conscience told me. I'm a *physician.* I never took the oath Papa took—not really. But I took that oath in my mind. I *will not* turn away any who need my help. Regardless of what they do. I can't *help* it." She hiccupped. Her face was streaked with tears, mucus under her nose where it ran.

He stood there helplessly, rage and sorrow mixing bitterly inside him and making him unable to speak.

Lucille looked away. "I am tired. I need to sit." She went into the office without another word.

Nicholas stood where he was on the road, speechless. Before he could speak, the door slammed shut behind her.

It took him a moment to calm down enough to notice that the sun beat down, making him sweat. A shy glance was all he risked taking, but he didn't spot anybody in the street. Not being witnessed didn't make him feel any less ashamed.

Turning back to the door, he considered whether to knock and if he had the courage to face her yet. He was still hesitating, about to touch the handle, when somebody spoke behind him.

"Sir, the prisoner's been taken back to the office," Glen said. Nicholas jumped, surprised to hear him. Chris with him. "Should we go back?"

Nicholas swallowed hard, shameful. He didn't know if they had seen how he shouted at her, swearing at her and almost at God Himself. "I guess."

He returned to his office.

Luke walked in to talk; his thin, youthful face was troubled, his brow lowered, eyes confused.

"Sir...the prisoner is in the jail. Glen and Chris brought him in. I apologize for calling you away."

"It's all right," he mumbled.

"Somebody tended to his wounds." Luke's eyes widened and Nicholas cut him off before he could say anything for or against what Lucille had perpetrated that morning.

"Don't say it."

"Um...yes." Luke frowned. Whatever he had wanted to say, he kept it to himself. "Um...sheriff?" he started carefully.

"What?" Nicholas asked, not really listening or thinking clearly; his mind was still blinded by his own shock at his own harsh response and wishing he could take it back. He wondered if it was something to do with the report from Mr. Elwood about the bar-fight that had seemed so urgent.

"I was thinking that... Well, it is midday."

"Yes? Well?" Nicholas asked, his own sadness and rage making him impatient with everyone. "What about it?"

"Well, it's dinnertime. And, well, we need to feed the inmate, too. Miss Wellford just returned from her parents' ranch, and said she could get some leftovers from her relative at the inn. Would that be acceptable?"

"Very well." Nicholas shrugged. Luke was right—they had to feed the man. He was no good as a prisoner if they didn't.

"Thank you, sir," Luke replied nervously.

Nicholas waved a hand at him. "Please, Luke," he said in a deep voice. "It'd be best if I just sit here by myself awhile."

"As you wish."

Leaning in his chair, the tension drained from him as Luke shut the door and his footsteps echoed in the hallway. Nicholas could finally stop and think about what had happened. He couldn't forgive himself for his outburst, for the rage with which he had confronted Lucille. At the same time, he still couldn't quite put aside the rage, not even to consider what to do about the bar fight that Luke had called him back to settle earlier.

Lucille had let his prisoner go. He knew that she hadn't done it on purpose. But whether it was purposeful or purely carelessness, she had still jeopardized him and the whole town. She had still risked them.

And for what?

He pushed that thought away. She was under oath. Whether she'd actually formally taken that oath or not, she was bound by it. As a physician, it was her job to treat all patients.

It just *felt* wrong. Those men had perpetrated such crimes and caused such suffering. Memories flooded him—the elderly folks with gunshot wounds, the injured men, the barns razed, and food taken—but he tried to see what Lucille saw.

All she had seen was a wounded man. Was she wrong?

"How must I know?" Nicholas groaned aloud, patience leaving him. Only one person he could think of would know, and that was the pastor. He turned to look out through the window, thinking that he ought to pay the fellow a visit. But he too tired and too confused to pray.

Lucille was right—she had done what was Christian and healed the man regardless. Nicholas knew that, but the act opened so many questions within him. They were complex questions, and he didn't know the answers. He didn't even know if he was ready to apologize to Lucille.

He stood pacing from a moment before calling down the hallway.

"Luke? Take care of things around here for a moment, will you?" he asked. "I'm going out."

"Sure, sir."

Nicholas limped down the road, the dust of the path coating his boots. He was weary and confused and the gray sand on the gray-brown street toned in with his mood. He hadn't walked this path for a while, he realized—he'd been to church once, since Lucille came to the ranch, but even then, he hadn't really wanted to. He'd just gone because the townsfolk expected it. Most understood the bandit problem took precedence.

As he'd expected, there was nobody in the church. The nave was empty, the bare rock of the wall dark and making the place like a cave. He sat in the back pew, the wood creaking under his weight. He had no idea how old the church was—it could have been a hundred years old, to judge by its appearance, or it could have been built a few decades ago. He had no idea.

He shut his eyes. "God," he prayed. "I know You're somewhere."

It was the first time in years he'd actually said that. For the first time in years, he felt with utter conviction that someone was there, listening to him.

Those questions—they had been the key to unleashing this new understanding. Having to truly wrestle with his faith made him realize there was something to wrestle *with*, some new, strange plant blossoming in his soul that had taken him by surprise and that he needed, finally, to address.

"God, I know You're somewhere. I know You're there because I have seen Your hand at work for the first time. I know You sent Lucille here. I know that You wanted her to stay. And somehow, when I look in her eyes, I know that there is something—something I have forgotten, something I haven't let in and have been denying. I know that love exists."

He stopped. Tears were pouring down his cheeks. He didn't feel self-conscious—at that moment, he was aware of nothing else apart from the ceiling soaring above him in the darkness with its blackened beams and the sense of the presence of the cross on the altar. Christ, figured in wood, transfigured on the cross, was gazing at him with compassion, and for the first time, he could receive that gaze and the love that was within it.

"I forgot my own heart. When my parents died, when the Radfords died, when I loved and was forgotten. I put my own heart aside and buried it, and I could not let You in. The heart is the door where You enter, and without that, I was empty, and I could not hear Your voice."

Nicholas stopped, sniffing. The realization dawned in his heart like sunrise. He had lost his faith in the instant that he buried his heart, and now that he had found the one, he could access, finally, the other. The tears were cold on his face and he was talking aloud, the empty church quiet around him.

That was quite something.

He felt almost as if the someone he was aware of—somewhere above the blackened roof-beams, all around him in the space—was laughing with him as he sniffed and wiped the mucus from his face.

He hadn't cried like that in years. Maybe not since he was a small child and his parents died.

Leaning back, he stared at the roof-beams. The emotions moved through him and, with them, the peace that settled on his heart was clean and true. He hadn't felt rest like this for years. It felt like he had been washed clean, like the pain that had been there, taking up so much space and energy, had finally worked through him and left him and he was fresh and new, washed onto the bank of his sorrow and with firm ground below him.

Chapter Twenty-Nine

Lucille stood in the yard, empty inside. It had been a long, wearying day and she'd done the most work she'd ever managed to do as a physician. She should have felt so proud, but instead, she was weary and tired.

"It wasn't wrong? Was it?" she asked the empty, velvety air around her. The ranch was silent, even the chickens roosting, the blueish dusk calm around them. She gazed to the distant hills, the outline inked onto the dusk-dark sky, wishing someone could answer her.

She had followed her oath. She knew in her heart that wasn't wrong.

The wall behind her was cool, but firm, the rough stone scraping against her coat as she leaned back. She'd ridden back to the ranch after sending Tom and Margery to the inn; exhausted and weary and barely able to see ahead. She was so tired; she was grateful she'd managed to reach the ranch unscathed.

And he'd think that was wrong, too—my riding alone through dangerous terrain without one of the men with me.

It had been foolish, and dangerous, but she'd done it anyway, trusting in beginner's luck and her confidence in the saddle to get her home. For someone who had only recently started riding and saddling her horse, she felt used to the sensation already and she'd adapted to it fast.

She stared at the sky, sad and confused.

I am the Way, the Truth, and the Light, and whosoever believeth in Me, shall not die, but have eternal life.

Swallowing hard, the verse from her recent afternoon reading of the Bible came to her. She had done as Christ would have recommended—she had no doubt of that. She had followed His Way, confident in her faith. How could that be wrong?

Lucille sniffed, the reassurance of that verse sinking into her heart, making her feel a little better. It was true—she had followed the Way of Christ. She had done as she knew was right.

Even if Nicholas could not see it, the Lord would certainly understand what she did.

More confident, she turned to go into the kitchen. As she went up the steps, cartwheels echoed as they rattled over the drive and toward the yard.

Nicholas drove the cart, with Luke beside him.

Daisie was in the back waving, her big smile bright in the dark. "Lucille! Hey! There you are."

Lucille grinned, spirits lifting. She waited while Luke helped Daisie carefully down from the cart, bringing her over to join Lucille. Lucille studied the younger woman's face, seeing how bright her eyes were and guessing that she had something important to say.

"Lucille?" Daisie said shyly. "Can we go inside? I need to talk to you."

"Of course," Lucille said, nodding. "Have you taken supper?" she added as they went up the steps into the kitchen, the men still crossing the yard after settling the horses in the stables. She looked at Nicholas, too shy and uncertain to say anything to him. He was also, it seemed, ignoring her.

"No," Daisie said. "We just came directly from the office."

"You should certainly eat something, then," Lucille suggested.

They went into the kitchen, where Mrs. Grierson was busy cleaning the counter. Once Daisie was settled at the table, Lucille fetched the bowls, ready to eat the evening stew.

"Evening, Mrs. Grierson," Nicholas greeted as he entered the kitchen. Lucille glanced at him briefly, noticing that he didn't meet her eye. She would have to wait until Daisie and Luke were settled somewhere before she could talk to him. She wanted to speak to him—to settle matters if they could. And if Daisie was going to share her bed-chamber, as she had on her previous stay, that was going to prove difficult in any case, since she would need to wait for a chance to see him in private.

"Evening, sir," Mrs. Grierson said . Lucille put the bowls of stew out—first for Daisie and Luke, and then for Nicholas and herself. Mrs. Grierson said she'd already eaten with Glen and the other ranch-hands.

They sat quietly at the table, focusing on the stew. Lucille reached for some bread. When she looked up, Nicholas' eyes were on her. He offered an apologetic smile, but she hastily looked away. Her heart pounded. She was still hurt, still angry, but that look made her feel as though he wanted to talk, to apologize. That made her feel more disposed to forgiving him.

She ate and was surprised when Daisie—who usually took time over a meal—rushed through her food and nudged Lucille hesitantly.

"Can we talk?" she asked. "Upstairs, in your chamber?"

"Of course," Lucille said. She'd eaten a small bowl of stew and could always come down later again if she was hungry. They excused themselves.

Lucille glanced back at Nicholas, sure that he'd forgiven her. She felt more ready to forgive him. She wanted to say something but Luke and Daisie were there and so she followed Daisie upstairs to the bedroom.

"Miss, there's going to be a raid in three days."

"What?" Lucille stared at her, jaw dropping. "A raid? What sort of raid? Where?" Her heart was in her ears. Daisie's wide eyes frightened. Lucille couldn't think about anything except her terrifying words.

"A raid on the village. Tegan said so."

"Who?"

"The man. The one in prison. The one whose arm you set."

"What?" Lucille gaped at her, unable to speak. "When did he say that?"

Daisie paused, looking at the ground sheepishly. "I took him a meal," she said. "I got some leftovers from my mama's cousin at the inn. I couldn't let him starve—not after you'd helped him like that." She coughed. "He wanted to speak to me. He said he'd seen me at the office, and he knew I knew you," she added awkwardly. "But he said I was to tell you—nobody else, just you—that there was going to be a raid. The bandit leader, Rider, wants to take control of the town. He's got thirty men with him, and they're all armed. He knows he can do it. Tegan wanted you to know."

"Why me?"

Daisie smiled, her blue eyes admiring and sorrowful at once. "So that you can escape," she sighed. "He said you'd done him a good turn, and he wanted you to run away. He said you and me, we should get away into the hills. If we hid there, he could come back and help us get to Pinewood where we could get a wagon to Prescott. He said he didn't want the men finding us. It'd be safer for us if we didn't go back." She shivered.

Lucille made a small sound in her throat. Fear tightened her chest, making it hard to breathe. She didn't want either of them getting stuck in a town run by thirty desperate men. But at the same time, they weren't the only women in Oxplains. The town...the whole town. It was small—just a cluster of houses with perhaps eighty people at the very most—but she couldn't possibly let them all be harmed. And what about Nicholas? They couldn't keep this from him.

She stared at Daisie. "We have to tell the sheriff."

"We can't," Daisie whispered. "The man said only to tell you. What if he finds out we told...?" She sounded terrified.

Lucille took in a breath. "We can't just keep this to ourselves," she insisted. "What about your relatives? We don't want any harm coming to them, either."

"Of course not, Lucille," Daisie agreed immediately.

They looked at each other. The fear on Daisie's face was clear, her mouth set in a thin line. They certainly needed to tell everyone. But if Tegan found out about what they'd done, he would surely want revenge. And besides, she felt a moment of guilt at using the information—he'd wished only to help her, not to lead to his entire gang being killed.

As she stood there, mind racing, an idea came to her. "I have it!" She grinned, the inspiration flooding her thoughts. She felt almost as though an angel had dropped the idea into her thoughts. "We tell the sheriff something, but not that. If he takes action before the raid, then nobody will ever need to know we knew. He might be able to chase them off before the raid ever happens."

Daisie whistled. "What a brilliant plan. But could he?" she asked, her delight replaced swiftly by a small, swift frown.

"Could he what?" Lucille began, then she guessed. "Chase them? I don't know," she shrugged. "I guess we'd have to ask him. And maybe Max could help..." An idea was forming in her mind, a plan that she would never have considered, but which grew so naturally from the idea that had just drifted into her mind.

"Max? Mr. Chaffee? The trading man?" her friend asked with her head titled.

Lucille nodded. She wasn't surprised Daisie had heard of Max Chaffee—all the ranchers and their families even further out than Prescott knew him, since he toured the ranches, selling things and sharing news from one house to the next.

In her mind, she imagined him carrying a message. But she had to contact him first.

"I might need to ride somewhere," she said, thinking aloud. Max's ranch was a day's ride away from this one, perhaps more. If she could manage to do the ride in a day, she could stay at Max's ranch overnight to recover—provided she took a chaperone. "Can you ride?" she asked Daisie. She wasn't really thinking about the question, since she didn't expect an answer—Daisie didn't strike her as a girl who could ride.

"Somewhat." Daisie shrugged. "I could get somewhere if I had to." She paused, seeming self-conscious. "We all learned, my brothers and sisters—my pa insisted that we had the skill, even as girls. Said it might be useful." She gazed up at Lucille, who almost cheered.

"Good," she said. "Now, I think the first thing we should do is to tell the men what we know. Not the actual news, but the suggestion that now is the time to get rid of the bandits. I don't know if they'll listen to us or not, but we need to convince them."

"All right!" Daisie giggled. Her fear had evaporated, replaced by sudden excitement. Her eyes were bright, and her cheeks glowed, as if she was embarking on some exciting venture. Lucille wished she could be as carefree, but if Daisie chose to see it as an adventure, it lightened her fear somewhat.

"We need to get them help," Lucille continued.

"Will we ride?"

"Yes," Lucille said swiftly. "But I don't want to tell Nicholas. He would never allow it. And if he thinks we've gone to get reinforcements, he won't want to go ahead. He'll insist on doing it himself and delay by three days."

"Yes," Daisie added, looking concerned.

"We'll have to do it ourselves."

"Yes," Daisie agreed.

"Let's go downstairs," Lucille said, gesturing to the door. "If I know either of them, they're still downstairs eating their dinner." The two went down the stairs. Lucille was aware of her heart thumping.

It might feel like an adventure, but she knew full well the kind of injuries the men might come back having sustained there, and she knew that the doctor's office was already poorly supplied with resources. Pushing aside the image of the tens of wounded men that would arise from their scheme, she tried to focus on planning. Supplies, men, weapons. They would need all of them and it would be her job to ride to get them. They only had three days, and if Mr. Chaffee wasn't at home, a big part of her plan would already need mending.

Taking a deep breath, feeling that she was being divinely guided and knowing that she would be shown the way, she went down the stairs with Daisie to find the men and tell them about their plan.

Chapter Thirty

Nicholas sat at the kitchen table, exhausted. When Lucille and Daisie quietly came back down from being upstairs, he could sense they wanted to say something to him. He glanced at Glen, who seemed to get the idea and stood.

"Goodnight, sir."

"Goodnight, Glen. Thanks for your help."

"It's nothing, sir." Glen went out into the yard, leaving Nicholas with the two women.

"Nicholas." Lucille cleared her throat.

"I wanted to say sorry—" he began, but she interrupted him.

"Thank you," she said, quite pleasantly. "But it wasn't that. It's something we need to say. Daisie and I... After tending that bandit, I have information. Daisie agrees with me."

"Information?" Nicholas frowned.

"The bandits are weak," Lucille said. "In number, they are strong, but having seen one of them at the office, I am aware of two things. Firstly, that they don't have enough food for their increasing numbers—despite the raids, that man is undernourished. And secondly, that they are...they have scurvy."

"Scurvy."

"Yes," Lucille assured quickly. "I had a chance to see his gums, and they were bleeding. Daisie can confirm that."

"Yes," Daisie agreed.

Nicholas scrutinized the women. *What were they up to?* His head swam. Why were they telling him this? And couldn't they tell him at breakfast?

"It's important," Lucille said urgently. "They are weaker than we thought. Isn't that something? Doesn't that mean it would be the right time to, well...do something?"

"Attack them?" Nicholas gaped. Was she not a physician, intent on preserving life? Here she was, though, inciting attack.

She nodded. Daisie's blue eyes were wide. Nicholas couldn't imagine why she agreed with Lucille—she was far too mild tempered for talk like this—but she was sitting beside her mentor, intent on convincing him.

"Yes," Lucille said.

He blinked. "There are more than twenty men up there, Lucille. It's not a good idea."

"Yes, but they are weak. They lack supplies. If you strike now, you could defeat them."

He drew in a breath, mind reeling.

"Attack now," Lucille repeated. "Within the next few days."

"It's the only way," Daisie added. "The best way."

It was dark in the kitchen, the fire almost out. The conversation stunned him. "There are so many of them," he said.

He didn't know how many, but considering that their raiding parties were often six or more strong, and Rider himself hadn't been on any raids lately, his estimate remained at over twenty men. Well over. Whether they were malnourished or not, he wasn't sure would help much—though he had to admit, it was advantageous.

"But there must be some hope against them," Lucille persisted.

Nicholas's brow furrowed at the two women. They were looking at him, eyes—so different in color, one pair like coal and one like water—staring at him with inscrutable looks. They were *pleading* with him to do this.

"All right," he sighed reluctantly. Daisie grinned, and Lucille remained serious, though she shifted in her seat, leaning on the wall. "But I need tonight to think about it."

"Of course," Lucille nodded instantly, looking thoughtful.

He wondered what was on her mind.

"You'll let us help, sir?" Daisie asked.

Nicholas raised a brow, surprised. "You ladies will be an immense help looking after the elderly and the little ones." He paused, frowning. "We'll tell them to gather in the church. That way, two men can stay and defend them while we take the rest with us." He imagined Lucille and Daisie safe in the church, where there were only two doors and a man at each door with a gun could defend it.

Nicholas shifted to take the weight off his sore leg. As usual, it was painful—it always did flare up when he was tired and worried. As he was now.

"I'll think about it," he promised. "But for now, we need to get to bed. It's late and we all have lots of work tomorrow."

"Yes," Lucille agreed.

It seemed she was no longer being mad at him, but he couldn't forget how he'd spoken to her. He wanted time to apologize. He glanced at Luke, hoping to persuade him to go to bed. Luke could sleep upstairs—there was another bed in the attic—and Daisie would share with Lucille, as she had done before.

"Do you want to plan now?" Luke asked him eagerly, but Nicholas shook his head.

"No, Luke. I really just want to go to bed. We need rest."

Luke nodded, heading upstairs. "Of course."

Nicholas stayed in the kitchen, worried and upset. He'd been planning to confront the bandits in their hideout for months now. Why was Lucille pushing that he did something now? She knew something; he was sure she did. He had to think so, or he would just feel that she shamed him for not having acted months before now.

His head ached for lack of sleep and he could barely think.

As he limped up toward his bedchamber, steps came from above. He tensed, thinking Luke had forgotten something and was returning to the kitchen, but the step was lighter and slower than Luke's. When he looked up, he saw Lucille.

She flushed, eyes moving hastily to her boot tops. "Oh! Sorry to get in the way," she murmured. "I was just going downstairs."

"I know." Nicholas could no longer feel mad at her.

Lucille seemed hesitant to meet his gaze as she played with a loose string on her sleeve.

Nicholas didn't move. Eventually, her eyes lifted to meet his and she gazed at him. Tension spread in his whole body. Her expression was eloquent, eyes a mix of wary questioning and shyness. He felt the same way himself, and he also just knew, with complete, untarnished knowing, that he loved Lucille. He had known it a long time, he realized—but now, it was so clear to him. Alone here, in the hallway, he wished he could cover her with kisses. She was so beautiful, and so distressed at the moment.

Her gaze was not unkind, just questioning in a way that made him realize how much he had left unsaid, how uncertain he had made her of him.

"I was stupid today," he said slowly.

She didn't say anything. The expression in her eyes softened, becoming compassionate, even loving.

"I said and did some stupid things," he reiterated. "I wish I hadn't. You were right."

"I did let your prisoner get away," Lucille said sheepishly. If there was a smile on her lips, he couldn't quite see—it could have been a play of shadow on her porcelain skin, but it might have also been a sorrowful grin.

"Yes, you did," he replied. "But he didn't get very far."

"He could have."

The warmth in their eyes became clear and soft on the shadowy stairwell.

"Listen, I understand what I did. I could not have done any differently—that man was my patient, and I am a physician, bound to help. It's who I am. But I know I should not have been so unthinking."

"Next time, don't let him sneak off unobserved," Nicholas said with a small smile.

Lucille was standing so close to him, her hand almost touching his. Without thinking, he clasped her soft, fine hand in his own, lifting it to his lips.

"Sir!" Lucille exclaimed, a low, urgent sound as she jerked away. He released her hand, not quite touching it to his mouth, as she turned and went hastily down the stairs.

Nicholas inhaled. He had been close to kissing her mouth as well. He drew a breath to say sorry, but she ran down the stairs and the next thing he heard was her deep voice talking to Daisie, leading her up toward her bedroom.

He'd gone too far and scared her. He seemed to keep on doing that.

Annoyed with himself, he walked down to the landing, hearing the two women already in their chamber, talking in low voices. He headed toward his own bedroom, shutting the door behind him. He undressed by the light of a single lamp; the fire burned down to a warm glow in the grate by the time he was in the room. It was warm and pleasant, and he ought to have slept well, but he knew he was going to be awake half the night, tossing, and turning, trying to plan an ambush while trying not to think about Lucille.

It only took an hour to fall asleep, his weary, numb mind instantly letting him rest. When the rooster called the dawn hour, he stumbled out of bed, dressed, and went downstairs. He expected to find Lucille and Daisie already in the kitchen—or at least Lucille, to whom he wanted to apologize—but instead, he found only Mrs. Grierson, with a note which said Lucille and Daisie had ridden off somewhere.

"Where?" he asked Mrs. Grierson.

"I don't know, sir," she replied.

Nicholas frowned as his stomach tightened in a knot. This was unlike her. If she'd just gone out for a brief ride, why the note? And why hadn't she told Mrs. Grierson where she was going? He didn't understand.

What was he going to tell Luke, too, when he discovered Miss Wellford had gone?

"Are you sure she didn't say?" Nicholas pressed.

"Sir, don't ask me," Mrs. Grierson shrugged.

Nicholas's stomach twisted uneasily. She knew where Lucille was, and she'd been asked not to tell; that much was obvious. But why would Lucille want to keep it a secret? If they'd just ridden to town to see to patients, that would be reasonable. He would hardly be angry.

"What time will they be back?" he asked.

Mrs. Grierson shook her head. "It doesn't say in the note."

Nicolas held out his hand. "May I see the note?"

"Of course."

Nicholas read it and put it down, his heart racing.

"She doesn't know when she'll come back," he groaned.

He clenched his fist, pain in his chest. He had scared her off, sent her away. He was a fool and now, what could he do, but as she had suggested? It was the least he could do to say sorry for what he had done.

Nicholas stretching, deciding he should go and talk to Glen and the other ranch hands. He'd need them to ride with the other men of the village.

He would need every last man to go with him to face them.

Chapter Thirty-One

Lucille and Daisie had vanished, and nobody knew where they had gone.

Nicholas rode across the desert, Luke beside him. He was furious and confused and sad. He had no idea what had happened yesterday morning and he had absolutely no idea what to do about it, either.

They had been gone all day, and Mrs. Grierson—whether she knew of their whereabouts, he didn't know—had not told him anything. She had only insisted that she was sure they would be back, though even she looked worried.

Nicholas had decided to put the plan into action—if Lucille and Daisie were not there, what could he do? He had to believe them that there was some urgency to all of this.

In almost all his intuitive senses, he felt their idea was ridiculous: he had just enough men at best to accomplish it and he risked throwing lives needlessly away. In his heart, he also knew that he could not refuse to do as Lucille had asked. Especially not now that she had taken Daisie with her and disappeared somewhere.

He glanced at Luke, who rode with an expressionless face. Fear and sorrow was in the younger man's eyes, and Nicholas didn't wish to add to his burdens or to expose himself as equally debilitated and confused. The women's actions had troubled them. Instead, he rode wordlessly, not allowing anyone to see the utter confusion he experienced.

"Chris will join us," he commented as they rode. They had ridden to town, where they had assembled a group of men—of all the inhabitants, there were only eight men in an age-group he would safely take with him to fight. He glanced back, where Glen, Albert, and Jackson rode with them. Chris would join them, which would raise their strength to fourteen. They were still hopelessly outnumbered—and that was if his guess of twenty was anywhere near accurate. He had no idea how many men might be up there.

"Yes, sir," Luke replied. While the others waited, Luke rode down the path to the ranch to fetch Chris. They could also count on Bert and his three friends, increasing their numbers to eighteen. But Nicholas was still unsure. Even if he had overestimated the numbers of the bandits, they would only be very narrowly in an advantageous position. He would have liked to have twice that number.

Luke and Chris rode up behind them. As Chris fell into step with Luke, the men talked among themselves. He tried to plan as far as possible; he couldn't let his mind rest, because if it did, he would focus on Lucille and he would be frantic, wondering what had happened.

She and Daisie could be anywhere! And why had they chosen to ride? In the village church, they would have been perfectly safe. He would have wanted them to be there and not just because they would be safe—Lucille could have been important to keeping the villagers' morale raised. She was the physician, and they would have felt safer with her there.

"Luke, when we get to the caves, this is what we must do." He and Luke had already been over the plan, concocting it together on the way to the town. It was a desperate plan, but he felt fairly sure it could work. Given the number of men he had, it was their only chance at success. "You take six or seven men—no more than seven, and ride down that path, there." He hated sending Luke into danger, but they had agreed Luke rode faster—he was lighter, and he could get his horse to a gallop that Nicholas couldn't achieve on account of his extra weight and his knee. "When they come after you, we shoot at them from behind. We take out as many men as we can, and then you turn, and take out the rest." He swallowed hard, resting a hand on his chest. It was a mortal sin to kill, even though he was sure God knew his duties and would understand. He would feel the weight of that sin, even though he knew it would be understood.

"Yes, sir," Luke agreed. "I'm going to take Bert and his friends since they're all lighter and faster. You choose three other men."

"Of course," Nicholas nodded.

The rest—Chris, Glen, and the stronger, slower riders, would wait with him. They would stay at the rocks, concealing themselves. To that end, they would have to stop and dirty their guns at the spring, covering the gunmetal with dirt so that it didn't shine. He glanced at them, glad that they were all dressed in leather trousers and faded shirts so that there was no chance of them standing out as a point of color in the landscape.

"Let's go," he said.

They rode on. Bert and the men joined them—Bert riding with no hint of pain in his leg—and approached the narrow path ahead of them Nicholas gestured to his men.

"Behind, men," he told them succinctly. "We wait behind the rock."

They all concealed their horses behind the big outcrop of rock one side of the road. A narrow road led directly under the bandits' hideout, and Nicholas hoped they would see Luke and his followers and be drawn to attack them. Those men—in contrast with his own—would ride loudly, shouting to each other, making sure to draw attention to themselves. Some of them had strapped saddlebags to their saddles, hoping the bandits would think they had pickings worth raiding.

Nicholas drew his horse behind the bluff and waited, watching Luke as he rode out with his men. They were laughing, talking, and making as much noise as they could. Luke sat straight but Nicholas could see he was terrified. He tried to remember each detail—white hat, checked shirt, his hands. He wanted to be able to remember that forever, in case he never saw the young man again. He swallowed hard.

Nonsense. Focus.

He couldn't let himself think about Luke. The other nine men with him had a job to do. He sat on his horse, sweating in the blazing sun, and waited.

When the bandits were upon them, Luke would fire twice into the air.

Behind him, a horse stamped and snorted. Chris swore, tugging a rein, but Nicholas ignored him. They didn't need to be that silent—the bandits were a good few hundred feet from where they hid.

Trying to keep cool in the achingly hot desert sunshine, they waited.

***

Time crept past.

After what felt like an age—and during which time, Nicholas was sure their plan had failed, that the bandits weren't going to pursue—he heard a shot. He frowned, wondering if it was Luke's signal. They had agreed to two shots, not one. A second or two later, he heard another.

"Is that him, sir?" Glen asked.

"I don't feel sure," Nicholas said carefully. Their horses' hooves were soft on the dusty sand below them. "Luke has a better gun than that. He showed it to me on the night we had the dance at the ranch."

"Who else could it be?" he frowned. "Two shots, like you said."

"But it sounds wrong." He paused, taking just one more instant to think. The path was rocky and any sound there was rendered strange, the weird echoes mingling and shifting the sounds. He couldn't be sure he could judge the quality of a gun from this distance. "Maybe it's the echoes. We can't waste time thinking about it." He gestured to them, and they rode ahead.

They rode on. Luke and the men must have got quite far ahead, he thought—the trail of hoofprints was wide down the path and he couldn't see a sign of them.

Then, shots rang out. Two more, urgent and swift, and then another two, the sound rendered impossibly loud by the weird echoes off the rocks around them. Fear surged within Nicholas. What if he was wrong? What if that hadn't been Luke? What was going on ahead?

"Careful, men," he called as more shots rang out. Three up ahead, and three he could have sworn came from their right. He decided it was echoes—it must be echoes, there was no path on the right where men could ride—but then Chris yelled.

"Sir! Men on the hill!"

Nicholas swore. Three men stood on the hilltop above them, firing down into the defile. As he watched, more joined them. *How many men were there?* If he looked at the tracks before them, he was sure there were at least twenty horsemen in the defile already. How many bandits were there?

"Turn!" he shouted to his men, horror filling him. Where were Luke and his companions? Had he sent them into a trap? He wheeled his horse, Starburst neighing loudly, as he tried to see to his right. "Men! Split up! Alfred, Jackson, go back!" he gestured to the path down which they had just come. "Try to get around them." He indicated up the hill, hoping the men on the hilltop weren't listening and couldn't hear his shouted orders. All they could do was try and get between the bandits and the cave, cutting them off. He looked at the men—Chris and Glen and the rest. "You come with me. We have to rescue Luke."

"Yes, sir!"

Nicholas galloped ahead, gunshots hailing around them from the men overhead. It was terrifying, but wasn't terrified for himself: after all, he'd been in a few firefights, but never one at such close quarters and never with so many men with him, all at risk. A bullet rattled onto rocks beside him and he squeezed with his knee, desperate to make his horse run faster. He could barely cling to the saddle, his knee burning like a coal was in it, but he could not ride slowly. He had to take the bandits by surprise.

Around the corner, there were ten of them, and he could just see Luke and his men up ahead. They had been pushed to the end of the defile, the perfect place for an ambush, except that it was filled with rocks. Luke and his men had used their senses and concealed themselves, firing at their ten opponents from around the jumble of stone. That could only last for so long, however—they had limited ammunition with them, while it seemed the bandits had plenty, and, having more men, could take time to reload.

Nicholas winced, aiming at a man on a horse, not focusing for longer than it took to pull the trigger. He fired again at another man, and again, and repeatedly. One bullet left. One before he had to reload.

"Luke!" he screamed in warning. A man was aiming straight at him, but Luke turned aside at the last minute and Nicholas aimed at the attacker, who ducked behind a rock.

More shots rang out, and Luke rode back toward him and then, abruptly, it was still.

Five of the bandits had fallen, the rest disappearing back among the rocks rather than stay to face the bullets and the riders around them. Luke and his men were emerging from the rocks, ready to take care of the rest, and he could at last shift his focus to loading and thinking about the other men. "We need to find Alfred and the rest."

He hoped they were taking care of the men on the hilltop, but as he paused to look over, someone yelled.

A terrified scream came from the rocks where they had first hidden—he would not have thought was human except that he knew it was.

"Alfred!" he should. "Jackson!"

There was no reply, but they were just in time. A force of bandits rode down from the hills, and if he had thought the twenty in the defile represented almost all of them, he had been sorely mistaken. Another twenty were on the hilltop, and as he led his men, desperately fast, out of the opening, the riders swarmed behind them into the small valley.

The bandits who rode behind them had fresh horses, unlike his own, and they were riding fast. Nicholas shouted to his men, desperate for them to keep up, as he led them back across the open desert, searching for a place of shelter. His men needed time to reload, and by now, their horses were badly in need of water.

Cursing himself, desperate to get the men to some semblance of safety, he rode. Raising the dust around them, their pursuers followed them.

Nicholas focused ahead, aware, dimly, of Luke riding beside him and the other men following, but he was unable to slow enough to turn and look. All he could think of was returning the remaining men to safety.

His mind calculated a track that would lead around the rocks near where they had found Tom and Margery. They could try to bluff, circling around the rocks before turning back, making a wide arc back to town. "Almost there," he whispered. He had meant to shout it, but he had no energy for shouting.

All he could do was cling onto the reins, not fall off, and focus on the rocks ahead.

"Left, men!" Nicholas shouted. He gestured, hoping his voice was loud enough for them to hear it. "Go left!"

He sighed with relief as Luke turned with him. Luke had blood on his shirt and Nicholas's heart twisted. Too many of his men were injured. If they managed to bluff, they should ride straight back to town.

"Go! Go!" he shouted. The bandits were closing on them and they had not more than a few seconds to evade them before they would see their maneuver and follow them anyway.

For a second, Nicholas thought it would work. Then, as the bandits closed the gap and his men appeared from behind the rocks, he gestured to the town.

"Ride, men! Fast!" he shouted. It went against everything that made sense—he would rather not lead the bandits to the town and risk the vulnerable townsfolk—but if they blocked the road before the office and aimed to make a stand? Maybe they could do it.

He set the course for the town.

"Men! To me! To the office!" Nicholas shouted, spitting out a mouthful of dust. He was exhausted and his mouth was sticky and dry.

When Luke rode in beside him, dismounting by the trough, Nicholas shuddered with relief. "We can give the horses turns, sir."

"How much time, Luke? Before they get here...? About ten minutes, I'd say." The bandits had been closing behind them throughout the chase.

"Could be," Luke said. "I'll warn the townsfolk."

"Get them into the church," Nicholas commanded. "Ring the bell. Summon them together. Someone will have to stay to defend them."

"I will," Chris spoke up.

"Me, too," another man said. Nicholas recognized he was one of the villagers, related to Mr. Burwell. But he couldn't think of his name. He smiled at him.

"Thank you," he said.

The two men went with Luke to the church. Nicholas focused on the men he had with him. Of the eighteen who had ridden out, he had eleven with him. He wanted to believe the other seven were simply too wounded to mount up. He didn't want to believe worse than that.

"Injured men, head into the office," he said, pointing. "You'll fire from the windows. Try not to hit us," he added with a weak grin. It was a weak joke to make, and he wanted to keep them calm.

"Yes, sir."

Alfred and Jackson might be among them too. Guilt twisted in his heart. He had sent his two men into danger. He would find it hard to forgive himself for that. He focused on the six men who were with him.

"All right, men. Two of you, guard the horses. We might need them later in the fight and I don't want them stealing or shooting them." He had no idea what would happen—if they couldn't make a stand here at the office, where they had ammunition and supplies, he had no sense of what they would do. The church bells were ringing the alarm, and the men had to speak up to be heard.

"Yes, sir."

"Luke?" Nicholas called. The man was a few yards away, bloodstained shirt stark against the beige and white surrounds. As he neared, Nicholas saw a scarf, blood-red in places, tied around his shoulder. He wished the bleeding would stop deputy needed help.

"Yes, sir?"

"Get up on the roof."

It was at once the safest and most risky place Nicholas could put him. Safe, because he could duck out of range behind the chimney and fire on the men, and dangerous because there was no safe way down from there. Nicholas handed him two cases of bullets and Luke walked briskly around the office, footsteps on the stone.

They were putting the last things in place when they arrived.

Luke was on the roof when he shouted. "Ready, men! They're here!"

Nicholas stood with the five men on the terrace, the big desks jammed onto the railings to allow some sort of cover, the chairs and the big bench and other furniture jumbled in front of him to allow him some patchy shelter from the oncoming shots. He lifted his gun.

Lord, if I die, please let me see Lucille before I go.

He knew it was selfish, but he couldn't bear it. She was out there somewhere, thinking he was rude and discourteous because he'd imposed on her by kissing her hand. He didn't want that to be the last sight of him she saw. He wanted to see her again and for those dark eyes to warm and for him to see her smile.

Once he spotted the first bandits, he lifted his gun and fired.

Their response was a hail of bullets. Nicholas dropped to his knees, sheltering behind the barricade. The men were mostly out of range—only six men had dared to ride that close—but even so, the bullets roared, and there was the hollow thud as two of them lodged in the wood of the desks, the other six rattling overhead to hit the walls.

"Careful, men!" he called to his own fellows.

Risking a peep over the barricade, the two men shot at them. He got off a round of his own but ducked instantly behind the furniture as more bullets returned.

He only had his eleven men, five of whom were injured. Luke was up there somewhere, and he made himself forget about the danger to the young man because if he thought about it too much, the worry would weaken him. He shot, ducked, and shot again.

One of the men beside him reloading frantically.

"Another good shot," he commented to the man on his left, who was using his ammunition sparingly. The man grinned. Nicholas recognized him as a nephew of Mr. Knapford, the store owner.

"Pa taught me, sir," he said.

"Good," Nicholas said. "He was a good teacher."

He had to turn left almost instantly, ducking as a bullet fired back toward them.

"Get ready to go inside, men!" he called. "That desk won't hold out long."

They had been crouched here for ten minutes, he reckoned, but already, they were being pressed hard. The bandits were still there, the rain of bullets more or less constant. Ducking out from around the chair, he fired, knew his shot would miss, and ducked back, angrily and concerned.

"Men, we're going to have to make a run. Alfred will open the door for us, and we'll pile in as fast as possible. Stay under the windows."

"Yes, sir."

Knapford's nephew, took a shot, hit his target, and ducked back. He needed men like that in a permanent defense: Earnest, kindly, and with deadly aim.

Nicholas's thoughts wandered, exhaustion stealing his focus. He had to remain present. If he got distracted, his men could all be endangered. They relied on his observations to keep them safe.

"Inside! Now! Alfred!" he shouted at the top of his voice. "Alfred! Open up. We're coming to join you fellows inside."

Relief flooded through him as he heard an answering shout, muffled from the thick walls, and then the scrape of the door opening.

"Sheriff!" Glen yelled at the door. "Come inside."

Nicholas ran, risking turning his back to throw himself in as Glen slammed the door behind him. The door rattled as bullets hit it. As he ran to the window, trying to keep low, he thought that God was looking after them all—though some of the bullets passed straight through the thin wood of the door, none had hit any of them.

He hoped Luke had enough ammunition, and that, should the bandits overrun them, he'd have enough time to get away. One of them should survive, at least. Nicholas kneeled on the floor, aiming out over the windowsill in the room that had once been the waiting room. Now, it was a dusty, echoing space where even the mat had moved, thrown over the door at the back to damp the bullets.

He lay on the dusty floor and tried not to think and listened to the bullets raining down on them. The glass in the window had gone, and he tried to avoid the shards that lay everywhere.

The noise stopped. Nicholas frowned.

"What's going on?" the man lying beside him whispered.

"I don't know," Nicholas admitted. He wasn't sure if it would be intelligent to risk standing up—the window was broken, giving the gunmen an ideal shot at whoever was standing in the window. When no gunshots rang out, even when he threw a stray hat through the window, he decided to stand.

"Sheriff Barnes!" somebody shouted. It was a man's voice, and not one he recognized.

Nicholas froze. It was coming from outside. One of the bandits was naming him.

He cautiously peered out of the window, staring out onto the outside path. Among the bandits, a general agreement seemed to be made to lay down arms. It also seemed to be agreed upon to make way, so that a man on a tall piebald horse could ride forward. The man had dark hair, was solidly built, and had a low brow and clever eyes. He sat hunched forward, his mouth firm. Though he was a stocky man and also had a massive horse, he still seemed excess in size in comparison to it.

Nicholas went cold. For all that, the man was not threatening him, he still felt a wall of hate and violence directed at him. The man on the horse seemed to breathe violence into the air, his presence dark and hateful and all of that was directed at Nicholas.

"Sheriff Barnes," the man repeated, mocking. "You know what? You're the one causing all this trouble here. It's you that caused my men to die. And your men." He gestured at the building where Nicholas could hear the frightened gasps of those who hid with him.

"All I have done is defend the town," Nicholas shouted firmly. He believed that. The bandits were the ones terrorizing his town, not the other way around. "I fight for the law."

The other man laughed. "And get lots of men killed. I see how that works. But if you believe that...?" he shrugged. "I guess I can't help."

"Help?" Nicholas scoffed.

"I can stop this raid," the bandit replied. Nicholas was sure this was Rider, the bandit leader. He'd seen him once or twice, but always too far away to see close detail. He had a piebald horse and wore a white hat, so it must be him. "All I need to do is tell my men here to stop. You're outnumbered. In return, you step down," he said, gesturing to the group. "I have a lot of men, and they need space. Homes. Food. We could live in this town. Of course, you'd have to get the townsfolk out for us. We'd want their goods, though." he grinned. "And then? Well, then, we'd let them get away in peace. No point shooting people for no reason, eh?" He narrowed his eyes. "But your men would have to disarm. Right now."

"And what guarantee do we get?" Nicholas demanded, sensing confusion around him. Some of the men seemed to agree with what the bandit suggested. In part, he agreed too. He knew their small force would not hold against so many. Already, two of the men who were with him had been hit by bullets and he had to get them out, and soon. Their chances were limited if they stayed here.

Rider grinned, seeming pleased. "Well, all we need is you."

"What?" Nicholas glared.

"Yes," Rider repeated quite calmly. "You're the one who's been a thorn, stabbing us for so long. If it weren't for you, some of my men would be alive who are now dead, and we'd have our own town by now. You have any idea how mad that makes a man?" His men muttered in agreement.

Nicholas went cold, his hands like ice. Terribly, unimaginably, part of him agreed with the bandit leader. Part of him knew it was inevitable. He would walk over there, and they would shoot him, and the townsfolk would go free. Luke could lead them to Mr. Chaffee's ranch, maybe, and they could all get passage to Pinewood or somewhere safe where they could find shelter. He could see it so clearly. It seemed to be the obvious choice, one he could make without hesitation.

"Sir? Sir!" someone yelled. He thought it was Alfred, or maybe Glen. He didn't know. A piece of him floated above the scene, seeing himself, disembodied, walking forward. The rest of him—the part that remained in his body—felt hollow. Every gesture was so precise, so rich. He could hear the dust under his feet, the crackle of glass, as he stepped forward. He could feel the cold doorknob. Smell the dusty air. Did things smell in Heaven? He had no idea.

Life was so precious. Rain smelled so good. Air felt so clean. It would be strange to give that all up. So strange.

He walked through the door, drifting, floating above himself, and out toward the bandits.

"Nicholas!" somebody yelled. He recognized Luke's voice. He was scrambling down the roof, reaching the ladder at the back, running over. Nicholas turned to him and smiled.

Luke gaped, blue eyes full of fright. Nicholas, who felt like he was already halfway dead, lifted a shoulder.

"It's what I have to do," he said gently. He cared for Luke, whose face crinkled with tension, the shock and pain making him seem even younger than his eighteen years. Nicholas felt no resistance.

He had to do this.

His mouth was dry, his feet were lead, and felt terrified. He didn't *want* to die. He imagined what it would feel like—the sudden impact of a bullet, the burning, searing rip of it. What was it like? He didn't think he could visualize it. But the rest of him was calm.

"Come on," Rider snapped.

Nicholas stepped forward. There were a few paces between the office and the bandits. It was late afternoon, now, the sunshine slanting at an angle that meant there were only two hours or more of sunshine before the sky turned vibrant orange and the shadows slanted eastward.

A sunset. Such a beautiful way to die, facing the sunshine and its warm rays on his face.

"Nicholas!" somebody screamed. The voice was a woman's voice coming from the path, and he turned, confused, scanning the surrounding area.

She was not here. She had run away. She had ridden somewhere far away and did not intend to return.

His eyes widened. Lucille was in the road. She was on the front seat of a wagon, and a man sat beside her. Behind her, just visible around her shoulder, was Daisie's blonde hair. And with them were ten tall and proud men, armed with guns and rifles.

Luke gaped. Beside him, the bandits glared.

Nicholas met Lucille's gaze. He stared at her, seeing love in her eyes. Love and care and wonderment and sadness and other emotions he could not name.

His heart shifted and grew, and deep within him, he said a prayer of thanks.

Though I walk in the shadow of the valley of Death, I do not fear.

He glared across the road at the bandit, whose eyes were utterly cold.

Chapter Thirty-Two

Lucille sat numbly in the front of the cart, her shout cold on her lips. She was trying, desperately, to make sense of what she was seeing. Nicholas stood there—proud, tall, and unarmed—before the leader of the bandits, arms at his sides. He had chosen to give himself up. She knew that without having to be told. Luke was there, at his side, unmoving, his face frozen with horror.

Lucille watched Nicholas. He was close enough for her to be able to see the expression in his eyes, the distant dreaminess of someone who is already halfway to the other side of life and knows and accepts that.

"No!" she gasped.

The man on the horse was still aiming his gun. He was shouting at her, at Mr. Chaffee, at Daisie, and all the others who they had retrieved. "Get back! Back where you came from, or I kill him right now. And all of them with him."

"No!" Daisie cried. "Luke!"

Lucille squeezed her hand. They were both in an impossible position. Nicholas was there, hostage, and Luke was too, surrounded by men with guns, all of them ready to shoot. Her stomach twisted. She had thought—had honestly believed—that they would arrive in time. That the men they brought—ten men recruited from Mr. Chaffee's small ranch and the neighboring outlying farmsteads—would increase the townsfolk's numbers for an equal fight against the bandits. But none of that happened.

"Ladies," the bandit yelled, making the term seem like an insult. "Get that cart backed up and get back to where you came from. This isn't your fight."

"It is!" Lucille hissed.

A few bandits laughed, but the leader's laugh was sinister.

"Get back home, girl." Now that he dismounted, he stood before Nicholas, his gun still held poised. He gestured dismissively. "This isn't your fight, so take them with you."

The men were already making the climb down from the cart.

"Wait, please," Lucille whispered.

"Hold on, men," he advised beside her. "Wait and see what Nicholas wants."

"Lucille!" Nicholas shouted. "Take them back. Get yourselves to safety."

"No!" she cried. Her voice was too tense for her words to carry, but she knew he heard, because he smiled.

He mouthed some words. When she sat, she realized what they had meant.

I love you.

She breathed deeply. Tears flowed down her cheeks.

"I love you!" she bawled. She didn't care what the townsfolk thought, what the bandits thought, what the silent and grim-faced men on the cart had thought. All she cared about was that she meant every word. She had for the first time put a name to her feelings—the intensity of how it was to look into his eyes, her longing to talk to him, the joy he made her feel. She wished she'd known.

Nicholas grinned. "Catch!" He threw something to her—she didn't see what, but the form glittered and shined. Whatever it was must have been somewhat heavy because it moved with the forcefulness of his throw, heading purposefully across the big gap, directly at her.

The bandit leader, who was distracted, watching the glittering object as it flew across the space between them, faced her. It only took that second.

Nicholas bellowed and threw himself at Rider. The bandit leader was stunned and, as Nicholas vaulted, wrapping his arms around the man, Rider tumbled backward. They were too close for the bandits to risk shooting, locked together as close as an embrace. They both fell, and Lucille screamed, gripping Mr. Chaffee's hand and Daisie held her arm and they all watched, terrified, as the men struggled on the ground.

"Somebody, shoot!" one of the bandits yelled. They lost their moment to act as Nicholas, grasping the bandit leader around the neck, held the gun up.

"If anyone steps forward, he dies," Nicholas shouted.

The bandits stopped. Nobody fired.

In his arms, the bandit leader was still wrestling, but Nicholas's arm was firm around his throat, elbow locked so that it squeezed against his vein. If Nicholas kept that going, the man would faint, his brain losing oxygen as he struggled and gasped and fought.

Lucille sat where she was, transfixed, as the bandits stared at Nicholas.

Rider was a larger man than Nicholas, built and strong. It was only a moment before he broke the grip on his neck, and then, she had no doubt, he would kill Nicholas. Someone had to act.

Standing beside Nicholas, Luke hadn't moved, watching the action unfold and seeming as unable to comprehend it as the rest of them. Running forward, Luke grabbed the bandit leader, his own pistol pressed to the man's forehead.

"Get down," he snarled.

"Luke!" Daisie whimpered.

Lucille knew how she felt, only her fresh-acknowledged love was rawer and aching and she longed to run to Nicholas, to kiss him and know he was safe. The two women sat helplessly, holding hands, as the men fought.

"Lay down your arms!" Nicholas shouted at the bandits. "We have no quarrel with you! Lay them down and you can go free. I will not prosecute any of you who give up your gun and swear you will not return here again."

Holding her breath, she was sure none of them would do it. They were still in the majority, and the only thing that had changed was that Nicholas threatened their leader. She had no idea how loyal they felt to him.

One by one, they dropped their guns and she stared, amazed. A few started it, but more continued so that, by the time she could have counted to five, only five of them out of the twenty, she guessed, had guns. Shouting, Nicholas gestured to the house, beckoning for his men to come out. Nicholas's men slowly emerged from the house. First Alfred, the ranch-hand, whom she knew, then some others. They went to Nicholas, who said some words she couldn't hear.

They stepped forward. Some confiscated the weapons, while others led the unarmed men to one side, assembling them near the inn.

"Now!" he growled. "You who are armed, you have another five seconds to put down your guns, or your leader is shot and all of you with him. You see those men there?" he gestured to the cart. "They can shoot you from there if they have to."

Chaffee's men climbed down from the cart, and Lucille tensed. Rider was thrashing, but Luke had him pinned, his gun at his temple.

The remaining five men gave up their guns.

"We have no fight with you," Nicholas said as his men recovered the weapons, carrying them back to the office so that the bandits could not use them. "We will escort you to the main road. You may take your horses, but you will each go different directions and none of you will remain within half a mile of here. If people wish it, they may hire you as ranch-hands. I will not hold you liable for your past crimes."

Lucille gasped. Some of the men with her gasp, too.

It is right, she thought. *What he does is right.*

She remembered her thoughts about Tegan, the wounded man, and knew that what Nicholas said made sense. They were mostly desperate men, people who knew no other way besides that of a soldier. They deserved a chance to live honestly and turn their lives to good works. There was a rumbling of disagreement among the men around her, but Max spoke forcefully.

"The man's right. Give them a chance."

The muttering fell silent. They went forward to join the men with Nicholas. He gave them orders and each group of two or three men escorted a group of five of the bandits. They took them in different directions, and Lucille nodded approvingly.

Beside her, Mr. Chaffee sighed. "Good man. Clever idea."

Proud, Lucille swallowed hard. The men dispersed as she sat with Daisie and Mr. Chaffee, the three of them huddled together in the cart, waiting as the bandits were led off. Her hope for all of them was that they were changed men.

She shut her eyes, sending up a prayer of thanks. Nicholas was alive. That was all right now that mattered.

As Luke and another man escorted the bandit leader to jail, Nicholas turned to her.

"Nicholas!" she screeched.

Without heed for the people who were watching, without care for her reputation or concern for their opinion, or her disheveled hair and travel marked dress, she ran across the street, running straight for Nicholas.

"Lucille." He wrapped his arms around her, pulling her against him. She gazed into his eyes and, without thinking, without either of them considering anything else, he pressed his lips to hers and her lips moved on his and they kissed, a deep, sweet kiss.

Lucille clung to him, breathless, as he gently lowered her to her feet. His green eyes were bright.

"Well, now I guess I have to make an honest woman of you."

She laughed. "Oh, Nicholas." Tension drained from her and made her want to laugh and laugh and never stop. "Oh, Nicholas. You are a funny man."

He chuckled and he took her hand. Staring into his eyes, she knew that she loved him, and he loved her, and that their lives were always going to be different from now on.

They found the shining object and he picked it up.

"My badge," he chuckled. The small silver star sparkled on his palm, winking through the thin layer of dirt that streaked it. He blew on it and passed it to her. "I guess it made a good distraction after all. I wondered where that had gone."

Lucille giggled. "Oh, you are dear." She studied the little star and as she did, she recalled looking to the heavens and she seemed to hear her father's voice, naming the constellations in the cold stars overhead.

The Bear. The Crown. The Polar Star.

She knew that her heart had found its true north, its constant, the one point in a tumultuous universe that she knew would always be fixed, safe, and certain.

"I love you."

Grinning, he put the badge away. "I love you, Lucille."

He wrapped his arms around her, and someone yelled, but Lucille ignored them, and Nicholas barely noticed, the shards of glass and dirt around them. They had a new life ahead, and it began the moment they walked through that office door together.

Chapter Thirty-Three

The warmth of the sunshine, tentative through the thick glass in her bedroom, fell on her face. Lucille stepped back, pausing as Daisie made room.

"Is this how you meant?" Lucille asked, frowning.

"No use asking me," Daisie said with a giggle. "Why not look for yourself? Mirror's over there."

Lucille nodded. She peered up at the glass and stood in silence.

The long white dress she wore was trimmed with lace, the bodice square and showing her neck, the sleeves puffs of thin fabric. The dress itself was fine silk and it whispered about her as she moved, thin and cold and breezy. She stared at the woman looking back at her.

Daisie had arranged her hair, curling it a little and pinning it in place, each pin decorated with pearls so that her hair seemed caught in a net of little sparkles. She tilted her head, admiring the effect.

Her face was a soft oval, and her eyes, which were deep brown, seemed large in its softened form. Her lips she had always described as over-pouted, were dusk red and her cheeks were pale. The hairstyle brought out the soft contours of her face, bringing a delicate lift to it. She stared.

"Daisie! I can't believe it."

"You should." Daisie grinned.

As Lucille looked into the younger woman's eyes, her heart melted. "Thank you, Daisie," she said softly. "I never imagined what it would be like to have a friend."

"Oh, Lucille," Daisie said, beaming. "You're the best friend I could imagine. You and Matty are the truest friends I ever had. Now, let's get that veil."

Lucille sighed, glad that her friend hadn't said more, or she would have started crying. She waited while Daisie fetched the veil, standing still so her friend could put the ornamental wreath on her hair. She breathed in, smelling the flowers.

"There!" Daisie said. "My, don't you look a picture! I'm going to start crying if I don't go outside."

Lucille smiled at her friend, and then drew a deep breath. It finally made sense.

This was her wedding day. She was going to go to the church and be married to Nicholas. She was really doing it, and this time, there was no doubt in either of their minds that it was nothing to do with the villagers—it was about love.

Daisie returned, carrying flowers. "Matty brought these."

Lucille gasped. The flowers were roses, and of all the people she knew, only Matty grew them. Her heart filled, seeing the fine blossoms with their delicate petals—pale pink and cream and purest snowy white.

"Oh, Matty," she whispered. Her voice was wobbly. If she cried too much, her face would look a mess.

She giggled, turning to Daisie, who stood beside her, her dress palest butter-colored fabric. She had her hair arranged stylishly, one or two tiny flowers decorating it.

"Shall we go down?" she asked Daisie, and her friend nodded.

"Yes. Let's go downstairs. The house is full of people, and I need to get them to the church."

Lucille laughed. Nicholas agreed that the ride from the ranch was too far and that her hairstyle would suffer the punishment of the wind if they rode all the way in the wagon, even with a cover. They were upstairs in the inn, and guests had been arriving all day, coming to decorate the church and cook and generally to visit. Lucille followed Daisie downstairs.

In the hallway, the townsfolk—those who could not be persuaded to wait until she arrived at church to see her—gathered. Lucille stood where she was, transfixed.

Five happy faces stared up at her. Gracie was there, with her son, and her neighbor. Matty was there too, and Rebecca. Standing with her squarish face strong and firm, her graying hair arranged in two bunches, was Rachel. Mrs. Grierson.

Lucille's heart ached. The older woman smiled, her gentle face lighting up as she saw her. Her dark eyes were bright. Gracie and some of the others were tearful with fondness, but Rachel just smiled. Her face was strong, and her expression was certain, her eyes softly glowing with a wisdom that touched Lucille's heart.

"Bless you, my child."

Lucille's heart ached as Rachel whispered the words, her eyes filling with tears. She took Rachel's hands, the joints gnarled, skin rough, and held them, looking into her eyes.

"Thank you, Rachel," she said softly.

Her friend just smiled. Lucille looked away, knowing she might cry.

She embraced Gracie and hugged Keith, Daisie shooing him when he tried to touch Lucille's hair. Though she wouldn't have really cared if Keith dislodged a curl or two from out of its place, Lucille understood. She was deeply touched that he was there. She took Rebecca's hands, and Jessie's, and then turned to Matty, who clasped her hands, kissing her cheek. Her friend smelled like lavender and roses.

"Bless you, my dear," Matty whispered. "You look so lovely."

"Thank you, Matty," Lucille whispered. She was crying, trying not to let tears fall. When she had her tears held back, she turned back to Matty. "Thank you for helping with everything."

Matty, who had organized the dress, veil, and cake, just grinned. "It's nothing, my dear. You're like a daughter. Now, off we go—the coach is waiting."

Lucille giggled. "What coach?"

She stepped outside to see Max Chaffee, sitting at the front of the cart. He had the reins in his hand and the oxen were yoked to it. He had—or somebody had—thought to give them wreaths of flowers. The whole wagon had a fairground air.

"Let me help you up."

Lucille laughed, allowing herself to be helped into the cart. She sat beside Mr. Chaffee, took a moment for arranging her skirts, and he shook the reins, moving them forward up the street toward the church.

The road from the inn to the church was short—no more than a minute or two on the cart. Lucille watched dreamily as the houses moved smoothly and slowly past, thinking that this was the village where she would spend the rest of her life.

The cart rolled to the church and Mr. Chaffee stopped outside, letting the reins fall. When he turned to Lucille, there were tears on his face. "Your father..." he could barely get the words out. "He'd burst right now; he'd be so full of himself."

Lucille had to laugh. She sniffled, too, pain in her heart, thinking of that one dear man who would not be there today. But somewhere, deep in her heart, she knew he was there. She was sure that, just sometimes, the veil of heaven rolled back and those in the realm of angels could look down and see, and know their loved ones were well. She gazed at the sky, blinking back her tears.

"Come on, then," Mr. Chaffee said gently. "Let's go into the church."

Lucille accepted his hand, and he led her in. The church was dark—she had been into it once, briefly, and she had noticed then that it was plain and unadorned, the walls stone that was rough, not plastered. She had thought it forbidding, then, but now as she looked to the rafters, she felt as though the entire space radiated with love. She surveyed the church.

The guests had somehow reached the place ahead of them—Daisie must have dragged them all off through some other entrance while she and Mr. Chaffee were in the cart. Daisie was in the front pew, Luke sitting beside her, with Matty and Gracie just back from them. Rachel was there too, and Rebecca, Bert, Glen, Chris, and all the others, occupying the pews that stretched from the doorway to the front of the church. Eyes landing on the altar, her eyes fixed only on the man.

She would have been content with a simple affair—just one or two witnesses—but Nicholas had insisted that, since they had the time to prepare and have something special, they ought to do it properly. It was just a month since the fight with the bandits—it was the least time she and Nicholas would be prepared to wait.

Nicholas's tall form was clad in black—a suit she didn't know he owned—hugging his firm legs and stretching across his big shoulders. His dark hair with its one or two little strands of white was shadowed in the dark space, but he seemed full of light to her, and she joined him, standing before the altar and its candles.

The pastor—a tall man with a softened face and big dark eyes—smiled at her warmly. Mr. Chaffee released her arm, and she looked at him, love and sorrow in her eyes, reflecting on his face. It was a sorrowful moment, sweet and tender. She glanced sideways as Nicholas looked down at her, eyes soft with love. She grinned, unable to keep the smile off her face.

The pastor cleared his throat to read the ceremonial words.

Lucille listened, each word deep in her heart. This was the most wonderful moment for her—she stood in the sight of the Lord, beside the man she loved more than anything in the world, and pledged her love for him to God, vowing to both that she would—and did—love him for all eternity.

The pastor's voice, lilting and musical, told them of the love they shared and how precious to God it was, and her heart glowed, knowing that was true.

She drew a breath as they reached the moment of the vows.

"Do you, Lucille Melissa Newbury, take thee, Nicholas Stuart Barnes..."

She smiled, learning his middle name was Stuart for the first time. She forgot the passing surprise as she heard the vow spoken, and then she replied, voicing the words with every bit of her. "I do."

The pastor beamed and turned to Nicholas. "Do you, Nicholas Stuart Barnes, take thee, Lucille Melissa Newbury..."

She shut her eyes for a second, unable to contain her delight as she heard the vow spoken. She listened to the low, resonant reply. "I do."

The pastor concluded the ceremony, and Lucille held her breath as he reached the end. Nicholas's hands were so gentle as they lifted the veil.

The light, silky fabric lifted from her face. She blinked a little, peering up at him. She had gotten used to the indefinite light behind the fabric, and the blinding, full candlelight was bright to her. Staring up into his face, a slow excitement built inside her.

Nicholas smiled down at her. His green eyes were warm. He rested his hand on her shoulder, and, so gently, he pressed his lips to hers. She shut her eyes, relishing the soft, sweet feeling that was the fullness of his mouth pressed to her own.

She was surprised and delighted, amazed by the feelings that ran through her. This sweet, slow kiss seemed different, something beautiful and gentle and exciting, something that called on her body and her soul. Lucille faced the congregation, her heart overflowing as she looked out at those dear faces.

Rachel was watching them, eyes full of love. Daisie was smiling, tears on her cheeks. Matty had a smile on her face, eyes damp. Beside her, Gracie and Keith and Matthew sat, Gracie smiling and Keith round-eyed. Rebecca, Bert, Chris, Glen, Alfred, and Jackson were all there. In the front pew, watching her with those gentle hazel eyes, was Mr. Chaffee.

Lucille drew a breath. She could barely contain all the delight and wonder that flooded through her, lifting her heart, and making her rejoice.

Taking Nicholas' hand, they walked out of the church together, out into the sunlight.

Nicholas lifted her, helping her up into the cart. As always, he was so gentle, his hands touching her soft and tender and full of love. He looked into her eyes, and she felt as though her heart would melt as she stared back at his own.

He wrapped his arms around her, and she rested her head on his and he set the oxen walking back to the ranch, where she and he would start a beautiful new life together, living side by side, spending each moment together, blessed in the sight of God and living each day joyously.

The Lord does work in mysterious ways, indeed, and His wonders are the light of our lives.

Epilogue

Lucille breathed in. The scent of the desert drifted to her, the familiar perfume of dust, rust, and heat that she loved so much. Even after four years of living on the ranch, she still loved standing in this particular spot, gazing out over the yard toward the hills. She was in the shade nearby the kitchen, and it was evening, the sunshine bright on the horizon, the clouds just touched with the orange and purple that would be the sunset—harsh and glorious—in time. She took a deep breath and smiled.

"Hey! Mrs. Barnes!" a familiar voice called.

"Hey," she smiled to Glen, who carried a heavy tarred rope past on his way to the barn. A new barn had been made—one to store the hay for the growing number of cattle. She waved as he wandered off, the heavy burden seeming light on his big shoulders.

Glen's wife, Marcie, lived on the ranch now too, in a small cottage near the stables, and Lucille recently helped her with a burn on her hand from cooking. Their three children—Bennie, James, and Lauren—were welcome additions to the growing ranch family. James was a newborn, Bennie was five, and Lauren was just three. Lucille couldn't help the warmth she felt toward them, especially when she watched them play.

Lucille went indoors. The kitchen was spotless—Marcie and Judi, the wives of the ranch-hands—looked after it now, though Rachel, who lived nearby, was a regular visitor and always welcome whenever she came to call.

"Mrs. Barnes?" Judi came out of the hallway with a basket on her arm. "I just brought the cushions in from outside." She gestured to the back of the house, where the washing could dry in the harsh desert sunshine. Lucille nodded. She'd recently cleaned the parlor, and the washing was ready to bring indoors.

"Thank you. I'm on my way upstairs now," she said. She frowned. "Is she sleeping?"

Judi grinned. "She is, Mrs. Barnes. She will likely wake soon, though."

"Certainly." Lucille nodded. She tucked a strand of deep brown hair out of one eye. She had two strands of white there on one temple—she was only twenty-three, but Nicholas lovingly said that they were so beautiful. She blushed, recalling how lovingly he brushed them from her face and touched her hair.

Lucille and Nicholas occupied the bedroom beside the parlor upstairs—she peered in, seeing that the bed was spotlessly made up, the white linen gray-touched in the darkening room. She smiled to see the brighter furnishings and curtains. She and Nicholas had agreed that the space needed some lightening, and the addition of softer colors was quite welcome.

The portrait of the Radfords still hung there. She had come to be fond of them, too—after all, they were the only parents Nicholas had.

She hurried across the landing, going upstairs to where the spare room had been transformed. She paused in the doorway; breath held. Sleeping in a crib was Gerard, and in Rachel's arms, Izzy slept. Her tiny daughter, just a year old.

"Izzy?" Lucille whispered.

"She's awake," Rachel said with a grin. "She was looking for you. I said we'd come down and find you, but I thought you might be busy studying," she chuckled, scraping a gray hair from one eye.

"No, I'm not busy. Thank you, Rachel," she added, gratefully lifting the small child from Rachel's arms. Her friend often helped with babysitting, and she appreciated it greatly—there was nobody she would have trusted more. The child wriggled and peered up at her, her eyes—soft brown, like Lucille's, with crinkles at the edges from smiling.

"Mama," Izzy said. "Out."

Lucille grinned. Her little daughter had recently started to say single words, naming the people she knew closely and asking for the few things she knew the words for. She loved to go outside, and Lucille lifted her, making her chuckle and grin.

"We can go outside in a moment, my sweetie," she promised. "First, we should wake your brother. He also needs to go out."

Gerard, just three years old, was sleeping, his small form reposeful, the regular sound of his breathing a soft sigh she could just hear if tried. She watched him for a moment, but Izzy wriggled, bringing her back to the moment.

"Outside," her daughter insisted.

"Very well, very well," Lucille said with a laugh. She set the little girl on her feet, letting her walk a few paces before sitting down promptly on her bottom by the fireplace. She could walk, but she was unsteady and fell down often. Lucille giggled.

"Look at you! You are clever little lady, you."

At a sound from the small bed by the door, she realized their giggling woke the boy. He yawned and opened his eyes, sitting up.

"Mama!" he said, sounding delighted. "You're here."

Lucille nodded. "I am. And would you like to go outside, my fine little boy?"

He grinned and nodded. "Outside!" he said. "Is Bennie there?"

Lucille nodded. "We'll go and find him." At three years old, Gerard could talk fairly well—at least, as far as expressing what he felt was concerned. He was firm friends with the other children on the ranch, and spent hours playing outside, watched over by Lucille, or Bennie's mother.

"You need some clothes, my fellow," she said, lifting him. He was wearing a nightshirt, one her friend Daisie had sewn. She kissed his pale brown hair and set him on her knee, reaching for some little trousers which she had made—Matty taught her patiently—and a tiny shirt that she'd received as a gift. She dressed him while he wiggled about with the need to be active and running.

"Now," Lucille said, setting him on the floor. "You just need your shoes—where are they?"

"There!" Gerard toddled over to the door, where his tiny shoes—made for him by a man skilled with leatherwork—lay. He tugged them on, and Lucille lifted Izzy into her arms, ready to take them outside.

"Let's go downstairs," she said. "Carefully, now. Hold onto my hand," she advised, as Gerard toddled with concentration toward the stairs, pausing to take her hand.

She led him down, Izzy propped on her side, and reached the kitchen. There, she took a blanket to sit on and went out to the yard. Near where the path led to Matty's ranch, there was an adequate space with some rocks—still warm from the day's sunshine—where they would sit. She let Gerard walk across the small space while she laid out the blanket and sat, holding the baby.

"Now, you can play nicely," she said, gesturing to the stones he loved to pile up and construct things from. He and Bennie spent hours playing there. She sat back, letting Izzy stand so she could explore a little. The sun was setting, but it was still bright and warm outside, and the heat sank through the thin fabric of her gown.

Nicholas came over from the stables, having just got back from work. She called out to him, and he grinned at her.

"Nicholas!"

"Lucille!" His limp slowed him a little as he joined them. He was smiling, his face—lined with work in the sunshine, bright with smiling—full of tender feelings for them. He lifted Izzy into his arms.

"Who is here?" he asked playfully. He kissed her hair, holding her against him. She rested her head on his shoulder and Lucille's heart filled with love as she witnessed his gentle care.

"Papa," Izzy informed him.

"Quite so!" Nicholas laughed. "And where is your brother, eh? Where's that little rascal?"

"Here!" Gerard toddled over, passing Nicholas a stone he'd found in the pathway. "Look! Round."

"It is, indeed," Nicholas said, grinning as he took the stone in his hand. He rolled it over in his palm, Lucille looking at the weathered skin of his hand with love. He put the stone in his pocket. "Can I have it?"

"Very well," Gerard sighed, reluctantly.

They both laughed. Lucille's heart raced as Nicholas sat beside her. He stretched his long legs, not dirtying the blanket with his riding shoes. She was aware of the unique scent of his body—musk and the dry smell of the desert. She nestled into the crook of his arm, and he held her close.

"How are you, my dearest?"

"Well." She grinned. "And you?" She looked into his green eyes. He smiled, deepening the folds around them. He had become more weathered in the last four years, the sunshine carving lines onto his brow and face, but she thought it made him all the more beautiful. He shrugged.

"It was a good day," he said. "I chatted with Kenley, and he's happy."

Lucille nodded. "Well, that's good."

Mr. Kenley, a relative of the banker in Pinewood, opened a new bank in Oxplains—a sign of growing prosperity. The town was thriving. New houses had been made, and apart from a bank, they had a post office and two new stores. It was a growing town.

Lucille felt Nicholas' strength as he held her, his arm tightening about her waist. She flushed. She had become used to being close to him—a delicious closeness that expressed the way they felt for each other and was a blessing for them both.

"How are you?" Nicholas asked again, his face next to hers. His lips were on her own, then, and she blushed and let him kiss her, body flooded with warmth. Her cheeks were burning, heart racing.

"I fare very well," she said, teasingly. "It was a fine day today."

"Good. Good," he said gently. He took her hand as they watched Izzy toddle uncertainly toward the house and Gerard play with stones. They could sit there for hours, but Lucille kept an eye on her little daughter, knowing she could rush off surprisingly quickly if they didn't pay attention.

"I spent the morning with Matty, and Marcie and I did some tidying. And I worked in the parlor for a while. Then, I came outdoors and saw a certain dead man walking up to the house," she teased him fondly, her hand squeezing his fondly.

"I was glad to see you there," he chuckled, pressing his lips to her ear.

She giggled. "And we should go indoors, I reckon. Izzy is about to try to find her way inside."

"Oh. Yes." Nicholas stood, running across the space to lift his daughter, who was, indeed, toddling with purpose toward the water trough.

Lucille fetched Gerard, knowing that it would take some time to convince him to come inside when there was a game with his stones offered. "We should go in," she cooed. "It's almost suppertime."

That was the one thing that could budge him—a strong interest in anything edible. Gerard peered up, stones lying on the dirt.

"Supper," he said.

Lucille giggled. "Quite so." She took his hand and went indoors with him, pacing herself to the speed of his short legs. She lifted him and they went into the kitchen together.

The community on the ranch customarily met in the kitchen for dinner. Judi was already cooking while Marcie minded the children in the yard, and Lucille sat at the table, helping Gerard up to sit beside her.

"I made a good stew," Judi said fondly, reaching for the pot and ladling the food into their bowls.

Nicholas grinned at Lucille where he sat across from her. Izzy was on his knee, and he would feed her while she helped to make sure Gerard ate his food. That, she thought with a grin, was an easy thing to do. The trick was stopping him from eating Bennie's too.

They all came into the kitchen slowly. Glen arrived next, bringing the children with him, and Albert, and Jackson and another youth who had joined them, named Jack. They all sat together at the table, the conversation rising and falling. Nicholas cleared his throat to say a prayer before they ate—it was tradition now, and each evening someone else took a turn.

As Nicholas said the words of thanks, Lucille's heart filled with feeling. She was so happy here, so grateful for every second. It was a beautiful, full, rich life and she murmured the words along with Nicholas, every word true.

Thank you, Lord.

She looked up as Marcie ran in. "Guests!" Marcie yelled, coming in with the egg basket on her arm. "There are guests on the way here. Do you expect anyone?" she asked Nicholas.

He shrugged. "I wasn't expecting guests, no," he agreed. He glanced at Lucille. "Were we expecting anyone?"

"Not till tomorrow."

Nicholas went outdoors, Lucille holding Izzy while he went to investigate. In a moment or two, he returned, a big grin on his face.

"It's Gracie and Matthew, with Keith. And Matty too."

"Oh!" Lucille stood, her heart full of delight. She couldn't be happier. Gracie and Matthew had remained friends of hers, and Keith was now thirteen and growing tall. She felt close to him—he often came into the house while she worked, and he watched her silently. She sometimes wondered if his experience—which he barely remembered—had sparked a thirst for knowledge. He was a studious boy, and she was already considering approaching his parents with a plan to send him to school in Prescott.

He had a great deal to offer.

"Lucille!" Matty grinned, coming in through the door. She was dressed in bonnet and coat and Lucille's heart warmed as Matty came to embrace her. The other three came in after her, followed by Emory, a new face on the ranch, who chuckled.

"Just stabled the oxen," he said. "My! You have a fine barn."

Nicholas grinned. "Thank you, Emory."

They both laughed. A rancher from Pinewood, Emory had met Matty when he came to the village to recover from a bad fall. Matty had visited him regularly, and the two had become friends. Since then, their friendship had deepened, and Lucille expected he would soon live permanently at Eastfield, the ranch beside theirs.

"There's a bench in the parlor," Nicholas said, about to stand. Matty chuckled.

"There's room for another five," she assured. She sat beside Lucille, and Gracie and the others crowded into the space at the end of the table. Lucille's heart flooded with warmth, looking into the face of her old friend.

"I'm so pleased you're here."

"I couldn't resist the chance to call," Matty said warmly. "I know we're close by. But you're always at the village and when you're here, these dear ones need a lot of focus." She ruffled Izzy's hair and the little one grinned up at her.

"Mmm," Izzy said.

"Matty," Matty told her, eyes sparkly. "I'm Matty. That's Emory."

"Emmrey."

Lucille chuckled. "That's good!"

"It's excellent," Matty encouraged. "She's talking so early."

Pride spread through Lucille. She had read so much about babies and seen them born, once or twice, but she had never imagined what they were actually like—how each day was a miracle from God, and every moment they seemed to be learning more. She had learned so much in the last years—of love, joy, pride, and wonder—and every day it seemed there were new lessons to be learned.

"She is," Lucille agreed. Gerard had started talking later, but then he'd taken to it soundly and seemed to be informing them of his concerns endlessly.

"How was the trip back yesterday?" Matty asked her.

Lucille shrugged. "Good," she said. She had taken the cart—it was still uncomfortable to ride, though she wanted to get back into the habit soon. She had worked in the village at the office yesterday—she and Mr. Simmons had an agreement. She worked one day, he the next, and on both days, Daisie helped as the assistant, learning from both of them. She had learned quickly, and Lucille was encouraging her to travel to California for her degree. Of course, Lucas would have to agree to move now they were wed.

"I think you're good," Matty said. "With all the new families here, you have to be on your feet all day."

Lucille chuckled. "It's no bother," she admitted. She loved it.

Many of the men who had plagued the town had settled nearby—they had been without work or hope, and Nicholas had helped them, finding many of them apprenticeships where they could learn new skills and discover new ways to live. Over time, one or two had raised enough money to buy land and become ranchers. The others either worked at the ranches or in the town, where a new leatherworking enterprise was growing, thanks to Tegan, the bandit who warned them of the raid and employed five men.

"It's good," Matty said warmly. "I have learned a lot just lately. A lot about forgiveness. About God's path for all man."

Lucille swallowed hard. She had to agree, having learned that, too. Seeing the bandits turn their lives to good had been inspiring. She had sensed, deep inside, they could achieve it.

The sunshine was a haze of red on the horizon, just visible through the windows, and the first stars were just showing on the darkening sky above them. Lucille leaned back, looking around the kitchen, feeling the warmth of Gerard's small body pressed to her, and watching Nicholas carefully feed Izzy with soup.

"It's good, isn't it?" Matty asked.

Lucille nodded. She didn't ask what Matty meant—the kitchen, the folk all gathered, the news from the growing ranches—it was all wonderful news.

She ate her stew, her mind drifting as she thought about the next day.

As the rise and fall of talk grew in the kitchen, she ate and drank and talked and it was a good hour before she and Nicholas excused themselves, feeling sleepy.

***

The following morning dawned bright, and the roosters woke Lucille, calling outside the window. She rolled over at the sound of Nicholas in the room next door. He kept his clothes and things there; the small space more like a pantry than a room. She thought of him trying to find things as she knew he didn't have a candle and the pantry-room had no windows.

A slow, warm smile spread across her face, comfortable and drowsy but at the same time thrumming with excitement for the day ahead.

Lucille slipped out of bed, washing her face in the porcelain bowl on the nightstand. Though they had added many small luxurious touches to the rest of the house, the bedroom was just as she recalled it from the first night she slept here. She had sworn not to change anything in it ever—the stark, functional beauty of it was so like Nicholas and she wanted it to be just as it was when she first met him. She dried her face on a linen towel—the towels were the only new thing in the room—and reached into the wardrobe for her dress. She had some new dresses, too—made with fine linen by the seamstress in Prescott—a gift from Nicholas and Matty.

She chose a white gown with a small black pattern—her new favorite dress—and was just unbuttoning it when Nicholas came in.

"Good morning," he greeted. He was dressed in a long white shirt and leather trousers. His hair was still tousled, and he grinned, a sleepy smile that lit up his eyes.

"Good morning," Lucille replied. She stood beside him, and he wrapped his arms around her, drawing her close to him, his body hard against hers through the thin fabric. She beamed up at him, blushing. He was so handsome.

"A fine morning," Nicholas commented. "And the best morning for organizing a party, I reckon."

"It is." Lucille changed from nightdress to smallclothes, cheeks warm, and Nicholas helped draw the dress up around her while she fastened it. The buttons down the back were tricky, but with a little help, she could manage it. She peeped into the crib where Izzy slept in their chamber. Gerard slept on a small bed in the corner. Glancing at him, she wondered if he was awake. She thought he was pretending to be asleep—his eyelids fluttered, and she bent, studying him.

"Are you awake, young man?" she whispered.

"Yes."

They all laughed. Lucille lifted him and he rested his head on her shoulder, cuddling close. She kissed his hair and passed him to Nicholas, who lifted him into the air, making him shriek. Lucille giggled, enjoying the moment before they all went down to breakfast together.

***

Nicholas went to the town, promising to return early that evening. Lucille stayed in the kitchen with Marcie, while Judi took the children up to the nursery—Izzy, Gerard, and

Marcie's three—to play while the other women got busy with preparing meals.

There was going to be a big party on the ranch that evening.

As they worked, guests started arriving—Matty turned up, a vast bowl of lettuce under one arm to contribute to the evening's celebrations. Gracie brought carrots and potatoes. Keith was with her, since it was a Saturday, and he stayed in the kitchen to help out for a while. When Jessie arrived, he quickly went off to play with his friends in the yard. He might be learning to lay bricks, but in many ways, he was still a child. Lucille focused on peeling potatoes, smiling as she heard the sound of children's laughter in the yard and hallways.

She could not have been happier.

That afternoon, Nicholas strode in. He brought more guests with him in the cart—Chris and his wife and children, and Mr. Simmons. Lucille greeted the old physician warmly while he set about helping in the kitchen—even he was happy to join in and prepare the salads.

"The barn's all ready," Nicholas agreed as he paused in the doorway. "I reckon the other guests should be arriving in an hour or so."

"Good," Lucille agreed. Her back was sore, but she hadn't noticed until she sat. Her feet ached too, but she was happy. She looked at the ceiling, saying a silent prayer. She had never imagined her life would be so full and so girded with love.

The guests started arriving as they put the last of the food out on the big trestles. Lucille turned to hear a friendly shout from the doorway.

"Daisie!" She ran to embrace her friend, who was wearing a white and blue gown and looking flushed and lovely. She hugged her, smelling lavender.

"Lucille!" her friend gushed. "You look stunning."

"Thank you," Lucille said shyly. "You, too." Her dress—the white one with the tiny black print of stylized lilies—was skillfully sewn and fitted in the waist, the neck high but with a beautiful lacy collar. Daisie's dress was patterned with flowers too, the neckline a little lower, the sleeves breezy puffs. Her pale face was a picture, framed with her soft curls.

"How are you?" Lucille asked as Daisie joined her at the table. There were only a few tasks left before the barn was ready: the dishes to be set out, the chairs and places set. Daisie laid out spoons as Lucille placed bowls, some borrowed from Matty for they were having so many guests, they would not have enough cutlery and dishes on the ranch for all of them.

"Well," Daisie grinned. "It was not too busy this morning. Mr. Burwell came in."

"How is his shoulder?" Lucille asked, reaching for a fork to place beside a bowl.

Daisie smiled. "He's almost cured. That way you strapped his shoulder really helped. He said he reckons it works better now than last year!"

Lucille giggled. Mr. Burwell had a minor injury, obtained when reining the bull to the cart. He had come into town to the office, and she'd strapped it three days ago. She was glad to hear it was progressing well. They chatted together about the progress of their various patients. Lucille made a mental note to raise the topic of her studies later. She glanced over as Matty and Judi came in, the food from the kitchen on trays carried between them.

"Daisie!" Luke called from the doorway. Lucille felt sure he was taller and broader than when she last saw him, though that could be the growing confidence within him that seemed to increase daily. He was taking on more responsibility in the sheriff's office, and Nicholas knew without a doubt that when he retired, he could trust the place to the young man.

"My dearest," Daisie greeted him warmly. Seeing the way, she looked at him, so admiring and loving, made Lucille's heart kindle. She took joy in the love she saw around her because it reflected her own. Her happiness was multiplied by seeing it in others.

"Can I help you ladies?"

Daisie giggled. "Please do," she said. "Lucille? Are there any jobs for strong men?"

Lucille smiled. Luke was red in the face, his blue eyes warm with pride and love. She spotted two ranch-hands at the door, struggling with something heavy.

"I think the fellows are bringing benches in, and they look like they might do with a hand." She gestured to the door. Luke nodded, hurrying over.

"He's so sweet and nice," Daisie gushed.

Lucille had to smile. She was so happy to see that the two of them were as much in love now as they were four years ago. They hadn't yet had any children, though she was sure that would happen soon. She looked up as more guests arrived—the Burwells and their neighbors. She was not surprised to see some faces she didn't know, but she was overjoyed by the familiar ones.

"Good evening, Mrs. Barnes," Mr. Burwell greeted her warmly.

"Good evening," she replied. "Are you feeling better?"

He nodded and told her about his shoulder, which seemed to be mending. Gracie came in, with Keith and Jessie and Jessie's children following her inside. She had the sandwiches from the kitchen, which meant they were all set to start.

"Everybody's here," Nicholas commented, coming up behind her and wrapping his arms around her. "Just the music still to arrive."

"Quite so," Lucille agreed.

She scanned the room. Mr. Elwood and his wife were at one table, Bert and Rebecca with them. The new banker was there, looking a little shy, he and his wife being introduced, and the ranch-hands and their wives were at another table, laughing and talking. There were so many happy faces and it seemed so remarkable that so many people were so blessed and happy and gathered here today.

She said a small prayer of thanks and, in Nicholas' wise gaze, she knew that he was thinking the same. As they stood there, watching their happy guests, someone moved at the doorway.

"Is the party in full swing?"

Lucille's heart leaped. It was Mr. Chaffee! She walked briskly over, weaving her way around the children and guests who milled in the entrance of the barn. She embraced the smaller, old form of the man she thought of almost as close as a father, and he held her, the familiar smell of leather and dust filling her nose as she stood there.

"Why, Lucille!" He stood back, looking up at her, hazel eyes bright. "Look at you! I swear you get prettier every time I call."

Lucille chuckled. "Now, I do think that's flattery, Mr. Chaffee. But thank you." She hugged him again, her heart fill with warmth. "It's so good to see you!"

He smiled. His face was weathered, hair white. "It's a party! You can't expect me not to come."

She smiled back fondly. He was busy, even though one of his ranch-hands was learning the trade from him and sometimes accompanied him on trading-ventures, now. He was not often in the area and so, having him here, unexpected, was a treat.

"Good. Trust you to get here," she said fondly. "It's such a long way!"

"I was on my way over this morning when I picked up some other people wanting a lift," he added, gesturing behind him. Lucille's heart flooded with warmth as she saw Rachel, along with the musicians. Her nephew was a tall youth now, far taller than Rachel, his long hair dark as night.

"Rachel!"

Lucille embraced her and greeted the youths warmly. Nicholas shook Mr. Chaffee's hand and directing the young men to where they would perform later that evening. Lucille chatted with Rachel while the guests organized themselves and settled at the places.

"It's so good to see you."

"And you, too," Rachel agreed. "How are the children faring?"

"Well," Lucille said smilingly. "Judi is upstairs with them. She'll bring them downstairs the moment the party starts. And how is your family faring?"

Rachel had become the center of her community, playing the traditional role in her tribal group now that she was retired from work. Lucille was delighted, and every day when they met, she learned more about Rachel's knowledge and shared some of her own. It was a strange, unacknowledged bond between them, a recognition that they might come from different worlds, but, for their people, they performed similar functions—not identical, but close enough to make them understand each other.

They watched as the guests settled and the music started.

Nicholas joined them, and once everyone was seated—Judi and the children close by the seats where Nicholas stood to say the blessing.

"Lord," Nicholas said, his voice loud and strong and warm as he stood at the table. "We thank you, not only for this food and this space, but for each other. We have learned so much—about faith, about love, and about Your Will for us. You have brought us all so many blessings, and you have given us to each other—a whole community that helps and loves one another. And for that we thank you, now and always."

As the group echoed in "amens," Lucille's heart melted with the love and truth of that.

She leaned against Nicholas as he sat, and, as the guests ate, and drank, and the sound of laughter rose around them, she snuggled close to him and watched the joy and happiness unfold around them all.

***

Later, as the guests danced and Judi and Marcie shepherded the children to a corner to play—or, in the case of the youngsters, to sleep—Lucille followed Nicholas outside, into the cool, clean air outdoors.

They stood together in the empty yard, the sound of the celebration as soft as the scent of dust and the traces of warmth in the air about them, the only light the stars overhead.

Lucille peered up at Nicholas, his face just visible in the darkness, his green eyes crinkled at the corners as he smiled down at her.

"A fine evening," Nicholas commented softly. He seemed shy and Lucille cleared her throat.

"It is," she agreed. Her voice was warm. She looked around, her hands in his, the warmth of his fingers heating her own, which were cool in the chilly night air.

"It's quiet here," Nicholas said. She laughed.

"It is. I can still hear Gerard asking for pudding. Listen carefully."

They both chuckled. His appetite was talked of on the ranch, but he was growing faster than any child Lucille had ever seen. He was already as tall as a child a year older was expected to be.

"He's growing," Nicholas commented.

They laughed. Tipping her head back, Lucille looked up at the stars. She could spot the Bear overhead and nearby, the Pole Star.

"It's a beautiful night," she said.

"Mm," Nicholas agreed. "And you are beautiful, too, my dear."

Lucille giggled. "I take that. And you're rather handsome as well, you know, you fine gentleman."

"Now that is flattery. But I accept."

Lucille stood on tiptoes as he took her in his arms and gently, so tenderly, kissed her. She held him close, her body pressed against his, and he wrapped his arms around her, holding her close in the starlit night, his body warm around her.

The stars looked down on them, and Lucille fancied that perhaps their loved ones watched from up there beyond the glittering heavens and were glad for them. She was aware, too, of God's love and His plan for them—a plan that had, it seemed, been written on both of their hearts since the time of their childhood. She had achieved her dreams, as did Nicholas, and in so doing, the whole community had prospered and men who had once been bandits sat in companionship with townsfolk and discussed their plans for uplifting their town.

Looking into Nicholas' eyes, she knew that God's plan is written in words of love, and that it is possible to hear whispers of it when one listens to one's deepest, truest heart.

"I love you," she whispered to Nicholas.

"I love you, too."

He held her close in the darkness and the stars shone on them, the light a blessing from heaven up above.

THE END

Also, by Olivia Haywood

Thank you for reading **"An Unconventional Woman to Restore his Faith"**!

I hope you enjoyed it! If you did, here you can also check out **my full Amazon Book Catalogue** at: https://go.oliviahaywood.com/bc-authorpage

Thank you for allowing me to keep doing what I love! ❤

Made in United States
North Haven, CT
18 October 2022

25618547R00192